Run Away to the Keys

A "Florida Keys Romance" Novel

MIKI BENNETT

Manufactured in the United States of America

ISBN: 0692695028
ISBN 13: 9780692695029
Library of Congress Control Number: 2016939402
WannaDo Concepts Publishing , Charleston, SC

To my large, big wonderful family——love you all.

"You could have your pick of any guy of means, if you would stick to your own kind of people. I mean, you chose a marine biologist. And then you are doing boat charters. You are a Cartwright. If you played your cards right, you wouldn't want for anything for the rest of your life. That is, if your parents could get their act together too." Skylar stood there, dumbfounded by Andrew's remark.

"Why, Dad? Why would you talk to him of all people?" she said, pointing to Andrew.

"I was only doing what I thought was best. Garrett, I'm sorry, but you aren't right for our daughter. She has such a bright future; plus, you are much older than she is," Mr. Cartwright said forcibly, looking Garrett in the eye.

"So you want to destroy my life like you are destroying yours and Mom's." Skylar said it before she thought. She was so hurt, but she never intended to air private information about her family. She suddenly looked around, and the whole ballroom was eerily quiet. People were speaking in hushed tones. She knew all eyes were on her.

"Personally, Mr. Cartwright, I think that if it weren't for Garrett, Skylar would have already been back here, where she belongs," Andrew said smugly. The next sound that traveled across the room was of the slap of Skylar's hand across his cheek.

1

"This feels strange. It's hard to believe that it wasn't too long ago I was helping you unload a moving truck. Now you are helping me pack mine," Garrett said as he took the two small boxes out of the arms of Abbey, his next-door neighbor. Zach, her fiancé, stood to the side, leaning on a cane with his leg in a brace. He was still recovering from a car hitting him months ago. As Garrett looked at the couple, who were now standing side by side, he was so happy for the two of them. Abbey and Zach had been through so much but had found their way back to each other—a real-life true-love story with a happy ending. For Garrett, though, past failed relationships still haunted him, one in particular, so he focused on his career. He loved his work as a marine biologist, working as a researcher on a coral reef study in the Florida Keys. It kept him so occupied that even entertaining the thought of dating was pretty much off-limits, which was fine with him. Love had only seemed to cause him heartache, something he really didn't want to go through again.

"Do you have everything?" Abbey asked, as Garrett shut and locked the doors to the back of the small trailer attached to his truck.

"I think so. If you guys find something of mine, just put it away for me. I'll pick it up next time I'm here."

"Which will be in seven months, if not sooner. You made me a promise, remember?" Abbey said, with her eyebrows raised.

"Abbey, give the man a break. You have already mentioned it five times. He probably knows the wedding date better than our parents do," Zach said laughingly as he came up behind his fiancé and put his arm around her waist.

"I'm just making sure he truly remembers, that's all." Abbey reached over and gave Garrett a quick hug. "Thanks again for being such a wonderful neighbor and friend. I'm really going to miss you. And maybe when you get to Key Largo, take some time for Garrett. All those fish in the sea will survive. I promise."

"That's girl talk for 'get a girlfriend,'" Zach quickly said to Garrett, and they both laughed, while Abbey just sighed.

"You guys take care," Garrett said as he got in the truck and started down the road. Before long, the city of Key West was behind him.

Garrett had packed his truck to full capacity. All his belongings were in every nook and cranny of the truck's bed. He had so much stuff stacked high on the interior seat that it blocked his view of the rearview mirror. He would have to rely on the side mirrors while driving. Thank goodness his trip was only one hundred miles or so. He had been in Key West for over a year, and now it was time to move on to his next location. Garrett was extremely grateful that it was still in the Florida Keys because he had grown to love the tiny islands so much.

He had grown up in Savannah, Georgia, only thirty minutes from the nearest beach. Garrett and his mom, Linda, had gone to the shore every chance they could. He knew from the time he was a little boy that when he grew up, he wanted to work somehow, someway with the creatures of the ocean. Now, years later, he was conducting his own marine research in the Keys, studying the possible causes of why the coral reefs were dying, and what could be done to save them. But Garrett also had a love for sea turtles, so he helped with research studies, tagging the magnificent creatures to track their wanderings along the East Coast and now watching the turtle population along the Florida Keys. His research grant would cover another year, but he had already applied for another grant to study the effects of marine algae for medicinal purposes. And he hoped that he could also conduct the new study here, in the Keys.

Garrett had already secured a small apartment in Key Largo, sight unseen. A fellow researcher had mentioned it, and once Garrett found out he could afford the monthly rent, he went for it. Since he usually wasn't home much, it didn't really matter what it looked like, as long as it was clean and had a kitchen, a bathroom, and a bed to sleep in. And that was just what it had, according to his friend. It also wasn't far from the marina where the boat was docked that he would be using for his offshore explorations. This made his new home almost perfect.

Finding the boat had been easy too. As a matter of fact, it was a fairly new company. The owner had just put the boat into service about a month before, and the woman he spoke to on the phone had offered him a great deal for the next six months. It fit perfectly into Garrett's budget, and he only hoped it would be big enough for his equipment. Even so, he couldn't beat the price, so as he had with his new apartment, Garrett agreed to the deal before even laying eyes on the vessel. The woman he talked to was very knowledgeable about the boat, giving him a lot of details about its use. But using the boat for research was the only thing he was interested in. The one thing Garrett hoped for was that the captain was pleasant. He had been lucky so far that most of the owners and captains of the boats he secured for work were nice guys, even though some had been stubborn on occasion. Garrett knew how to work around those situations, but he was bothered that he hadn't had a chance to speak to the captain before agreeing to the deal. He was told they would hopefully be able to talk in a few days, before they went out to sea for the first time. If not, Garrett kept his fingers crossed that this would work out and hoped for the best.

2

The boat was beautiful. Every time Skylar Cartwright walked down the dock to where she had it moored, she still was amazed that it was hers. She walked from bow to stern, looking over everything, as she had done so many times during the month since she started charters for scuba diving groups and snorkeling tours. In her first month as a boat captain, Skylar was already having success, having taken scuba and snorkeling trips three times that first week, and the business had been building every week since. Now she had a six-month standing rental for the boat with a marine biologist and his assistant while they did research along Florida's coral reef. They would need the use of the boat for those months, but according to Mr. Holmes, the researcher, they wouldn't need it every day. This was music to Skylar's ears because she would also be able to keep booking other groups around his schedule.

Skylar was determined to make this business work and validate that a woman could be a boat captain. She had one year to prove to her family, especially her father, that this was a viable business. If not, she would have to make good on her promise—to go back to work for the family—which was something she didn't enjoy but didn't hate either. But knowing she would keep her commitment gave Skylar the determination to do whatever she had to do to be successful and stay out on her beloved ocean instead of being stuck behind a desk.

The sea was in her blood. Skylar loved the ocean, with its clear deep-blue water. And her love affair with boats had begun when she was only a little girl. It was natural that when she was older, Skylar would do something involving her passions for the water and boats, and it was a fact that did not please her parents. Jonathan and Sadie Cartwright wanted all of their four children to work in the family's real estate business, so when Skylar declared one Sunday during the weekly family dinner that she was buying a boat, she took them all, including her siblings, by surprise.

Skylar's family was a very prominent part of Miami's real estate market. Her grandfather had begun selling land and homes during the 1950s, and over the years, he grew his tiny one-man operation into a very large, very profitable business, with many offices and employees in the south-Florida area. When Skylar's father and uncle were old enough, they followed in their father's footsteps, asking no questions. And the business had been kind to the entire family, as now the third generation of the Cartwright family was joining the business model. They were part of Miami's social elite, something her parents or siblings reminded Skylar of daily. But she couldn't help it. It was the sea that called to Skylar, not the land.

How could anyone blame her? She had grown up right on a beautiful lagoon with a canal that led to the ocean and beyond. Her family had access to boats that they could take straight out to the Atlantic Ocean. Every spare minute she could find, Skylar would sit by the water, often spotting stingrays, barracuda, hordes of colorful fish, and the occasional manatees that would swim up to the dock at her house. She always carried her sketch pad, drawing everything she could as a reminder of what she had seen that day. Instead of dolls, she had stuffed sea animals to sleep with. She even insisted at a very young age on decorating her room with starfish and sea turtles—two of her favorite ocean creatures. Her two brothers and sister thought Skylar was carrying the ocean thing a bit too far, but she didn't care. She loved the sea, and each time she sat by the water or was swimming in its warmth, Skylar felt as if the sea loved her back.

As she grew older and started going out in boats with her parents and friends, Skylar learned everything she could about them—sizes, shapes, styles, motors, and more. Even at the time when most teenagers were saving money for their first cars, Skylar told everyone that her money was going toward her first boat, quick to let people know that she still had a bicycle to use to get around on land. So it should not have surprised anyone that when she went to college, her major was biology, not business and marketing as her father had requested. The business world bored Skylar, but she took to marine biology as though she had known it her entire life. Her grades were excellent, and she graduated with honors. Though her parents were proud, they still insisted that she join the family's business. In fact, they used guilt to make her cave in and become the real estate agent she had sworn she would never be. They said little things that made her feel as if she owed them because of the luxuries she had growing up, even though being a part of the elite had never felt comfortable to her. Skylar had been much happier when she was with Grandma Cartwright, who had lived in a small home not far from Skylar's. Grandma still insisted on having a garden, sewing her clothes, and cooking her own meals. She lived a much simpler life than the one Skylar had had with her parents, with its galas, events, and social parties that seemed to be weekly occurrences. After her grandfather passed away, Grandma Cartwright had come to live with them, to Skylar's delight. They spent much time together then, and Skylar learned so much from her grandmother, especially an independent attitude, which would serve her later.

At twenty-two years old, Skylar began working as a real estate agent for her family's business. Though it wasn't what she wanted, she excelled in sales. She was especially good at selling any oceanfront properties they had, which was why her father put her in charge of those homes. She could sell a beach house better than anyone he had ever seen, and Skylar knew it was all because of her love of the ocean.

But now at twenty-nine years old, Skylar wanted more. She wanted something different. Skylar had started looking for a boat she could purchase for chartering scuba and snorkeling trips. She had a grand idea of owning a fleet of charter boats out of Key Largo and Islamorada.

Skylar kept her plans hidden, not telling a soul except her best friend, Kimberly. They had met in college and formed an instant bond. But they were definitely from different types of families. Kim's family lived paycheck to paycheck, but that didn't keep the two roommates from forming a solid, fast friendship. And one thing Skylar envied about Kim was the fact that her family didn't dictate what her life's path would be. They encouraged their daughter to be curious and to try new things. Yes, Kim had gotten her bachelor's degree in English, but right now, she was working at a very popular local coffee shop and freelance writing in her spare time. Skylar craved that type of freedom from her family, even though she loved each of them so much.

She knew that her parents were doing what they thought was best for their daughter by insisting she work with them, but Skylar felt unfulfilled. That is, until she hatched her plan to acquire boats and do daily tours to the Great Florida Reef that runs along the Florida Keys. Skylar's goal was to buy used boats and restore them to like-new condition, similar to what her parents did with older homes. She would just have to keep it all secret till she had every detail worked out. Only then would Skylar be able to face her family and answer the multitude of questions she knew they would bombard her with. Little did she know that her younger brother, Chase, had found out about her business plan after she accidentally left some notes laying on her desk at work. He was so excited about Skylar's plan, not knowing that she hadn't shared it with anyone, that when he asked about it in front of their father, Skylar cringed at the look on her father's face. She was furious at first with Chase, but it was her fault for leaving the documents where he could see them. But in a way, Chase helped her that day. It was the catalyst for where she was now—the captain of her own boat in Key Largo. But that had only happened after some heated discussions and a compromise with her parents.

So today was the big day. Her first long-term paying client would be on board all day. Skylar looked over the paper work he had e-mailed to make sure she had all the information correct: Garrett Holmes was a marine biologist whom she would be taking to the reef to dive and do research. Skylar and her only employee and first mate, Max, were ready. Even though Mr. Holmes wouldn't arrive till around eight o'clock, she had been at the marina at six o'clock, making sure everything was just right. Max even arrived a bit earlier than planned, his excitement almost matching hers at the thought of having a real marine biologist aboard.

"Thanks, Max, for helping out. I wish I could pay you more."

"This is great. I'm working out on the water and still going to college, so my parents aren't mad—it's the perfect scenario for me. I should be thanking you!" Max said, giving Skylar a big hug. He was her best friend Kim's little brother and Skylar had grown fond of him these last ten years, watching him grow up. Max felt like a baby brother to her. His personality was infectious and with his good looks, he was already a hit with the local tourists on the snorkel and scuba trips they had already taken. Just then, Skylar looked toward the parking lot to see a man carrying two large bags, one slung over his shoulder.

"This must be our marine biologist coming right now," Skylar said, and if it was, Skylar was a bit taken aback.

"Is this the *Sea Gypsy*?" the man said to Skylar as he approached the boat.

"Yes, it is. Are you Garrett Holmes?"

"Yeah. Who are you?"

"Skylar Cartwright, your captain. Welcome aboard." To say that Garrett Holmes was just handsome did not do him justice. This man temporarily took Skylar's breath away. His short, wavy dark-brown hair was a bit unruly but gave him a rogue look that was intriguing. The muscles that she could see since he was wearing a tank top and shorts were taut and tanned. He's gorgeous, Skylar thought as the man continued to stand on the dock, looking at her as if she had lost her mind.

"You are the captain. No way!"

The way he spoke brought Skylar back to reality very fast. "Is that a problem?" Skylar asked as diplomatically as she possibly could. How dare he think she was incapable of being a boat captain.

Garrett looked at the beautiful dark-haired girl standing defiantly on the deck of the boat. So this was a first for him. He had never been to sea with a female boat captain, much less one that was so attractive and young. There was no way she could have much experience with boats or being out on the ocean.

"Are you sure you can handle this boat?" Garrett asked the woman, whose face became hardened at the question.

"Mr. Holmes, I am Skylar Cartwright, owner and captain of this boat. I have grown up around the ocean and boats my entire life. If you do not have confidence in my abilities, then you are most welcome to move on to another boat with a male captain, for I presume that is what you were expecting. But you won't find a better boat or a better price, I can guarantee that." Skylar couldn't believe the words had flowed from her mouth as easily as they had, but there was something about him that made her defensive She had known from the beginning of this adventure that she would encounter men like Mr. Holmes but hadn't thought it would be her biggest client so far. But this is where her experience in the real estate world came to her rescue. She was a Cartwright, and they were strong. She would stand firm, knowing she was the best captain with the best boat and the best price this man would be able to find. If he walked away, she had the means to find other clients. She would make her boat charter business a success.

Garrett stood there for a second, sizing up the situation. This woman, Skylar, was right, and apparently, she knew it. He wouldn't be able to find a better price, that was for sure. He had already scoured the ads and had been shocked at the price she had given him. But now he knew why. She was young, new, and a woman. He had to give her props for jumping into a world mostly dominated by men. And for the fact that the boat looked almost brand-new. How could she afford such a luxury? Garrett didn't ask any of the questions coming to his mind because he knew he really had no choice but to work with the beautiful woman.

Garrett threw one bag onto the boat, and it landed on the deck near Skylar's feet. With another hop, he was on board, standing only a very small distance away from her. Even though their first meeting was proving to be somewhat confrontational, Skylar found herself a bit breathless as she was able to look at him even more closely now. His eyes were blue like the sea, and he had just enough stubble along his chin to accentuate a very sensual face.

"Okay?" Garrett said.

"I'm sorry, what?" The voice suddenly pulled Skylar back into the world.

"We will see how things go today, and then I will make up my mind. Your secretary, assistant, whatever, didn't tell me all the details about you and your boat." Garrett wanted to be upset, but the situation in which he found himself intrigued him. But he didn't want or need the distraction of an alluring woman on board the boat. Garrett quickly reminded himself he was only there for work.

"That wasn't a secretary, Mr. Holmes. You were talking with me. Anyway, I'll agree to your terms because I already know what the outcome will be. Max, let's get ready. Where to, Mr. Holmes?" Skylar said confidently, while still shaking a bit inside.

Garrett stared at her for a moment, and he finally gave her directions to the part of the coral reef he wanted to observe today. He then went quietly to find a place to store his equipment and change into his gear, all the while watching as Skylar and her first mate expertly maneuvered the boat from the marina and out to sea. He was finding it hard not to stare at her, but he had to stay focused, he told himself. Although, he finally admitted silently that this research trip might be a little more difficult than any other he had done in the past.

3

"We can anchor here," Garrett said, pointing to an area on the port side of the boat. Skylar slowed down, eventually shutting off the engine, while Max dropped anchor, making sure they were far enough away not to damage any coral.

"We are about thirty feet from the reef, which is good. I have the dive flags—" Garrett said, but he was cut off suddenly.

"I have the flags ready to go, Mr. Holmes," Skylar said in a businesslike tone, wanting to come across as the strong woman she knew she was, even though the first encounter with this man was still a bit unnerving.

Huh, Garrett thought to himself. Maybe this girl really does know a thing or two about what she is doing. She handled the boat like a pro, and when given directions, she went exactly to the correct spot. Still, something had him feeling a little on edge about the entire situation.

"Uh, thanks. And by the way—call me Garrett. Mr. Holmes makes me feel old."

"Then Garrett it is. You can call me Skylar, and this is Max," she said, motioning to the young man who had just dropped the anchor.

"I'm going to go have a look to make sure I have the right reef spot and then come back and make notes. We will probably be here for five hours or a little more."

"Are you diving by yourself?" Skylar asked, knowing that having two divers was the usual protocol.

"Yes, today I will be. Tomorrow, I have an intern from the university that will be working with me for the next several months. I will be coming up regularly, so there shouldn't be any problem." Garrett knew this was really against everything he had been taught, but the intern couldn't start till tomorrow, and he was ready to get in the ocean and begin his work. His dives would have to be done in short intervals today.

"Do either of you do any diving?" Garrett asked.

"We both do," Skylar said quickly, making sure she sounded like a boat captain.

"Great. If it is okay with you, please time my dives. That will be an element of protection. If I don't surface within five to seven minutes of the scheduled time, come find me." Okay, this will throw her for a loop for sure, Garrett thought.

"No problem. We'll make sure to have the dive gear ready, just in case you are in need of a rescue."

Damn, she's good, Garrett thought. His head was swirling with many thoughts, none of which were about the reef he was getting ready to look at. This woman, this girl, was certainly unusual, not like any other woman he had met before. Skylar had his attention, something he wasn't used to, and it left him feeling out of step. It had only been an hour or two, but Garrett felt an immediate attraction to Skylar, one he was trying to deny. She was definitely stunning and very independent. But Skylar had to be much younger than he was, leaving him wondering just how old she really was.

After looking at his watch, Garrett then glanced back up at her. "I'll be back in fifteen minutes. I have set my alarm. Does that sound okay?" he said, watching her set a timer on her phone and nod. Then he let himself fall backward into the blue water of the Atlantic Ocean.

"Way to go, Sky," Max said as soon as Garrett was in the water. "You sure put him in his place. That was so cool to watch."

Skylar was just starting to take regular breaths. Though she may have seemed like a confident boat captain, Garrett had completely unnerved her. But she had kept her wits about her and proved to the man that she could pilot a boat and that she knew her way around these waters. Little did Garrett know that she had grown up in this area, but she was sure he would eventually find out.

"Well, the day isn't over yet, Max. Let's just make sure he comes up in one piece. Diving alone is dangerous, as far as I'm concerned. I will be glad when he has his intern with him, except I feel sorry for whoever it is. Garrett seems like a very arrogant know-it-all." Taking a quick look at the phone to see only five minutes had passed, Skylar headed to the small galley and grabbed a bottle of cold water and a bag of grapes she had packed that morning. These, along with her iPad, she took back to her chair, and with the phone beside her, she brought up the sketching app where she created her digital artwork. Though she should have been reading a few of the books she had downloaded to the tablet, she always seemed to find herself drawing, sketching, and painting on the device. She loved this new medium when she couldn't create her mixed-media pieces with her hands in paint and glue. She loved using scraps of paper to create artwork. She had sold pieces in a few galleries in Miami, courtesy of her parents knowing several of the owners.

What was even more amazing to her about the artwork she created was that people loved it. The gallery owners were always asking her to make more pieces, but she loved the water too much. But when she found she could create digital art on the tablet, especially in downtime like now, she was beyond excited. So even though boating was her first love, digital art was growing on her daily.

Suddenly, the sound of the alarm on her phone broke her concentration on the stormy ocean scene she was painting. And as soon as she had put everything down by her chair, she heard Garrett's voice calling up to Max, who had been looking over the side, watching for their client.

"So far, so good," Garrett said to the young man, with Skylar listening from behind. "Tell your captain I'm going back down for fifteen minutes, then I'll be on board to make some notes and work a bit."

"No problem," Max said, waving to Garrett as he sank below the surface once more.

"I heard," Skylar said as Max turned to tell her.

"I'm going to make sure the table is available to him," she said before moving into the boat's enclosed cabin space.

It was spacious for a boat but not like the many yachts she had been on over the years with her parents, when they attended parties or had the occasional weekend excursion over to the Bahamas. But for her, Skylar thought the layout was perfect. On one side, there was a table that was large enough for Garrett to work on. The opposite side had a two-burner stove and a small double-basin sink. The captain's seat was in front of this area, where she had intended to work on her art. But not with Garrett in the same spot. She would have to sit outside under some shade to work. Plus, she needed to write notes of the phone calls to make once they were back ashore. These were calls that would probably lead to future bookings for her boat, so they would be a priority once she was home.

Skylar was always environmentally conscious, but now there was a pull between making this business of hers a success and not visiting an area for diving and snorkeling too often. With so many places to choose from, she was sure it wouldn't be a problem. But she also hoped that Garrett would be able to work while others enjoyed the ocean for fun, because right now, she was double-booked on a few occasions.

Garrett climbed on board, tossing his gear onto the floor of the boat. Skylar couldn't help but watch him—wearing only his diving gear and swimming trunks, Garrett was what Skylar would consider an almost-perfect male specimen, except for his attitude, which immediately put a slight damper on the sight before her. Garrett was dripping wet, tan, muscled, and oh, so sexy.

"So, is it okay?" Garrett asked again, staring at Skylar.

"What?" Skylar couldn't believe she had done it again.

"Is it okay to sit at the table while I'm wet? I should be dry soon. I'm going to get my notes and computer." Garrett stood there, looking for an answer to his question.

"Uh…yes…uh, it's fine. I'll just get my stuff out of there."

"You don't have to move. I'm sure there is enough room for the both of us," Garrett said as he quickly went to pick up one of the bags he had brought aboard earlier. This time, Skylar could tell there was a hint of kindness showing through the earlier arrogant exterior. Maybe a little time in the water to think had made him realize that she was capable of handling this boat, even if she was a woman.

"I think I'll just sit out on the deck for a bit."

"Suit yourself," Garrett said, toweling off after he sat the bag down. Then he scattered papers on the table that was apparently his research information. He also brought out a laptop, notepad, pen, and a bag with food.

"If you need anything, let me know." Skylar had been watching Garrett's every move since he stepped back aboard the *Sea Gypsy*. This man unnerved her in a very good way.

"Will do," Garrett said looking at the papers spread before him. There definitely wasn't room in the cabin for the two of them. And not just because of the papers and the computer he had. The tension between the two of them filled the small area.

"You're working outside. Wouldn't it be cooler in the cabin?" Max said to Skylar as she sat in the outside chair under a cover.

"I think Mr. Holmes needs his space," Skylar said defiantly.

Max began to laugh quietly and came to sit close beside her.

"What is so funny, Max?" Skylar said, looking up at her young friend.

"You like him," Max said very quietly, with a big smile on his face.

"You have got to be kidding, Max. First of all, I just met him. And he is definitely not my type. He is a client only for the next six months, which I hope goes more smoothly than this first day. I can tell he doesn't think I'm capable of handling this boat, but he will. And on top of all that, he is arrogant. What is there to like?" Skylar said the words so fast that Max just stared at her, still smiling.

"Yep, you like him." Max said it quickly and then went to make sure the anchor line was still secure. Then he dived into the water to cool off for a minute before Skylar could say anything back to him.

Skylar peeked through the window at the man sitting at her table where the cooler air was. Garrett looked immersed in his papers, and he was typing furiously on his computer. She had to admit that he was very alluring. And he couldn't be that much older than she was. Turning her attention back to her sketch in front of her, she tried to concentrate but found herself glancing through the window much too often. Ugh! she thought to herself. It was only their first day together, and this marine researcher named Garrett entranced her.

He was more unique than any other man she had ever met. He seemed to be totally committed to his research, never taking a break from the papers and computer before him for three hours. Skylar worked on her sketches, made lists of things to do and people to call when they got back to the marina, and had some lunch. Then she decided to take a quick swim to cool off. It was warm outside, but not as hot as it could be at times. Since Max was back on board, she decided a quick swim was just what she needed.

Garrett finally looked up from the papers surrounding him and the laptop that had seemed to make his eyes crossed. He was recording every detail that he remembered of what he had seen in the water below, referencing it with the data from dives around Key West. He had made lists of things to check on, people to contact, and more. When he finally looked at the time on the computer, he couldn't believe how long it had been. And the growling of his stomach let him know that lunchtime had come and gone. He was thankful that the captain and her first mate hadn't disturbed him the entire time. Hopefully, this was how it would be for the entirety of his boat reservation, even though the contract had mentioned the possibility of other passengers at times. It wasn't something he was too keen about, but once again, he couldn't beat the cost of renting this boat over the others he had checked on.

Garrett sat back, rubbing his neck and then his eyes, stretching a bit as he looked around. What caught his eyes about took his breath away. Skylar had just removed her shorts and was taking her T-shirt off, revealing a coral one-piece swimsuit that beautifully complimented every part of her. It showed her toned body, with just the right curves, and her smooth lightly tanned skin. She then proceeded to pull her dark-brown hair into a high ponytail. After saying something to Max that Garrett couldn't hear, she climbed onto the side of the boat and gracefully dived into the water below.

Just watching her completely took his mind away from the work he was doing. And for some reason, Garrett instantly wanted to join her. He did have to go back in the water once more before heading back to land, and maybe this was the time to do it.

"Hey there," Max said as Garrett walked toward the side of the boat. "Are you getting ready for another dive?"

"Yeah, I'm doing one more quick check on a few things. I'll be able to accomplish more tomorrow, especially if that intern shows up. Where's your boss?" Garrett asked, knowing full well where the pretty captain was.

"She decided to take a quick dip in the water to cool off. There's not much breeze today making it a bit warm, but it's not as hot as it could be." Max was cleaning up items around the deck as Garrett assembled his scuba gear.

"You're going in the water one more time." The female voice came from behind Garrett. He spun around so quickly he almost became tangled in his own equipment. Skylar had wrapped a towel around herself, but she still couldn't hide her beauty. And for the first time in such a long while, Garrett found himself thinking about something else—or should he say someone—while on a boat at sea. This woman, who was beguiling and also his sea captain, had totally captivated him on his first day aboard, but it was not as if he would admit it to anyone.

"I was just telling Max here that I need one more dive to gather a little more info, and I'll be done for the day."

"Sounds good. How long will you be down this time?" Skylar asked, watching Garrett as he assembled the gear. She kept her wits about her, though it was difficult, as she watched the man in front of her.

"Time me at twenty minutes this time." Garrett then sat on the edge and tumbled once more back into the sea.

The laughing that came from behind Skylar brought her back to reality. "Man, I love this job. I had no idea it would be this fun!"

"Now what are you talking about?" Skylar said, exasperated.

"You both are walking on eggshells around each other. He's staring at you—you're staring at him. It's freakin' funny! I can't wait to see who breaks first."

"Explain yourself if you want to keep your job."

"It's like I said earlier. You guys are really into each other, but neither will give in. And I can't decide who will be the first one to finally admit it."

Skylar was flustered now with her employee. "How in the world did you come up with this? It's our first day at sea with this researcher! And when I say 'our,' I mean the three of us," Skylar said, while making a circle with her hand in the air. "And it's only been a few hours. Anyway, think what you will. I have a company to run, and I'm not interested at all. I'm done with men for a while." When she finished that statement, Skylar's memories of Andrew surfaced in her mind.

She would never forget the look on her now ex-boyfriend Andrew's face when he had told her he wanted to break off their relationship. She had been in love with him, or so she thought. Skylar later learned that Andrew had just wanted her for her family's money, although his family was as wealthy as hers. Andrew hadn't liked the fact that Skylar wanted to strike out on her own. When he found out her idea for the boat charter business, the next day he told her their relationship was finished. No explanation. But three months later, she had seen him with someone new by his side—Alicia Tanner, another woman from a very wealthy south-Florida family. That was when Skylar had realized how shallow Andrew really was. She had to be honest and admit that she'd had feelings for him, but now they were long gone. Andrew and Alicia were going to get married, so she had heard, but she wasn't sure when since she had lost track of the social gossip since moving to Key Largo. But it wasn't really a wedding for love. Skylar knew it was more like a business deal. One that would benefit both parties, and it sickened her. Skylar promised herself that when she did marry, it would be for love, and not because of a bank account.

But for now, Skylar focused on her boat. And the fact that it was time for Garrett to pop up out of the water. As she and Max watched, Garrett came to the surface just on cue and climbed the ladder to get back on board.

"Are you ready to head in for the day?" Skylar asked, watching him as he toweled off.

"I think so. It was beautiful down there though. I haven't dived here in a while." Garrett watched as Skylar expertly got things ready to go, while Max brought in the anchor. And before he knew it, they were gliding softly back into the marina. Skylar expertly guided the boat into its place among the others, and Max quickly secured the boat to the dock.

"What time shall we meet tomorrow?" Skylar asked as Garrett got off the boat with both bags he had brought aboard that morning.

"Let's say eight o'clock again. The intern from the university should be with me then." Garrett watched Skylar, who was all business and wondered whether she ever loosened up.

"That sounds fine. We will see you in the morning," Skylar said and turned around to get her own things to leave.

"Listen, I'm sorry if we got off on the wrong foot this morning. It just took me by surprise that you were the captain and owner of this boat. To be honest, you are the first female boat captain I've been out to sea with. So I apologize if I came across a bit rough." Garrett really did mean it. Skylar had done an excellent job today, as good as any man that he had known that had piloted any research vessel he had been on.

"Thanks. I really appreciate that." The compliment made Skylar smile inside, but she didn't want to let her guard down too much. But staring at Garrett was making her weak in the knees. So she took a deep breath and smiled.

"See ya tomorrow," Garrett said as he walked down the dock, while Skylar watched with a smile on her face.

4

Who is Skylar Cartwright? Garrett thought as he drove to his little apartment. She was certainly beautiful and most definitely did not look like a boat owner or captain, but by the way she handled the boat today, she was a pro. Maybe her family owned boats, or she grew up by the water. A little Internet search when he got home would be in order. There was certainly more to Skylar, and for the first time in a very long while, he found himself wanting to know more about a woman, a subject he usually avoided for so many reasons. Mainly the painful memories of a girl from his past.

As Garrett pulled up to the house on the canal, he parked his truck to the side. He had been extremely lucky to find this place. An older couple owned the house and lived upstairs. They rented the downstairs area, which consisted of a kitchen, bathroom, bedroom, and small living room. And he couldn't beat the price. He was close to work and had canal access if he ever came across a boat he could use on his own. Garrett also told the couple upstairs, Mr. and Mrs. Driggers, that if they needed any small repairs done here and there, to let him know, since they offered the monthly rent at such an affordable price. All they asked in return was for a quiet tenant, which they didn't have to worry about with Garrett. If he wasn't in the water, he was researching or asleep, he assured them.

Garrett put his gear on the floor and went to rummage in the refrigerator and kitchen cabinets. As he examined the contents of both, he made a mental note to go grocery shopping soon. He had just enough food for a turkey sandwich, to which he added a few chips from the bottom of an old bag, and a bottle of raspberry ice tea. As he sat down on his sofa, instead of turning on the TV, he reached for his laptop. Now would be the perfect time to see whether he could dig up any information on Miss Skylar Cartwright.

As he typed in the name, city, and state, her name and picture were suddenly on his screen. There was a real estate company named Cartwright, and it showed her as an agent. Garrett continued scrolling down the search page. After reading more and more, Garrett was piecing the information together. Her family owned one of the largest and oldest real estate companies in the south-Florida area, dealing with million-dollar properties. Skylar's picture was coming up on many websites, all dealing with Miami's social elite and celebrities. There were pictures of her parents, a sister, and two brothers, all of whom were involved in the family's business. But it didn't make sense. Why was Skylar the captain of a charter boat?

He quickly set the laptop down and reached for the papers on the coffee table in front of him. Garrett finally found what he was looking for—the rental agreement with the boat company. The name across the top was Largo Bay Boat Rentals. But this company wasn't mentioned anywhere in the Internet articles he'd found about Skylar and her family. Damn! According to the Internet, this family was like Miami royalty. But Skylar was piloting a used but really nice boat, and the girl in these pictures and the one he had seen today were totally different. Instead of cocktail dresses and high heels, today she wore a T-shirt, shorts, and sneakers, with her hair pulled back in a ponytail.

Garrett sat back, digesting everything he had read. His mind was full of questions, and he knew that tomorrow he would have to talk to her to clarify a few things for himself. Namely, how and why Skylar Cartwright was piloting a boat if she was as wealthy as it seemed from all Garrett had read.

As he took a quick shower and headed off to bed, he began thinking that his stay in Key Largo was becoming very interesting, and he had only been here for a week. And he found himself very much looking forward to tomorrow. Not only to talk to Skylar to find out what was the real story but Garrett found himself thinking about the captivating girl with brunette hair, gorgeous green eyes and that coral bathing suit that accentuated everything about her perfectly.

Skylar was at the boat early the next morning. Just like yesterday, she wanted to make sure everything was prepared, but she was even more anxious now that she knew more about her passenger. She was going to make this work, and even though Garrett was her only long-term client at the moment, she acted as though she had a slew of clients and a fleet of boats. This helped her stay on track with her goal to make sure that this charter business would be a success. She could feel the stress trying to take her over both physically and mentally, but Skylar stood still on the deck of the boat, taking deep breaths to help her calm down and think more clearly. And as they had done before, the cleansing breaths helped her to feel more relaxed.

"You are here early again," Max said as he climbed into the boat. "Do you ever sleep?"

"Yes. I just wanted to make sure things went as smoothly today as they did yesterday. Oh, and by the way——thanks for assisting Garrett yesterday. You were a big help." Skylar meant that sincerely. Max was turning out to be one of her best decisions in this new venture of hers.

"No problem, boss."

"Oh, that sounds weird to hear you say that," Skylar said as she smiled over at Max. "But I have to admit—I like it."

"Hi there," said a female voice with a distinct accent from behind them. "Is this the *Sea Gypsy*?"

Skylar and Max both turned to see a very pretty redheaded girl standing on the dock, with a large tote bag on her shoulder. Max couldn't get to the side of the boat quickly enough.

"It sure is. Who wants to know?"

"I'm looking for someone I'm supposed to be working with—a Mr. Garrett Holmes. Is he here, or does he own this boat?" the girl asked, being very businesslike.

"He definitely doesn't own the boat. She does," Max said, gesturing back toward Skylar. "But he should be here shortly. Let me help you on board." Max reached over to the cute girl, who instead grabbed the boat's rail and came on board with no assistance at all. She completely ignored Max, walking straight to Skylar.

"Hi. I'm Casey Powell, Mr. Holmes's assistant for the research he is doing. Do you have a place I can put my gear and go through some paper work to get ready before Mr. Holmes arrives?"

"Sure. You can put your things here," Skylar said, motioning to a spot on the deck. "And you can use the table in the cabin if you need work space."

"Here, I'll show you," Max said quickly, trying to help Casey. But as Skylar watched the younger woman, Casey acted as though Max was a nonentity. She was very rude from Skylar's perspective since Max was going out of his way to be of assistance. As she watched the girl, Casey reminded her of someone, but Skylar couldn't quite figure out who. And from Casey's demeanor and attitude, it seemed to suggest that she probably thought she was better than Skylar and Max, especially Max. Skylar had grown up around girls like this——maybe that's why Casey seemed so familiar to her.

"Wow, things just got better around here," Max said as he returned to Skylar's side.

"I'm not sure whether she is your type, Max. Things seemed to have gotten a bit chilly when she came on board, and you are just the opposite—happy and friendly. But knock yourself out if you think there is a chance," Skylar said, giving him a friendly punch in the arm.

"Good morning!" Another voice came from behind them, but this time Skylar knew who it was. She turned around to see Garrett, who was looking just as dreamy as he had the day before.

"Good morning to you, Mr...I mean...Garrett. You are here just in time. You have a visitor in the cabin. She says she is your assistant."

"She..." Garrett said, with a puzzled look on his face.

"She's definitely a she. Just ask Max over there. I don't think his eyes have popped back into their sockets since she came on board."

"She...I thought my assistant was supposed to be a guy."

"Once again, don't you think a woman is up for the job? You are beginning to sound a bit chauvinistic," Skylar said, with a sarcastic grin on her face.

"I didn't mean it like that. It's just that I've always worked with guys and this is my first assistant. This is all a bit out of the ordinary for me, but I'm not complaining." Garrett smiled back at her. "I was wondering...sometime before we leave to-day, could I have a chat with you? I have some questions."

"About what?" Skylar suddenly felt worried, wondering whether she might lose the contract with Garrett.

"There are just a few things I want to ask you about your boat and your previous experience with charters."

"You signed a charter agreement for the next six months. I hope you aren't planning to back out. There is a penalty."

"No, it has nothing to do with that. I would just like to talk to you later, okay?"

"Just let me know when." Skylar was perplexed and confused. Did Garrett not see her as a capable boat captain? It is just a talk, nothing more, and certainly nothing to worry about, she told herself. But she couldn't shake the small feeling of paranoia. It was times like these when this business venture shook her confidence.

Garrett set his gear down next to the bag he supposed belonged to the new intern that was to be his assistant for the next few months. What was his name? Crap, her name. Garrett couldn't remember. Then he looked inside to see a girl with long red hair sitting at the table with her laptop in front of her, typing furiously while looking at the screen.

When he walked into the small area, the girl's head snapped up so quickly that she startled him.

"Sorry! I didn't mean to alarm you," Garrett said quickly. "I'm Garrett Holmes. And you must be the new intern from the university."

"I'm Casey. Casey Powell." She stood up quickly, extending her hand, which he shook. "I was just reviewing the work on the coral reef that you have turned in so far. I'm making sure I'm up to speed on everything."

"That's good. Well, we are going to head out now. You do scuba dive, correct? I need someone with me below. Then I'll be writing notes, and you will be putting them in order for me. This is a bit unusual for me because I normally work alone."

"It's no problem, Mr. Holmes. Just let me know what you need," Casey said, thinking about just how lucky this assignment was after seeing the sexy man she would be working with and who the boat captain happened to be. This is going to be great, she thought to herself.

"Just call me Garrett. Mr. Holmes just doesn't sound right."

"All right, Garrett," Casey said in a voice so sweet that it seemed to drip with honey.

"Are we ready to leave?" Skylar said, popping her head into the cabin before making her way to the captain's chair.

"I think so," said Garrett, his mind still swirling. It seemed like this research endeavor would be different from every other project he had worked on before. For the first time, he was working with a female boat captain, who was very beautiful and apparently very wealthy. And now he had his first assistant who was a woman who wouldn't quit staring at him for some reason and was following him around like a puppy on a leash. He was used to just doing his work and then relaxing at night. But he could tell that this time, things were going to be very different. He could feel it. But just what other changes were to come, Garrett wasn't sure.

5

"The water is gorgeous today," Casey said, as she and Garrett suited up to take their first dive.

"They are calling for great weather all week," Max chimed in quickly, still in awe of Garrett's intern, who had joined them and according to Garrett, would be working with him for a few months. Max smiled at that last thought, stealing glances at the cute girl with her porcelain skin and chocolate brown eyes.

"We will see you guys later. Ready?" Garrett said to Casey, who eagerly nodded and they both fell backward into the water.

"You can wipe the constant drool from your face now," Skylar said to Max while laughing.

"Laugh all you want, but I saw the way you looked at Casey. Do you think she could be some competition?"

"What in the world are you talking about now?" Skylar looked at Max incredulously.

"Skylar, you can't hide it today any more than you did yesterday. You're attracted to Garrett. Your body language gives you away. And from the way he's looked at you yesterday and today, I think he must be into you too. I wouldn't even worry about the age thing," Max said, as he moved toward the bow of the boat with a rope in his hand.

"Max, I think you are a little drunk in love with Little Miss Redhead. I'm not interested in Garrett at all except for the fact that he is a paying client—that's it. I have to make this business work, so that is my priority. Anyway, I'm taking a break from relationships. You know how my last one ended up." Skylar suddenly saw in her mind a picture of Andrew and Alicia from the internet article she saw last night announcing their engagement. Even though she was over the shock of how quickly he had found someone to take her place, it still made Skylar wonder whether she was relationship material for anyone. Everyone always said she was all work and no play. And now it was true, as this boat was her baby, and she seemed to be at the marina practically all the time.

"Just because Andrew was an idiot doesn't mean all men are. Take me—can't get any better or sweeter," Max said, bringing a much-needed smile to Skylar's face. And he was right, Skylar thought as she looked at Max, standing well over six feet tall with his sandy blonde hair and boyish good looks.

"I have to say, Casey is pretty hot, but she seems to have eyes for Garrett, and she has only been with him for a couple of hours. What's this guy got that I don't have? Two women and they are both drooling over him. Just using your words" Max said as he looked at Skylar with a smile.

"I'm not drooling over him! You sure have come to some big conclusions awfully quickly about our researcher and his assistant. We just met Garrett yesterday and Casey today." Skylar shook her head.

"I'm good at reading people. I always have been, my mom even says so. You never know—I just might ask Casey out."

"Well, lover boy, keep an eye on our two divers below. I've got to do some paper work and write some e-mails," Skylar said as she went into the boat's cabin.

The day progressed almost the same as the day before, except for the addition of Garrett's new intern. Skylar watched from afar, and it seemed she could almost sense that Garrett was a little irritated at Casey's constant attentiveness. Skylar even caught him once rolling his eyes at something Casey said or did, and she couldn't help but laugh. These next few months could prove to be very entertaining, Skylar said to herself.

As Max tied the boat to the dock, everyone was ready to disembark.

"Casey, I'll see you Thursday. I have to talk to Skylar about our dive schedule," Garrett said as they were standing on the dock, close enough for all to hear.

"Are you sure you don't need me tomorrow?" Casey asked earnestly.

"I'm positive. Be ready to work on Thursday." He turned his back on the girl and came back on board. Then he turned around again to make sure that Casey was indeed on her way to the parking lot, which she was. Thank goodness, Garrett thought to himself.

Skylar had watched the whole exchange, and once again, she couldn't help but chuckle lightly. Garrett had his hands full, and by the look on his face, he wasn't too thrilled about it.

"Hey, Max, thanks again. See you tomorrow, right? We have two snorkeling trips scheduled, so be prepared. Come early to make sure all the gear is ready."

"Yes, boss lady," the young man said before jumping to the dock. "Bye, Garrett. See ya Thursday." And he quickly started running down the wooden planks.

"I think he is trying to catch up to Casey," Skylar said, with a grin on her face.

"Why? Oh," Garrett said, as the realization hit him.

"He has been watching her like a hawk all day. It has been pathetic but funny. Max is the ultimate optimist, and I think he really has a crush on that girl, even if he has only been with her for a few hours. And from where I stand, Casey has had nothing but eyes for you. Then you seem to be a little frustrated with your new assistant."

"So, do you enjoy watching and analyzing people?" Garrett said, smiling.

"I was just observing, but I have to admit it was very, shall we say, fascinating." Skylar tried not to laugh, keeping a slight smile on her face. "Now, what did you want to discuss?" she said, trying to sound assertive and in charge, but the man standing before her was so intriguing that it was hard for her to concentrate. Skylar hadn't really felt like this before so her emotions made her feel unsure of herself. She couldn't even describe what was happening in her mind as she stood there looking into Garrett's eyes.

"I was wondering if you would mind telling the real truth behind your boat charter business," Garrett said in such a matter-of-fact manner that the words shook Skylar back into the present moment.

"What do you mean?" Skylar said, immediately coming to her own defense.

"Is this really your boat, or is it your daddy's? Yesterday, I couldn't figure out how a girl your age could own such an expensive boat and be its captain. So when I got home last night, I did an Internet search, only to find out you aren't just the average boat captain. It seems you have a rich heritage in Miami. Do you want to give me the real scoop on what's going on here?" Garrett said, waving his hand at the boat they were standing on.

Skylar was at a loss for words as she stood looking at Garrett. Instead of being dreamy eyed as she was just seconds ago, now she was angry, defensive, and hurt.

"Did we not do a good job for you yesterday and today? That should tell you that you have hired the best out here. I don't have to explain my family and their business to you." Skylar was trying to keep her cool, but the words tumbled out so fast that they sounded like an attack.

"I didn't mean anything negative. Sorry for my poor choice of words, but you have to admit, there aren't many boat captains like you," Garrett said, as he thought she was the best-looking boat captain he had ever seen. "Plus, this boat is very pricey. Most that I've rented before were like rundown johnboats compared to this one, for the same price."

Skylar went and sat on one of the cushioned benches, anger still coursing through her while Garrett followed close behind.

"I've loved boats my whole life, but my family loves the real estate business. If you did your research *correctly*, I'm sure you read online that I am a realtor, or *was*, but it was only to satisfy my parents. About a year ago, I had this idea to start my own boat rental business, which didn't go over so well with the family. Then I found this boat and put a deposit on it immediately which really sent my father into a tizzy. I knew it needed some work but I was willing to fix it up. After a long talk, mostly with my dad, he agreed to help me fund my venture with a couple of stipulations. So for now, I'm a boat captain instead of selling beachfront homes."

"What stipulations?"

"You sure are getting pretty nosy, don't ya think?" Skylar said, finally letting her guard down some. The way he smiled back at her melted her inside and some of the anger she had felt only moments ago was fading away. "I have one year to make this business work and pay back the loan. If not, I promised to go back to selling real estate and working along with my parents, brothers, and sister."

Garrett could tell by the way she told her story and the look on her face that working in real estate wasn't what she wanted to do. And he didn't blame her. Plus, she was a natural on the water. But as he sat listening to her story, he couldn't help but realize just how beautiful this woman was. He could feel an instant attraction to her that he hadn't felt in such a long time that it actually made him a little anxious. He had only a brief summary of her situation, and he already wanted to make sure her dream came true.

"Well, it looks like you are off to a good start. I know that I didn't book the boat for tomorrow, but do you mind if I come along? You're taking snorkeling trips, right? Are you going to a different place along the reef?" Garrett asked for two different reasons: the first was to scout another location along the reef for diving, even if others would be there, and the second was so he could spend more time with Skylar to get to know her better.

"That's no problem. It's just a party of six in the morning for two hours, and then the afternoon is booked for seven people. There will be plenty of room." Skylar suddenly felt so comfortable with this man and was secretly glad that he was coming along tomorrow.

"Thanks for telling me your secret." Garrett grinned. "I think you are going to do well. Hell, you are in a great place for diving and snorkeling. Have you ever thought about fishing trips, since you are in the best fishing spot in the world? I have a feeling that your charters are going to keep you very busy."

"I sure hope you are right," Skylar said, as she made sure she locked everything tight for the night, and then she hopped down to the dock to walk to the parking lot.

They walked together in silence down the wooden planks, the atmosphere feeling quite awkward but also as though there was a bit of electricity flowing between them. They both could feel it as they each headed for their vehicles. Then they waved good-bye.

Garrett watched as Skylar got into an old yet beautifully restored pickup truck, expecting a much more luxurious vehicle, given her family's wealth. Hopefully, she would tell him more about her family in the coming days and weeks. There had to be more to the story she had just shared with him. Garrett genuinely wanted to get to know her, even if that uneasy feeling continued to follow him. The anxiety brought up some very hurtful memories, but remembering Skylar's lovely face seemed to partially ease the feeling.

Skylar looked in her rearview mirror to see Garrett getting into an old truck that looked at least thirty years old. It seemed to be in great shape, but she couldn't be sure. At least they had the same taste in vehicles, she thought, smiling to herself.

As she drove to her house, she could think of nothing but the man who was only the fourth person she had told the origins of her business. And why had she? Skylar could have come up with a number of ways to answer his questions without revealing all that she did, but she had felt comfortable talking to him. It was as if they were old friends instead of strangers who had just met for the first time the day before. This unnerved and excited her at the same time. No man had been on her radar since Andrew, and she had kept it that way purposefully. But Garrett was unusual. And she didn't care that he was ten years older than she was—something that Max had brought to her attention. To Skylar, when she was talking to Garrett, she felt as if she was talking to a friend.

And as she thought about tomorrow, she was secretly happy Garrett was coming along for both outings. She loved snorkeling tours more than dive trips because of the excitement that seemed to shine from people's eyes as they saw a fish or ocean creature in its own habitat for the first time. But Garrett being there would make it even better she thought, smiling to herself.

But then she recalled the conversation about her family. Skylar was surprised that none of her family had shown themselves in Key Largo during this first month. She had thought her father would make an appearance for sure, but the family almost acted as though they didn't want to be associated with an errant member. She wished she could say that it hurt her feelings, but it didn't. She had always been the oddball growing up in her affluent family, something she had come to terms with long ago. Plus, Key Largo was a little more than an hour away, and if business was as busy as her sister had said when they talked last week, Skylar probably wouldn't be seeing them for a while, which again was fine, even though she did miss them, especially her grandma.

As Skylar pulled up to her small house, she breathed a sigh of relief. They had survived their second day with Garrett and his intern. That was an accomplishment in her book. When he chartered the boat for such an extended period, she wasn't sure what to expect. Now it was time for some rest and a shower. And maybe she would read a book on the back porch by the canal where her own little boat was tethered. It was her very first boat that she had bought when she was only a teenager. But really, a book couldn't distract her from thinking about the handsome dark-haired man that would be joining her out on the sea once again tomorrow.

6

So she came from money but didn't act like it. Skylar was just the opposite of the opinion he had formed the night before after his extensive Internet search. The news that she had struck out on her own was very interesting. So far, Skylar was handling the boat well, but she was doing it with just two passengers. Tomorrow would tell whether she could handle a group of people, especially tourists that usually didn't know the difference between a snorkel and a fin. Garrett wanted to believe that this woman could handle it all, but he still hadn't made up his mind.

He plopped on the couch and shut his eyes, promising himself it was only for a few minutes, but the next thing he knew, his phone's alarm was sounding loudly. As he tried to focus on the phone, he finally saw that it was seven o'clock. He had slept through the night, without even eating dinner. Yesterday had been a long day, but he hadn't realized how tired he was. But he immediately thought of Skylar and the trip today without Casey, and energy surged through his body to get up and get to the dock to see whether he could be of any help. Maybe, just maybe, she would open up to him again. Max would be there, but he was usually busy. Though Garrett could have used a day to work on the computer, he found that he was looking forward to a day off, so to speak, and a day to spend with the beautiful dark-haired boat captain.

As soon as he drove into the parking lot, he spotted her truck. Garrett found himself walking quickly toward the boat and slowed down, not wanting to appear too anxious.

"Hi there," he said as he spotted her wiping down the seat cushions, with some music playing in the background.

"You're here early. We don't leave for another two hours," Skylar said. Her heart had begun thumping hard in her chest as soon as she saw him standing on the dock.

"I thought you might need some help. Have you ever taken out a group of tourists for a snorkeling trip before?"

"We've done quite a few and have done fine so far. Maybe there was a fin lost here or there, but on the whole, we did great. Meaning me and Max," she said quickly, trying to sound as confident as possible.

"I have taken lots of groups snorkeling before. I'll give you a few pointers, if you want." Garrett wanted to help but didn't want Skylar to think he was trying to say she didn't know what she was doing.

"So, what do you recommend?" Skylar said, watching as Garrett moved toward the equipment which still looked brand new.

Skylar followed Garrett as he talked about snorkeling, equipment, what she could do to make things go more smoothly, and more. Then he started talking about the fish and sea life they could probably see if they went here instead of there. She could tell that Garrett was very passionate about what he did because he kept talking. Skylar could barely get a word in, but it amused her too. She loved seeing people get wrapped up in something they loved, as she did when she talked about the ocean and boats. So here was a great-looking guy, who had been nice to her so far and loved his work. And best of all, he was going to be around for a while. Slow down, girl, Skylar thought to herself as ideas of romance started flooding her mind.

"I'm sorry. I just start rambling and sometimes, I can't stop. I've been accused of being married to my work. Kids have even called me the Fish Man" Garrett said, smiling and looking toward the dock. "Here comes your helper."

"Hey, Max," Skylar said as the young man came on board. "Garrett is going out with us today to snorkel with our groups. He showed me a few things we can do for our customers today."

"Good because I'm still a bit uncomfortable with big groups. I snorkel all the time with my friends, but with tourists, it's different. So, what do I do?" he said, looking at Garrett. Then Max suddenly had a look of excitement come across his face and asked, "Is Casey with you today?" Both Skylar and Garrett could hear the hope in his voice.

"No, she has the day off. She is only required to work three days per week but is insisting on working whenever I do."

"It's because she likes you!" Skylar said.

"What?" Garrett said, with a shocked look on his face.

"Oh, come on, Garrett. She followed you around like a puppy dog yesterday. I bet if she knew you were here today, she would be on deck, ready to go."

"No, it's nothing like that," Garrett said. "She is just an intern. Plus, she is Max's age and not my type."

"So, what is your type, Garrett?" Max said, looking over at Skylar.

If there had been something in Skylar's hand, she would have smacked her employee in the head.

"I'm not sure what my type is, Max, but I will try to steer Casey your way if I can. I'm not making any promises," Garrett said.

"Well, good luck with that. I already told Max that I'm pretty sure she has a big crush on her boss."

"There is no way. We have only worked together for one day!" Garrett said.

"It doesn't take long for the love bug to bite," Skylar said, laughing as she picked up her iPad with today's passenger list and walked into the cabin.

The day turned out to be gorgeous—there was a beautiful blue sky, and a perfect wind kept the ocean calm with small swells. Skylar loved days like this, wishing each time they went out to the reef that it could be like this.

Garrett had turned out to be a huge help. Both groups Skylar had taken to snorkel that day were a mix of those new to snorkeling and those with some experience under their belts. Max was great with the gear, Garrett described to the passengers what they could possibly see, and Skylar just made sure to answer any odd questions. She almost felt guilty that they were bombarding Garrett with so many questions, but he seemed to be in his element. When the passengers asked him about what they had seen below the surface, he gave them such detailed and passionate explanations that Skylar could tell he was a true marine biologist. The love for his work showed in how he could make the most mundane question into a fantastic story full of information and leave people wanting more.

As they cleaned up the boat from the day's excursions, they were tired, but Skylar was so excited that the day had been a complete success. With Garrett's help, she had learned a few things that she needed to do differently, and Max was the best first mate she could have ever asked for. For the first time since she purchased the boat, Skylar felt as if she was truly on the right path.

"I'm outta here, guys. See ya tomorrow, but Friday is off, right?" said Max as he hopped onto the dock.

"Yep! We have a tourist group on Saturday. This time it's scuba diving, so be prepared." Skylar smiled and waved as Max ran down the dock.

"Well, I would say that you had a very successful day, Skylar. And thanks for letting me tag along. I got to see another spot along the reef that I would like to check out, if we could go back there again." Garrett came and sat beside her.

"No problem. And thanks for all your help today. Both groups had such a great time with you. I couldn't have answered a quarter of the questions they asked about the fish and such. Thanks," Skylar said, as she glanced at Garrett. He looked mesmerizing in the setting sun, his hair disheveled from the seawater and wind, and his chin stubbly from having not shaved in a few days. Just looking at him made her heart race a bit. Secretly, she was so glad he had come along today. Not just to answer questions and help—she liked being around this man.

"You are welcome. I'd love to come Saturday too, if you don't mind. Are you going back to the same place again?"

"I think so. It will be an instructor with his new group of students. He will have his own helpers, so I'm just taking them to the reef. I had planned to work on some artwork while we are anchored. If you want to, you can dive with them. I don't see a problem with that." Unless you want to stay on board with me, she thought to herself.

"Fantastic! I can get some more info without Casey being there. She is helping me, but I didn't realize how much I like working by myself. I only agreed to the intern program to help a friend, but I feel like I'm babysitting. I'm sorry to complain. She is a nice girl but a bit clingy, and we have only worked together for one day! But she called me on the way home last night to make sure everything had gone like I expected, and she kept talking till I was walking into my apartment. Then she called this morning to make sure I didn't need her today." Now, if you had been the one calling me, I could have talked to you for quite a while, he thought to himself.

"Do you remember what I told you about the love bug earlier? She has a big crush on you."

"Well, she can crush on someone else," Garrett said, with a sigh. "So, what are you doing now?" he asked, the words coming out before he gave them any thought. But he knew why—he wanted to ask Skylar out. This was so unlike him that it startled him, but in the few short days they had been together, Skylar Cartwright was occupying more of his thoughts than any woman had in such a very long time, even though she was much younger than he was.

"I'm going home to a hot shower, a little dinner, and some TV."

"Do you want to grab a bite to eat instead?" Garrett asked hopefully.

Skylar immediately wanted to say yes but didn't want to sound desperate either. So she hesitated just a bit and then casually said, "Sure." Excitement pulsed through her body. "I look a mess, so nowhere fancy."

"I think you look perfect, and I also know the best place, since we are both covered in sea salt and a bit windblown."

Skylar just smiled at the compliment. "I'll follow you then."

The bar and grill Garrett led them to was just down the street from her house. She had been several times and loved the rustic atmosphere and savory food. But during the entire ride there, Skylar couldn't think about anything but the words Garrett had spoken: "You look perfect." The happiness and excitement that filled her was hard to describe.

7

As they walked into the bar and grill, they both decided on a table out back overlooking the water, even though they had been outside all day. The weather was still nice, and the sun was beginning its descent for the evening. They both ordered something to drink and sat gazing out over the water.

"I love the sea. You would think that after being on a boat all day, sitting by the ocean would be the last thing either one of us would like to do. I know salt water must run through my veins. It has to be in yours too," Skylar said, opening the conversation.

Garrett sat there quietly, staring at the water too. But not only because he loved the scenery—he found himself so unsure of what to say to the compelling woman sitting with him. He felt so awkward because he was usually the first to start talking, especially when it came to the water and his work. But as he sat across from Skylar, he wanted to know more about her instead, so he took the plunge.

"If you don't mind sharing, tell me more about your family. And about yourself."

At first Skylar was unsure that she should share any details but since Garrett had already researched her on the internet, she figured it didn't really matter. "I was born and raised in Miami. I already told you about my family's business and the deal with my dad. I have one year to make all this work, or I'll go back to selling oceanfront homes."

"From what I read on the Internet, your family is pretty prominent around here. I mean, I saw lots of pictures of you at high-society events. The person in those pictures looked totally different from the woman sitting across from me," Garrett said.

"Wow, you say that like it's a bad thing."

"No, I didn't mean it like that. It's just that the woman I saw on the Internet and the one sitting in front of me seem completely different."

Skylar sighed because Garrett was being very perceptive. He was right.

"Because she is. I love boats. I almost think I would live on one, but there are a few creature comforts I don't want to give up." She laughed, making Garrett smile too. "Do you know that instead of buying my first car, I bought an old boat? My brothers and sister thought I was loony. But I fixed it up and made it seaworthy. I had to ride a bicycle everywhere or hitch a ride, but I had my own boat. Then once I went to college, I studied marine biology. That really annoyed my parents because, of course, they wanted me to study business like my siblings. I did just enough to get by." As Skylar was telling her story, she realized that she was actually enjoying her time with Garrett. She couldn't get over the fact that no matter how he dressed, whether he was fresh in the morning or had been in the ocean all day, he always looked so handsome.

"Right now, though, my priority is to make sure this business is successful," Skylar said, with a heaviness in her voice.

"Why would you make a deal like that? Why can't you just go and do what you want to?" Garrett asked. He couldn't believe that a parent would demand such a thing from a child. This made him think of his mother and how she had always encouraged him to live out his dreams, if possible.

"According to my parents, I was born into privilege, and with that comes responsibility. I'm supposed to be like my parents—marry someone in my so-called social circle and follow in their footsteps. It's a complicated situation, which I'm hoping to sort out during this year away on the boat. I feel stuck and a bit guilty because I love my family. I don't want to disappoint them, but then, being in an office and going to social events almost every weekend is not the life I want. I'm so sorry for all the complaining. I am really blessed compared to so many others. I haven't discussed this with anyone except my friend Kim. But you are so easy to talk to. So now, it's your turn. What is your story?" Skylar looked over at Garrett, who was now looking at her instead of the water in front of them. But before he could answer, the waiter brought the burgers and French fries they had both ordered.

"My story is that I'm just a guy who loves the ocean...a bit too much, most people tell me," Garrett said, as he finished a bite of his sandwich. "I've been told that I talk too much about my work, but I love it."

"That's it?" Skylar said looking at him with raised eyebrows. "Come on. I told you mine. Details please."

Garrett had never talked much about his past with anyone because it was a mixture of good times and painful memories. "I grew up in Savannah, Georgia with my mom. When I was just a little boy, suddenly one day my dad left my mom and me. Just disappeared without even a note. I was so angry for the longest time but my mom was the positive one. I knew that she was so hurt because I could hear her crying at night but she was so strong in front of me. After I watched her for several years, working two jobs to make sure we had a roof over our heads and food to eat, I promised that when I got older, I would take care of her." Garrett stopped as he relived the painful memories and Skylar could see a hint of sadness in his eyes. She almost wished she hadn't pushed him to talk.

"But just before I graduated from high school, she met a great man named Gene. They instantly hit it off and before I knew, they were married. He has been wonderful to her and me. He has been the real dad in my life all these years."

"Did you ever hear from your father again?" Skylar asked apprehensively.

"No, never heard from him but found out later he had died somewhere out west. Apparently, he still had my mom listed as an emergency contact, after being gone over eight years. So that's how we found out he had passed away."

"I'm so sorry."

"Oh, it's okay. I can't say I wasn't mad at first but my mom was my real hero. We were like a team and thank goodness she loved the beach and ocean as much as I did. I think my love for the water really came from her because we went to the shore practically every weekend. It was a way for her to relieve the stress of our hectic life."

"Now you sound like me," Skylar said with a smile.

"So when I decided to go to college, I studied biology at the College of Charleston in Charleston, South Carolina. That way I wasn't too far from home. My friends thought I was weird because they were all going to schools to get away from their families. I wanted to stay close to take care of my mom but as time passed I could see that Gene was the best thing for her. Anyway, I got my Master's Degree in Marine Biology at the college too and began doing any kind of marine research wherever I could. I've been all over the world, even though at times I was barely getting by, staying wherever I could and sometimes eating next to nothing. But I loved the research I was doing."

Skylar was fascinated by his story and it felt so opposite of hers. Garrett had come from a broken home, made his own way and just scraped by at times. Here she was, with so much at her disposal. But they had one thing in common: they were following their dreams, determined not let anyone stop them.

"I've been in the Keys for almost two years now, and I have to admit, I love it down here. The coral reef restoration they are doing is amazing, and I am thinking about staying here to help after I turn in my research. It is so fascinating, and..." Garrett stopped when he realized that he was just about to go into one of his ocean talks. This was new to him—catching himself before saying anything. But for a reason he still couldn't explain, he wanted to impress the woman sitting across from him. And Skylar probably didn't want to hear about coral.

"And…"

"And what?" Garrett said, once again at a loss for words.

"You didn't finish your sentence," Skylar said, before taking a bite of a few french fries. She found his work interesting, especially since she had studied marine biology too.

"Doesn't it bore you?" Garrett said before he continued to eat.

"It wasn't boring at all."

"No, I have been warned about how I can get carried away when I start talking about my research, so I'm doing my best to catch myself so I don't put people to sleep," he said, with a smile.

"I think you just haven't been talking to the right people."

Skylar's last sentence sealed the deal for him. This girl was special. She was rare. And Garrett could admit to himself that for the first time in so long, he felt a genuine attraction for this woman. He really wanted to get to know her, letting his past heartaches be just that—in the past.

"What is it? Do I have ketchup on my face or something?" Skylar asked as she looked at Garrett, who seemed to be staring at her.

"No, you're fine. Sorry," he said quickly, almost stumbling over his words.

As the sun continued its descent over the horizon, they both finished their meals, mostly chatting about work. Skylar felt as if she had found a kindred spirit in Garrett. His love for the ocean seemed to match hers. For the first time, except for when she was in college, she had met someone who loved the water and its creatures as much as she. Skylar could feel a pull toward him, and she wanted to follow it. But she didn't want to seem like a little schoolgirl with a crush. Was she telling herself she had a crush on a man she had only met days ago? Without hesitation, her answer was yes.

"Here you go. You can pay up at the bar," the young man said as he laid their check on the table. They both reached for it, but Garrett got to it first.

"My treat tonight, Captain," he said, looking at her.

"I insist that we split it," Skylar said, but she knew that she had lost this tiny battle because he was already up and walking toward the bar.

"Hey, thanks for the dinner," she said as they each headed toward their own trucks. "It was nice to sit and just relax. It seems it's been a while since I've done that. Thanks again, and I'll see you tomorrow, bright and early."

"No problem. See ya tomorrow," Garrett said as he watched her get into her truck and drive away, thinking to himself that even though she was younger than him, and they definitely had completely different families, he was going to get to know Skylar as more than just a casual friend and the captain of the boat he rented for work. She was the woman he had been looking for even though he didn't know it.

8

Once again, the weather was perfect for a day at sea. Skylar was at the boat early, as usual, to make sure everything was ready for the day. And it wasn't long before Garrett was there too. They talked and laughed as he prepared his gear and she double- and tripled-checked the equipment after yesterday's snorkel trip.

As Casey walked up the dock toward the boat, she slowed down so she could hear the lively conversation and laughter. When she saw that it was Skylar and Garrett whose voices had carried down the dock, her blood pressure shot up. Skylar will not do this to me again, she thought to herself.

"Hi, everyone," Casey said as she boarded the boat. "It sounds like you guys are having a party."

"Hey, Casey," Garrett said, as he continued to look at the scuba equipment. "I'm glad you are here. I need help double-checking the gear to make sure everything is prepared for today."

"Of course," Casey said almost too sweetly, rushing to set her bags down to help Garrett.

"Good morning, Casey," Skylar said to the girl as she watched her. Skylar had to stop herself from giggling because it was beyond obvious that Casey had developed a serious crush on Garrett after working with him only one day. It seems Garrett is having that effect on me too, Skylar thought to herself.

"If you would, finish going through the gear while I talk to Skylar about where to drop anchor today," Garrett said, oblivious to Casey's infatuation with him.

"No problem," Casey said while looking over at Skylar with a stony face.

What is her problem? Skylar thought to herself as she watched the exchange. It was evident from the look Casey gave her that she didn't like Skylar in the least. Skylar didn't know why this was happening, but she still had that nagging feeling that she knew Casey but for the life of her, she couldn't make the connection.

"Hey, guys. Sorry I'm the last one here," Max said as he hopped on board. "Hi, Casey."

Casey acted as though she didn't hear Max, even though Skylar knew she did. Wow, this girl was a piece of work, she thought.

"Skylar," Garrett said.

"What?" she said as she suddenly saw Garrett standing beside her. "Sorry—I'm a little distracted."

"Let's look at the map to make sure we get the right spot for today's dive."

"Of course. Max, I've already checked out the boat, but give everything another look over before we leave. Thanks!"

They went into the small cabin area and looked over the map on the table. They were standing so close that Garrett could feel the heat coming from her body. It seemed as if small electric shocks were being delivered to his arm that was closest to her. He looked at her and saw her mouth moving, but he couldn't comprehend the words. It was as though Skylar had taken part of his reasoning mind and thrown it into the sea.

"If that sounds fine to you, I think we are ready to go," she said to Garrett, looking up into his eyes, which left her feeling as though she was hypnotized.

"I think so," Garrett said softly as they both continued to look at each other, not moving an inch.

"Garrett, everything is accounted for and ready," Casey said, suddenly breaking the awkward silence between the two of them.

"Great! Let's go," Skylar said as she rushed out of the cabin past Casey. Garrett stood there, watching her walk away and feeling out of place, especially with his intern watching him.

"Garrett, are you okay today?" she said, coming up to stand very close to him. She was really too close, as far as he was concerned.

"Yeah, sure. Let's go get ready." He walked out, with Casey following right on his heels. She could see what was happening between Garrett and Skylar. But she wasn't going to have it. Garrett might be older, but she really liked him. She wanted to get to know him as more than a boss, and she wasn't about to let Skylar get in her way and ruin this for her like Skylar had last time. Anyway, she knew Skylar's family, and they would have a fit if they knew their beloved daughter had fallen for a lowly researcher. But Casey would keep this bit of information to herself.

As promised, the weather and seas were beautiful, creating a great ride to the reef. Garrett and Casey were in their gear and ready by the time they dropped anchor. Garrett had even made a spot in the cabin for writing and note-taking once they came up from below. Skylar tried not to watch but couldn't help herself. Garrett was so intriguing to her, and watching Casey's major flirting attempts was making for a bit of a show. Skylar laughed inwardly because she knew there was no way that the dark-haired, sexy researcher would have eyes for either her or Casey. He was an admitted workaholic and older than both of them. Plus, Skylar knew that she couldn't get involved in a relationship at this point of her life—she had to put all her energy into this business.

As for Garrett's intern, Skylar didn't know Casey's agenda, and it wasn't Skylar's business. But she did feel a little sorry for Max. It was very clear that he liked Casey. As Skylar mulled over this situation, it was beginning to feel like a soap opera.

"What is so funny?" Garrett said as he walked up to her, with flippers in hand.

"Nothing. I'm just thinking about how beautiful it is out here." Skylar recovered as quickly as she could. But once again, her breath caught as Garrett faced her. He was making it hard for her to think straight as he looked back at her with his beautiful blue eyes.

"I guess you know the drill. We will be down about thirty minutes and then back up for some notations. If this proves to be a good site, I would like to contact my team while we are here," Garrett said as he checked his gear once more.

"No problem. We will be here," Skylar said as she sat in her captain's seat, watching him.

"See ya in a bit. Ready, Casey?"

"Of course!" the younger woman said while admiring her boss.

Before Skylar and Max knew it, the pair were once again falling backward off the boat and into the blue seawater below. Skylar loved to dive herself, but it had been a while because she had been working on starting this business while taking care of real estate deals. But suddenly, she wished she was the one diving with Garrett.

"So, what are we going to do? Is there anything you need done, Captain?" Max said, with a smirk.

"I think we just wait, you know that. And I know that if there was anything that we needed to do, you would have already done it. That is why you are the best employee ever," Skylar said, giving Max a great big smile.

"Man, I wish you would go ahead and admit you like the guy," Max said, shocking Skylar.

"Haven't we already been through this, Max? He's nothing more than a client and friend."

"Whoa! The other day you said he was just a client. Now he is a friend. I can see it when you talk to him. When he is around, you turn into someone I've never seen before. Just admit it—you like the guy. We men know these things."

Skylar let out a heavy sigh. "He's just a client, and he's nice. He loves the ocean as much as I do, or maybe more. He's all work and no—I'm not interested like *that*. I hate to tell you this, but I think Casey would like to have him to herself. She even gave me an nasty look this morning when I was talking to Garrett in the cabin. I'm not quite sure what to make of her yet, but I get this feeling like I know her. It's really weird."

"Yeah, I noticed that she is really into Garrett. But it doesn't mean I have to stop trying. She's pretty hot, and I love redheads," Max said, with a positivity in his voice that Skylar loved. Max had been this way ever since she had known him—he always saw the bright side of life. She loved the fact that he could always see the good in a situation. Right now, it seemed that he was determined to get Casey to notice him, one way or another.

"Good luck, Max. And I don't mean to judge, but she looks like she could be a handful, so prepare yourself."

"That doesn't bother me," he said as he walked away to look over the side of the boat, where Casey and Garrett were checking out the waters below.

Skylar brought out her iPad and began to work on the art piece she had started earlier in the week. But her thoughts always seemed to wander back to Garrett. Max was right, she told herself, but she wouldn't let him know. She did like the hunky marine biologist. What was she thinking! He wasn't interested in her. He was all about work, and besides, they were from completely different worlds, even though Skylar preferred Garrett's to hers. The thought made her suddenly feel guilty.

Her family had always been there for her, even if they had been controlling at times. When her father offered to help her start a business, Skylar had been beyond excited, but she knew in her heart that he didn't think she would succeed. And if she didn't, he could write off the whole affair as a loss and never lose sleep. He would have proven his point to his wayward daughter. Suddenly a small bit of fear seeped into her mind. Had she been crazy to strike out on her own? What if she did fail? But Skylar didn't have long to mull it over before she heard voices beside the boat.

"It's beautiful down there today! We saw fish, several sea turtles, and a big-ass shark. Casey, you were a great help today. Let's get in here and take notes before we forget," Garrett said, apparently in full work mode, which actually appealed to Skylar. He quickly got out of his gear, dried off, and set to work, with Casey so close behind him that it was a wonder she never ran into his back. Skylar and Max just stood out of the way, watching the pair work.

"Let's get a snack and sit on the bow," Skylar told Max, as she continued to watch Garrett and his charge.

Garrett and Casey did three more dives, working more furiously than the previous trip that they had been on, Skylar noticed. It was as if Garrett was in a zone all of his own. She didn't even think Casey realized that Garrett was thinking of nothing other than the work before him. He was like a man on a mission, and Skylar loved seeing him work so intensely on something he was fiercely committed to. He went at his research with all that he had while loving every minute of it. That was what Skylar wanted in her life—she wanted what she loved to do to absorb her completely, to the point that if she had to do it for free, she would do it gladly, no questions asked. From the way Garrett focused on his work, this must be his thought exactly.

The ride back to the dock was quiet, each person watching the ocean and scenery around them. They passed a few other diving boats and a few snorkeling groups. It was busy this time of year, Skylar thought thankfully, as she went over in her head the different trips she had planned during the next several weeks. If the weather was cooperative, hopefully each trip would be a success. But her main client was Garrett, whom she worked around as she scheduled more snorkeling and scuba tours. A tiny part of her wished he was on every trip she and Max took out to sea.

"It sounds like you had a pretty good day," Skylar said to Garrett as everyone loaded their gear into bags.

"It was actually. I have enough work to keep me busy for a few days now. I guess we will see you again next Monday. How is your work schedule?" Garrett asked, hoping he might tag along as he had the other day.

"I have two scuba trips on Saturday. Tomorrow is an errand day, and Sunday we take off, if at all possible."

"I would love to come on the scuba trip on Saturday, if you have room," Garrett said softly, while looking at Skylar. Even though he had been in total work mode today, he had noticed her every time he came up from a dive. She had pulled her chestnut-colored hair back in a ponytail, which showed her slender neck and slightly tanned, creamy skin. And her eyes—they were like emeralds, and they captured him every time Skylar looked his way. All these feelings for a girl he had practically just met overwhelmed Garrett a bit, but they also made him feel a different kind of happiness that had eluded him for so long.

"I would love to come too. It would be nice to dive for pleasure instead of work," Casey said quickly as she slid right next to Garrett, so close that they looked like a couple instead of an employee and an intern.

"Well, actually, I only have room for one more person, and Garrett did ask first," Skylar said, knowing that she was telling the truth and so glad that Garrett had asked. "If anyone cancels, you are more than welcome to come along, Casey. I'll have Max call you if something opens up." Skylar was looking at Casey straight on and could tell by the pursing of her lips that this news didn't sit well, but Skylar couldn't help being secretly glad Casey wouldn't be coming. The girl was beginning to get on her nerves, and even though he hadn't said anything, Skylar could tell from Garrett's body language that he needed a break from his eager intern after only two days.

"No problem," Casey said, once again using a voice that seemed to drip honey. "Garrett—could you help me carry this gear to my car?"

"I would be glad to, if that's okay," Max said before Garrett could utter a word. "I was getting ready to leave anyway, unless you need me to do anything else, Skylar."

"Uh, okay," Casey said weakly, knowing that there was no way out of this situation. And Max had no idea what he had just done. As for Skylar, she stifled a small smile, and as she glanced over at Garrett, he seemed to have no clue as to what had just happened.

"See you Monday, Casey, and at the same time. Have a great weekend," Garrett said as he watched her and Max walk down the dock. Casey looked back at him with a look of irritation.

"What is her problem?" Garrett said as he finished packing his things.

"You still don't get it. That girl likes you, not just as a friend or boss but *likes* you. I tried to warn you the other day, but you didn't listen. I bet she was ready to ask you out or something when you walked her to her car. I just hope she doesn't break Max's heart. He is such a sweet guy."

"Do you mean that Max likes Casey that much?" Garrett looked at her with confusion.

Skylar started laughing. "You are totally oblivious to what is going on around you unless it's a sea turtle."

"It just sounds too complicated to me," Garrett said, shaking his head. Maybe that was why his past relationships had never worked and why he should try to stop forgetting that the captain of his rental boat was messing with his mind and possibly his heart.

"I agree with you there. For some reason, she certainly doesn't like me, and I can't figure out why."

"Don't ask me. I seem to be clueless in this whole thing."

"Well, at least you know now why Casey sticks to you like glue. But if you aren't interested in her, you need to let her down as gently as possible since you two will be working together for a while."

"I'm certainly not interested in her at all. She works with me—that's it." I can't quit thinking about you, Garrett said to himself.

"Then I'll give you some friendly advice. You might want to talk to her soon. Let her know where you stand about relationships on the job. Then for the rest of the time you are working together, it might be a bit easier on both of you. Nip her crush on you before it grows too big."

Garrett offered his hand to Skylar to help her off the boat and onto the dock. "Y'all are complicated."

"Who do you mean by 'y'all'?" Skylar said quickly.

"Women!"

"We could say the same for men. You guys confuse the hell out of us sometimes."

They both started laughing just as they reached Skylar's vehicle.

"Skylar, I need to tell you something," Garrett said before she could open the door.

"What is that?"

"When I first met you, I really didn't think you had a clue what you were doing. I'm just being honest because I had never been out with a female boat captain. But you have done a great job this week, so I apologize." Garrett looked at her with sincerity that made her heart melt.

"Thanks, Garrett. That means a lot. So, I'll see you on Saturday?" Skylar asked silently hoping he would say yes.

"Definitely. I wouldn't miss it!"

9

Skylar's Friday was full to the brim doing errands, fetching supplies for the boat, getting groceries, confirming boating trips, and so much more. But even though she was busy, she couldn't stop the thoughts of Garrett that were constantly in her mind. She could see him standing by the side of the boat. His dark hair was wet and slicked back. A little bit of stubble shadowed his chin. Those piercing blue eyes. The muscles of his arms and chest, both taut and strong. And the slight tan he had seemed to highlight his huskiness with each move he made. Skylar couldn't forget the way Garrett sounded when he talked or how he now considered her capable in a business field that consisted mostly of men. All of this made her feel good, and she couldn't help but finally admit that she was attracted to this man. But she also had to remember that he was a client, and that came first and foremost. But as Skylar fell asleep that night, tired from such a busy day, thoughts of the handsome researcher filled her head.

The next morning, as per her routine by now, she was at the boat early. It was almost as if the water vessel was part of her family, and each time she saw it, it made her smile. If only it had the same effect on her parents, then everything would be almost perfect in her world.

"Good morning!" Skylar heard a voice coming from the dock and immediately knew it was Garrett.

"Hi there," she said, turning to see Garrett, holding two cups and a paper bag, along with a huge tote on his shoulder.

"I thought you might like some coffee and a muffin. I wasn't sure what kind you liked, so I bought a few different ones."

"Thanks. I'm not much of a coffee drinker, but the muffins sound wonderful!"

"You have your choice of blueberry, banana, or apple cinnamon—you pick first. As for the coffee, I'll drink it. I stayed up a bit late last night going through papers and making notes for a report I have to turn in." And also thinking about you, Garrett said to himself as he watched Skylar walk toward him. Damn, she was beautiful. The contrast of her glossy brown hair and bright-green eyes was stunning, but he also noticed everything else about her—her soft skin, the sway and sexiness of her walk, and her smile that seemed to bring joy to everything around her.

"That works out well. I have my own drink here." Skylar smiled at him so innocently, and he couldn't help but smile back. But it wasn't till she heard a third voice that they both realized that they had been standing there, just staring at each other.

"Hey, guys! I thought I would take a chance and see whether there was any room. Maybe someone won't show up today." It was Casey—Skylar could recognize that voice anywhere by now.

"Hi, Casey," she said as nicely as she could, as she turned to see her waiting to come on board. Skylar then turned back to Garrett, who was standing there with an I-don't-know-what-to-do look on his face.

"The first group should be here in about an hour, and then, we will know."

"Then I'll just hang out with both of you till then, okay?"

Garrett could suddenly feel the frustration building. He had come to the boat early, knowing that he would probably have some time alone with Skylar. But if Casey was going to wait to see whether anyone canceled, then this would be an awkward hour.

And Garrett finally saw what Skylar had been trying to tell him all week. From the moment she stepped on board, Casey talked nonstop only to him, not letting Skylar say anything. So Garrett watched as Skylar moved to the bow of the boat, checking on things by herself till Max could arrive.

It wasn't long before Max and then the group of fourteen divers and their instructor showed up on the dock. Garrett watched as Skylar greeted each one so professionally. He couldn't help but smile as he watched. Then he felt someone standing extremely close beside him, and he didn't have to guess who it was.

"Whatcha looking at?" Casey asked in a sickly sweet voice.

"I'm watching the other boats. It seems like everyone is going out today since the weather is so nice." Garrett wanted to keep the conversation as sterile as possible because now he was afraid that one wrong move, look, or word could give his intern a very wrong impression about their working relationship.

"Hey, Casey," Max said as he joined the two divers watching the other boats leaving the marina. "I'm really sorry, but Skylar told me to let you know that everyone has shown up, and there won't be room for an extra person. I'm really sorry because I was hoping you could go with us today. I have my own boat, though, if you would like to go out tomorrow. There are a few of us going out to snorkel." As Garrett listened, he could hear the nervousness in Max's voice, and he realized that Max truly liked Casey. It seemed that as each minute ticked by, the situation was getting more complicated.

"Well, that's a shame I can't go today," Casey said, while contorting her face into a pout. "And I'll have to let you know about tomorrow, Max. It depends on whether Garrett needs me." Garrett felt a hand on his arm and looked down to see Casey caressing his forearm. He quickly moved to the side, out of Casey's reach.

"No, I'm fine. We don't work again till Monday, so go snorkel with Max and have a good time." There. Hopefully, she might take the hint.

"I'll let you know, Max. I still have your number from the other day. I guess I'd better go. I'll see you later, Garrett." Casey gave him a sly smile and a delicate wave and then turned to disembark. But not before giving Skylar an icy glare.

"Thanks, Max, for telling her. She certainly doesn't like me, but I know I shouldn't have done that to you. I promise that next time, I'll speak up," Skylar said to her young friend. She had been too busy to deliver the news to Casey but glad that she didn't have to be the one to do it. She had a feeling that she and Casey would not become best friends anytime soon.

"That worked out perfectly," Garrett said, coming up behind her.

"Did it? How so?" Skylar said, with a quick smile.

"Uh...now...uh...I can dive and not be bothered. And... uh...I can help if you need it." Garrett was quickly trying to come up with reasons as to why he was glad the redheaded girl had left, potentially leaving him more time with the real woman he wanted to get to know better. Garrett didn't care that there were fifteen other people on board. He only knew that each day, the desire to be with Skylar and learn all he could increased tenfold. Even the negative memories of his past weren't enough to shove these growing feelings aside, as he watched Skylar expertly guide the boat out of the marina toward the ocean.

Both scuba trips of the day were so successful that Skylar's confidence in her business and herself was growing. She would have much to talk about at her family's dinner tomorrow. Each week since starting this business, she seemed to be the topic of conversation at the Sunday gatherings at her old family home. And she was sure that tomorrow would be no different.

She had watched all day as Garrett was once more the hit of both trips. Even the scuba instructor and his assistants were amazed at the information he shared and loved his enthusiasm. Even Max, who had been on board with her while the others dived, listened closely, once everyone was back onboard, as Garrett explained everything they had just seen in the waters below.

"Miss Cartwright, you have a great boat, and this was such an enjoyable experience. I've rented other charters, and this is by far the nicest. I will contact you next week about my upcoming schedule, and I would like to talk to you about contracting all my scheduled classes with you, if possible," said Mike Gibbons, the dive instructor, before turning to Garrett. "Also, thanks so much for the information you shared with everyone. It was a wonderful treat to have a real marine biologist with us today."

"I enjoyed it," Garrett said, with a big smile on his face.

"Thanks, Mike. We will talk next week, and I would love to work with you. Take care, and have a nice weekend," Skylar said, barely containing her excitement as she watched Mike walk down the dock. As soon as he was out of earshot, she turned and impulsively hugged Garrett with happiness. But she quickly realized what she had done and backed away.

"I'm so sorry! I was just excited about another possible contract for the boat! Yes!"

"I'm not sorry," Garrett said, with a sly smile.

"Um…is it okay for me to leave? Everything is in place, and I think you have everything under control here," Max said, trying not to laugh.

Skylar's cheeks were heating up and surely becoming blood red. She had hugged Garrett out of excitement, but the feel of her arms around him caused her to feel weak from head to toe. Especially when he had put one hand on her waist.

"Of course, Max, I'm sorry. Thanks for everything, and see you on Monday."

"Enjoy the family dinner tomorrow," Max said before jumping off the boat and running up the dock.

"What family dinner?" Garrett looked at her quizzically.

"My family has dinner each Sunday where I grew up so we can all get together. My two brothers and sister come, along with their girlfriends and Mara's husband, Paul. We just spend some time together and talk about what happened during the week. We might work together, but we don't see each other as often as people think. My mom started the Sunday dinners when we were in college, at the insistence of my Grandma and it has stuck ever since. Although I'm the first child to step out of the nest, so to speak." Skylar's description of dinner and her family sounded so nice to Garrett since he had never experienced a big family, but he could hear a little apprehension in Skylar's voice.

"You don't sound too thrilled, and you should be excited. Look at what you have accomplished this week. Your parents will be ecstatic," Garrett said, trying to cheer her up.

"But you don't know my mom and dad. I love them dearly, I truly do, but they really believe that I'm a rebellious child throwing a temper tantrum," she said, motioning to the boat around her. "That's why I want to prove to them that this is where I belong. And just because I charter a boat, or possibly one day a fleet of boats, doesn't mean that my love for them is any less. Or that their friends won't still appreciate them."

"What about their friends? Do they worry about what they will think? Because you have a boat business?" Garrett asked, trying to understand.

"It's a Miami social thing. These parties, events, gatherings—it always seems everyone is trying to one up each other instead of being true friends. I grew up in it, and I have been the dutiful daughter, but once I found my best friend in college, who wasn't born into a prominent family, I got to see the type of family life I wanted. Don't get me wrong. I loved the trips we took and some of the luxuries that others never get to experience, but I guess I just want a simpler life." Skylar sat back on the cushioned seat, while Garrett sat down beside her, so close that she shivered inside. "I think that is why I was the oddball kid growing up. No one could fathom my love for the beach, the ocean, or boats. Sorry, I've talked too much. I probably sound like a spoiled brat."

"No, you don't. You sound like someone who wants to make her own way in this world, even if you might fail. To me, that is someone who is brave, especially since you have so much at your disposal. Not once have you ever come across as spoiled. A spoiled person would be someone who bought a boat and hired a captain. And someone who was driving a Mercedes instead of a used truck." Garrett was smiling at her, which once again gave her a sensation inside that she had never known before.

"There's one thing I do have to ask, and I hope you don't think it is too personal," Garrett said.

"Sure!"

"Is there a boyfriend in this mix?" he said, glancing sideways at her.

Skylar hesitated, looking at the deck of the boat. "Well, there was till he found out about my grand boat charter plan. Then for some reason, he decided that he was going on a trip to Europe for a few months with friends and that it would be best if we broke off our relationship and reevaluated everything when he returned home. The timing was just a little too convenient, so I knew that he thought this business was beneath him." Skylar had looked down the whole time she recounted the story to Garrett, not wanting to see any pity in his eyes.

"He sounds like an idiot to me. If he could just see you out here in your element and your expertise with the boat, he would change his mind quickly." Garrett said it to cheer her up but felt a small pang of jealousy. Each day, he was coming to think of Skylar as more than a friend, even though neither of them had ever said anything. They hadn't even been out on a proper date. Plus, she was so much younger, maybe ten or eleven years. He had tried to see her as a little sister, but to no avail. All he could see was a beautiful, bright woman sitting next to him, who seemed to speak to his heart. She spoke his language about life and shared a similar passion for the sea. There was no way this was a coincidence. And never had he felt so free to be himself. When he found himself talking on and on about his work, she didn't complain but seemed genuinely interested. But then he would catch himself changing the subject to something completely different. This was out of character for him, but he found it so easy to do with Skylar.

"I found out a few weeks ago, at a family dinner, that he is back in town," Skylar said, rolling her eyes. "And that he is already engaged to a girl named Alicia, who used to be a friend of mine. She is very much into the Miami social life, something Andrew—my ex-boyfriend—loves. I think he lives off of the attention."

"Sorry. I didn't mean to bring up such a sensitive subject." Garrett hated that she was reliving something hurtful, but he was glad to know that she was unattached.

"So, what about you, Mr. Fish Man, as the people called you today. Is there anyone special in your life, waiting for you on land?" Skylar said, laughing and giving him a slight punch in the arm.

"Nope. It's just me. I'm working too much to get very involved. I had some past relationships, but things never really panned out," Garrett said.

"Oh do tell," Skylar said. "I told you my secrets."

"It was a very long time ago. Just something that didn't work out. She went her way and I went mine. Not much to tell," Garrett said. Skylar could see in his eyes there was much more to the story but decided not to push him any farther for details at the moment.

"Can I ask another personal question?" Garrett asked.

"I guess."

" How old are you?"

"How old do you think I am?" Skylar asked, already knowing his age from the papers he had signed to rent the boat—thirty-nine years old.

"Aww, don't do that to me. That is such a trick question for a guy. Okay—are you twenty-six?" he said, wincing slightly.

"You are so sweet. No, actually, I'm twenty-nine, turning the big 'Three O' this year. Why do you ask?"

"I was wondering whether you would like to go on an official dinner date with me. I would like to spend more time with you off the boat," Garrett said, with a smile, his nerves jittery and his palms sweating. He had never before been this nervous when asking a woman to go out on a date.

"I think that would be nice, but I have a pretty full plate till next Friday. Would that be okay?" Skylar said as calmly as she could, but the excitement welling up inside of her could hardly be contained. She didn't care that he was almost ten years older than she was. She liked being around him. They shared so many of the same interests, and he made her smile and laugh. Garrett was easy to talk to and what made it even better, he was so easy on the eyes.

"Then next Friday it is. There is this little restaurant on the water in Islamorada called the Lorelei. Have you been there before? It's a bit of a drive, but it's a casual place with great service and good food. Plus, they are on the beach."

"I love it there. It sounds like fun, and I would very much like to go."

"And just where are you two going that sounds like so much fun?" Both Skylar and Garrett looked up to see Casey standing on the dock, apparently listening to their conversation.

Skylar was speechless, so Garrett took control of the situation.

"What are you doing here? I thought you would head off to Miami since we weren't working," Garrett said as nicely as he could while he strode over to the edge of the boat. Skylar got up quickly to get her tote bag and secure the cabin.

"I decided to stay with a friend in Key Largo for the weekend. I just happened to be driving by and saw the boat was docked. I wanted to make sure everything went okay today." The artificial sweetness of her voice made Skylar almost sick to her stomach. She knew that this girl was up to no good, and Skylar wished she could remember why she was so familiar.

"It was a good day—great weather, calm seas, and a bunch of people who got to scuba for the first time, with Garrett giving them plenty of info about what they had seen below," Skylar said as nicely as she could to the younger woman, who was now standing on the boat with them.

"That sounds just wonderful! Maybe next time, I could come too. That way your passengers could benefit from both our knowledge," Casey said as she slid up next to Garrett, getting as close as she could as seemed to be her habit by now. She was so close in fact that Skylar thought she would suddenly wrap her arms around him. From the look on Garrett's face, he was very uncomfortable.

"So, where are you two going?"

"Right now, I'm heading home," Skylar said. "It's been a long day, and I have to drive to Miami tomorrow to spend the day there. Everything is locked and secure. See you both on Monday." She looked at Garrett with a smile, then back at Casey. Suddenly, the thought of spending the next few months with her was sounding a little hard, but at the same time, she consoled herself with the fact that she would be spending more time with Garrett.

Garrett watched as Skylar walked down the dock, giving her a small wave when she looked back at him on the boat. "Well, what are you doing now?" Casey said, looking up at Garrett like a love-sick schoolgirl. Garrett remembered Skylar's words about Casey and decided to take this time to clarify their relationship.

"Casey, I think it is time that we had a talk," Garrett said, motioning to her to sit on the cushioned bench.

"Why don't we go to the bar and grill down the street. Maybe we can have a drink."

"I don't think that would be such a good idea." Boy, this was going to be harder than he had imagined.

"What's wrong?" Casey said very innocently.

"I just feel that we need to keep our time together as professional as possible. I don't usually work with an intern, and I took you on as a favor to a friend. He said you needed the experience for school." Garrett sighed, hoping that he was saying the right thing, because he felt as if he was jumbling his words.

"I don't see why we couldn't go out for a bite to eat. That is, unless you don't want to," Casey said.

"I just think it is better to keep this as only a working relationship. You make a great assistant, and I don't want to confuse things." Or give you the wrong idea, Garrett thought.

Casey stood up quickly. "I'm sorry that you feel that way. I thought maybe we might have had a connection, but I can see I'm wrong. Does Skylar have anything to do with this?"

"Skylar. We are friends, but really, that is between me and her."

"So, you like her, don't you?" Casey said, sounding hurt and a bit angry.

"Casey, that is my personal business." Garrett didn't mean to sound cold, but the girl was quickly frustrating him.

"Thank you for clarifying things for me. I'll see you on Monday, Mr. Holmes," Casey said and quickly jumped off the boat and walked down the dock.

"This is why I have avoided women for so long," Garrett said to himself. But he quickly replaced the conversation he had just had with Casey with the thought that Skylar had agreed to go out with him. It had been so long since he had had a real date that even though it was a few days away, he could feel himself getting excited already. He would even have to go through his closet to see if he had anything decent to wear for a date. Since he was actually taking a day off tomorrow, he would look through his clothes then. A day off was unusual for him and he wasn't sure what he was going to do, but he knew one thing was certain: Skylar Cartwright would be a constant thought in his mind—that was a given

10

Skylar walked into the huge, beautiful house on Key Biscayne that her parents had owned since before she was born. It was built in the early seventies, but no one would ever know because her parents always kept everything in the house up-to-date and modern, just the way her mom liked it. If Skylar had her way, she would have kept some of the old-Florida charm that the house once had when she was growing up, but she had to admit it was a stunning piece of real estate. She had even had a client at one time ask about buying the house, not knowing that she was living there at the time. Skylar now had her own apartment nearby that she was currently leasing while she stayed in Key Largo for the next year. That was one thing her dad did praise her for—she was at least making some money on her property while she was on hiatus from the family's company. "Hi, Maggie," Skylar said as she rounded the corner into the spacious kitchen that was filled with wonderful smells.

"Hello, Skylar," the older woman said as she hugged her tightly. "I sure have missed you."

"I just saw you last week," Skylar said, smiling as she reached over to take a piece of warm bread that Maggie had just pulled out from the oven.

"Mmm, these are divine. Try as I might, I still can't get mine to turn out as good as yours."

"You are a sweetheart!"

"So, what is for dinner today?"

"Your father has decided to grill steaks with Paul out by the pool. The rest is salad with honey-mustard dressing, roasted green beans with a hint of garlic, baked potatoes with your choice of toppings, and Lyla talked her grandfather into homemade ice cream with wafer cookies." Maggie told Skylar the menu as she continued to work, smiling the whole time. She was always so cheerful, and Skylar loved being around her.

"It sounds a little basic but good compared to what Mom usually wants for Sunday dinners. And I'm glad that Lyla is here. She likes the little things, like I do."

"You always have, my dear, since you were a little girl. I have to say, that's why you are my favorite!" Maggie whispered into Skylar's ear when she hugged her again.

Skylar continued to walk through the spacious house where she had grown up. Most people would have considered it a mansion, but to her, it was her childhood home. As she went through the French doors that led to the patio and pool, a set of little arms wrapping around her legs greeted her. Skylar looked down to see her sweet niece, Lyla, looking up at her with a beautiful smile and big blue eyes, while her long curly blond hair fell down her back. Lyla was a sweetheart, and Skylar told her sister, Mara, that Lyla would make the perfect child model. Now her adorable niece had graced the cover of several magazines and catalogues.

"So, how is my favorite little person in the whole world?" Skylar said, picking up the small girl and giving her a squeeze.

"Fine. Pop-Pop is making hamburgers. Do you want one?" the four-year-old asked while wrapping her little arms around Skylar's neck.

"Let's go see if he will make one for me," she said as they walked toward the grill, where Skylar's father stood with tongs in hand.

As she looked around, today's gathering seemed to be more of an outdoor barbecue instead of their normal family dinner, but the spring weather was good for it. The next-door neighbors were here today too, along with her sister, Mara, Mara's husband, Paul, and her younger brother, Chase, with his girlfriend, Blair. Her brother Harris had yet to show. She figured he, along with his fiancé, Tracey, would have been here already since they owned the house around the corner. But just as she thought the words, they both popped through the door. Everyone gathered around the pool and the grill.

"Hi, Dad," Skylar said, giving her father, Jonathan, a quick kiss on the cheek. "Where is Mom?"

"Upstairs, I think. Even though we are keeping it a bit casual today, you know how she likes to get dressed up. How is the boat? How are your bookings?"

That was her dad—always thinking about business, at least most of the time. And she surmised that since he had a small stake in her boat, he had every right to ask.

"Actually, the business is really good. The marine researcher signed a six-month contract, and thanks to his help, a local scuba instructor wants to talk to me next week about being his main charter boat for his students. Plus, local hotels and businesses are helping by letting me put up flyers and business cards." Why was she so nervous as she talked to him about her business? Skylar knew in her heart that even though he didn't want his little girl to fail, he wanted her back under the family's umbrella. But this little taste of freedom had let Skylar know that even if her boating business didn't take off as she hoped, the taste of freedom from her family was wonderful. But that thought also made her feel guilty. Her family was precious to her, but Skylar just didn't have the same dreams as her siblings and most certainly not her parents. Why did she have to be the one out of sync with the rest of the family? Or was that really such a bad thing?

"That sounds promising. I'll have to come down soon so you can take me out on the boat."

"Anytime! Just let me know!" Skylar said, excited that she could show off her skills to her father but a little intimidated at the same time.

"Hey, little sis!" Harris said, hugging her. He was so tall that the top of Skylar's head barely reached his shoulder. Tracey was close behind, giving Skylar another hug. "It looks like that ocean air is agreeing with you. It feels weird, though, not having you around the office."

"It's a little strange for me too, but I love it in Key Largo. I feel so at home on the boat. Now I can just imagine my own fleet of charter boats. How does Cartwright Boating sound?" Skylar laughed with her older brother. But then she looked at

Tracey. "How are the wedding plans coming along?" She was a wonderful girl, and Skylar thought how lucky Harris was to have Tracey after the shenanigans he had pulled during his teen years and twenties. But he was settling down now, and soon, her older brother would be married. According to both Harris and Tracey, they were ready to start a family right away, which would make her parents very happy and give Lyla a cousin to play with.

"Really, everything is planned and ready. I have a feeling it is going to be hectic during those few weeks before, but I'm leaving it all to the wedding planner. I'm just not that organized, unless I'm at the art studio," Tracey said sweetly. Tracey was an exquisite jewelry artist, and she sold her creations around the world. She was also a favorite with a few celebrities. Being creative was something that she and Skylar had in common, but they had also become friends while she had dated Skylar's eldest brother.

"Let me know if I can help. I know I'm not close by, but I'll do what I can."

"Thanks, Skylar, but as long as you are there with your bridesmaid dress on, that's perfect."

"We just have to have a bachelorette party," Mara said, joining the conversation. Skylar had to admit Mara was the perfect older sister and the two got along great. Except for differing hair color, the two sisters looked very much alike. "Please have one. I need some girl time that does not consist of mommy-and-me classes," she said, leaving all three women laughing and nodding their heads in agreement.

"Who is having a party?" Chase said, as he and Blair walked up to the ever-growing group near the barbecue. Even though Chase was Skylar's little brother, his light blonde hair and blue eyes made it seem as though they were from different families.

"It's a party where Blair is invited, but you are definitely not. It will be a night of fun for us girls to celebrate before Tracey decides to make herself a Cartwright."

"Then that means I get a bachelor party, right?" Harris said.

"I trust you," Tracey said before kissing Harris on the lips.

"Uncle Harris, I want a kiss too!" said Lyla adamantly, who was now in the center of the group.

"I think I can manage that," he said, picking up the small girl, giving her a kiss on the cheek, and then proceeding to tickle her.

"Everything is ready in here, if the steaks are done."

Skylar turned to see her mother standing in the doorway, looking beautiful as ever but prim and proper too. Though she loved her mom, she and Skylar couldn't be more polar opposites. Skylar was fine without makeup, keeping her hair in a ponytail and wearing T-shirts, shorts, and flip-flops. Her mom, on the other hand, had to be dressed to the nines each day, her hair neatly in place and her makeup on. It was the way her mother was brought up, and Skylar accepted that, though there were times when she wished her mom would just relax a bit. But Skylar had learned long ago to accept her just as she was.

Everyone headed to the big dining room, where all the other food was beautifully lined up on the table, waiting for the steaks her dad had grilled, along with a piece of chicken for Skylar and a hamburger for Lyla. Maybe her little niece would follow in her footsteps and be an out of step Cartwright as she was, Skylar thought. The dainty girl definitely had a mind of her own already.

As everyone sat down and started passing food around the table, Skylar took a minute to take it all in. Though she had seen her family at dinner these last few weeks, she had been used to seeing them every day for the last twenty-nine years of her life. She didn't know whether she would call it homesickness, but as she watched everyone, Skylar did miss being with her family each day. But then she quickly thought about her boat, the beautiful waters of the ocean, and now, most of all, Garrett. Thinking of Garrett made her wonder how he would fit into the people around her today. She wasn't sure, but then, she might find out one day. Goodness, they hadn't even been out on a date, and she was daydreaming about him meeting her family. She quickly shook her head at the silly thought.

"What's wrong?" Skylar's mother said.

"Oh, nothing. I'm just thinking."

"It must have been something good because you were in some very deep thought with a smile on your face."

"It's been a very busy week." Skylar was trying hard to steer the conversation away from her errant thoughts.

"So, how is it down in Key Largo?" Sadie, her mom, asked.

"It's great so far. The charters are coming along nicely. My little rental house down there was available, so I fixed it up and decided to stay there. It's on the canal, so I have my small boat moored outside behind the house. The business has been keeping me pretty busy, but I'm not complaining."

"We have already named Skylar's empire—Cartwright Boating. How does that sound, Dad?" Harris said.

"We'll see," her father said in a monotone that let everyone know that this topic of conversation wasn't sitting well with him.

"I haven't even seen the boat or your house," Harris said.

"I have a few pictures on my phone. I'll show them to you after we eat."

The conversation quickly turned to other topics, letting Skylar off the hook and allowing her to relax just a little. There was no way she wanted to talk about her boat and Key Largo during dinner. Everyone knew what a rift this had caused, even if they didn't want to admit it, so why Harris brought up the company name was beyond her. She was only glad that she was no longer the center of attention.

As they scooped out homemade vanilla ice cream from the ice-cream maker and added assorted toppings to their bowls, Skylar heard her baby brother say, "I want to see the pictures of the boat."

Skylar squeezed her eyes shut to quell the slight anxiety rising up from the pit of her stomach and found some photos on her phone. She was so proud of her boat and her little house in the Keys. She hoped and prayed her siblings and parents would love them as much as she did, even though she knew she didn't need their approval.

"Wow, Skylar, the boat is awesome!" said Chase as he flipped through the pictures, with Blair by his side.

"I love the house too," said Blair. "Hey, who is that?"

Skylar took the phone from Chase and looked. She had accidentally taken a picture of Garrett, shirtless and standing in what seemed to be a model's pose on the deck of her boat. Though seeing the picture sent a shiver through her, she tried to remain calm.

"That is the marine researcher who has leased the boat for the next six months so he could work out on the reef."

"He could research me anytime," Mara said quietly, looking around to see whether Paul was nearby before giving the phone back to her baby sister. "You did pretty good with him!"

"Mara, he is just a client."

"If I had clients like that, I would want to go to work every day too!" Tracey chimed in and also, like Mara, looked around to see whether Harris was nearby. "Damn, he is good-looking."

"Let me see." Skylar's father was suddenly at their side and thumbed through the photos, not saying a word or showing any reaction except for a bit of hesitation at the picture with Garrett.

"The boat looks good. But make sure you are staying on top of the accounting." And with that, he walked away. That was her dad—again all business.

"I'm next," said her mom. This time, there was more reaction, as her mother had something sweet to say about each picture. But when she came to the photo of Garrett, all she said was "Oh my." All the other women in the group started giggling, which broke the ice with Skylar, who finally let her guard down to enjoy the group of women ogling the good-looking man in the picture.

"He looks like he could be in one of those calendars of men. You know, the male strippers," Blair said, now that all the men had gone out to the pool.

"You have to give us more details, Skylar," Tracey said, as Blair and Mara furiously nodded their heads in agreement. Her mother only sat and smiled.

"His name is Garrett, and he is a marine biologist. He is renting the boat about three to four days per week. He is very much into his work and also, he's pretty much a loner."

"How can a man look like that and be a loner?" Mara said.

"I think Skylar is probably wrong on that fact. There's no way this guy doesn't have a girlfriend. Wow!" Tracey said.

Blair and her mom sat, saying nothing, but smiling.

"I didn't even know this was on there. I was taking pictures of the boat for a brochure I'm making."

"If you put him on the brochure, I'm sure you will have the female tourists lined up, and possibly have a waiting list." Tracey started laughing, with everyone following suit except Skylar's mom.

"I'll keep that in mind," Skylar said, smiling and shaking her head at the women in her family. But she had to admit that Garrett would look pretty good on the front cover of the brochure. If his picture caused this much commotion at a simple family dinner, she could only imagine the response from the tourists of the Florida Keys.

11

Her ride back to Key Largo later that afternoon was slow and relaxing. The scenery was beautiful, even if she had seen it a thousand times. Skylar was so drawn to these small islands because this was where she felt most at home.

She wanted to go by and check on the boat, but she knew that everything was fine. The marina had wonderful security, and she had to allow herself some time away, but it was hard. That was her passion, her baby, sitting in the water. But Skylar made her way home, just in time to watch the sunset on a rocky area on the water near her house. The sunsets were magical in the Keys for some reason; she didn't know why, and it didn't matter. She was glad she had brought along her camera because tonight's show was especially spectacular. As she reviewed the sunset pictures at home, she thought again about her brochure and how one of those would look great on it. But then, so would that picture of Garrett. She smiled to herself, remembering how everyone—no, the women—had reacted today.

As she arrived at the *Sea Gypsy* the next morning, Skylar was taken aback that she was not the first to arrive. Garrett was there, already sorting gear, with various objects holding down his notes against the gentle wind.

"Good morning," Skylar said as she stepped aboard her boat. But Garrett was so focused on his task that her words startled him. The piece of the snorkel he had in his hand flew in the air, threatening to head for the water, but it landed safely back in the boat.

"I'm so sorry. I thought you heard me step on the boat," Skylar said, unable to contain her laughter as she watched this extremely attractive man try to regain his composure and then start to laugh himself.

"Damn, you scared the hell out of me," Garrett said, turning around to see her smiling and laughing at his expense. But he didn't mind. Skylar looked radiant this morning. The look on her face made him want to kiss her, something that he had thought about so many times yesterday when he was trying to concentrate on writing reports. Now he couldn't help but laugh along with her. "So, how was your family day yesterday?"

"It was all good. The same ole thing, except I was the topic of conversation because of the boat. As I'm the first person in the last three generations to step away from the family's business, it kinda makes me the target of many conversations. I just can't figure out who is betting against me and who is cheering me on. I guess I'll have to wait and see." Skylar unlocked the boat and started organizing her things as she talked, not knowing that Garrett was watching every move she made.

"What?" she said when she turned around to see Garrett just standing there.

"What?"

"You were staring at me. Is something wrong?"

"No. I was just lost in thought. Are we still on for this Friday?" Garrett said in a softer tone, continuing to look at her.

"I'm looking forward to it," Skylar said, feeling flushed from head to toe as he continued to gaze at her.

"You two are going out this weekend? That's sweet." Casey. How did they both miss her arrival on the dock? It seemed she always had a way of showing up at just the wrong time.

"Sorry. I just happened to overhear your conversation," she said as she daintily stepped aboard the boat. Casey might have sounded nice, but the look that she gave Skylar was full of pure contempt. But for Garrett, she was all smiles.

Garrett stood there awkwardly, trying to find the right words. "Casey, that's our personal business. And as for you and I, we have a lot of work today. That is why I'm here early. Let's go over a plan I mapped out yesterday that I want to accomplish over the next few days." Casey quickly put her stuff down, and Garrett went into researcher mode, discussing the details of his plan which Casey seemed over eager, hanging on every word Garrett spoke like a little child listening to a mother telling a bedtime story. The only thing Skylar could think of was how glad she was that Casey's internship would only last a few months.

"I'm not late, am I?" Max said as he climbed aboard with a box of muffins in his hand.

"Not at all. Whatcha got there?" Skylar said as her stomach growled.

"I brought some homemade organic muffins. A few are even gluten free! They're courtesy of my mom," he said proudly.

"Yum! Your mom is the best!" Skylar said as she reached for a blueberry muffin.

"Hey, would you guys like a muffin?" Max asked the two people intently looking at papers scattered all over the cabin's table.

"Do you mind? We are working," Casey said flippantly.

"I would love one," Garrett said, totally dismissing the redhead by his side.

"They are homemade. I thought it might be a nice treat this morning." Max looked at Casey, but she didn't budge, totally ignoring him.

"Are you guys ready to go? We can get an early start if you want, since everyone is here, and the boat is ready," Skylar said as she finished the last bite of muffin.

"That would be great! Let me get these papers together so they don't go off into the water."

"I can do that!" Casey said quickly, and before Garrett knew it, the papers were in a neat pile, and Casey was handing them to him, once again with that schoolgirl smile.

"Thanks," Garrett said uncomfortably.

"Max, grab the ropes. Let's get out of here," Skylar said, still keeping an eye on the intern because now she seemed to be the target of Casey's anger. Garrett might not be able to see it, but this fiery girl was in an odd mood. Skylar's best guess was that the conversation Casey overheard about Garrett and Skylar's upcoming evening together was causing her annoyance. It was apparent that Casey wanted Garrett for herself, and Skylar wouldn't put it past her to do everything she could to get what she wanted. As much as Skylar felt a strong connection to Garrett, she didn't have time for childish pranks with this girl. She had too many other things on her plate with this business, but she couldn't help feeling a little miffed that this girl was treating her like the enemy. Skylar had a kind heart, as her grandma had always said. Grandma had always called her an old soul because she liked simpler things than the rest of her family did, whether it be material things or relationships. Skylar had always seemed to look for the bright side of things, but with Casey, she was having a very difficult time at the moment.

As they made their way out to the reef, the sea was a bit choppy, making for a rougher ride than last week. But the routine of the day was the same, and this continued into the next day as well. Garrett and Casey worked side by side; Garrett was like a workhorse—single-mindedly focused on his work. Even though he and Skylar didn't talk hardly at all during the day, he was mesmerizing Skylar more with each passing minute. She also found him staring at her occasionally, or he would catch her looking at him. But it was something she hid from Casey. She didn't want to give her any more fodder to work with, as she seemed to make up her own unpleasant thoughts.

As they all exited the boat that evening, Skylar reminded them of her scuba trips the next day, telling the two researchers that she and Max would see them on Thursday. As they stood there in the group, Garrett's eyes locked on Skylar's. She immediately knew he wanted to come but didn't want to say anything in front of Casey.

"Garrett—could you come to the truck with me? I have some papers I need to go over with you about your boat rental for the next few months."

"No problem." Garrett turned to Casey. "If you can put that info I gave you into a small report, say one or two pages, that would be great. I'll get it from you Thursday."

"I can do that, but I would love to come tomorrow. You know—to be able to dive without being on the clock." This time Casey almost sounded sincere, but Skylar knew better.

"It is filled, Casey, but I will let you know when we have availability. Garrett," Skylar said as she walked toward her truck. "Good night, everyone." She looked back to see Max walking happily to his car, while the younger girl was walking like a mad bull. As she and Garrett neared her truck, Skylar did indeed pull out his rental papers, at the same time watching Casey leave the parking lot just a tad bit too fast.

"I thought all the papers were fine," Garrett asked, concerned.

"They are, silly. I was trying to help you out of an uncomfortable situation. Unless you don't want to dive with us tomorrow." Suddenly Skylar felt awkward. She had assumed that he wanted to come with them, or at least she hoped so. "I had one spot left."

"Of course I want to come. Sorry! Casey is driving me a bit nuts. I even sat down and talked to her the other evening after everyone was gone, telling her that this is just a working relationship. I thought everything was clear. Today, I felt like I had an octopus on me. I wished I had never agreed to an intern." Garrett's tone sounded like he felt defeated.

"It can't be that bad. You definitely have an admirer!" Skylar said, with a smile.

"She's not the admirer I was hoping for."

Skylar's skin immediately started to tingle as she understood what Garrett was saying and the way he was looking at her.

"Well, the empty spot is just for you, if you want it. That's why I was able to say the trip was full without lying."

"I wouldn't pass up a dive with other people. But I also like spending time with the boat captain," Garrett said, with a wink, before turning to walk to his truck.

For Skylar, the next morning couldn't come fast enough. All she could think of the evening before had been Garrett's wink and the flirty comment he had made. With each passing day, her fondness for him was growing more and more. She found herself thinking about him almost nonstop, which had her perplexed and a little rattled. She kept reminding herself that she had a business to build—that was first and foremost on her list of priorities. But Garrett was slowly working his way into her heart. She loved his nonstop chatter about his work. And he genuinely seemed interested in her passion for the charter business she was trying to bring to life. They had some casual conversations that just seemed to flow like the water they were usually on. It all felt so right in her soul. Skylar didn't imagine when she started on this journey that she might meet a man who was in sync with her, but in reality, it was too early for her to be thinking about such things.

"Permission to come aboard, Captain," Garrett said in such a jovial way that Skylar couldn't help but look up, laughing.

"Granted," she said. "Good morning. You are in a really great mood."

"Anytime I'm going diving, it's a good day." Plus, the fact that I'm here with you, he thought, but he kept that to himself.

"Everything is ready to go. Max got here early, and I have to say, he is just about the best decision I have made in this little venture of mine."

"Thanks, boss!" Max yelled from the stern of the boat.

"And he has good hearing!" Skylar shouted back.

As Garrett and Skylar stood close together, double-checking things before the first dive group arrived, there was an almost-palpable electricity in the air between them. He wondered to himself whether she felt it too and wanted so badly to ask. It wasn't like Garrett to hold back something he wanted to say or ask. But this situation was completely out of the norm for him. To feel this way about a woman had him out of his comfort zone and feeling like he was on shaky, wobbly ground. For a man that prided himself on being strong and steady, this had him taking baby steps when he usually just leaped into a situation. This woman was changing him.

"Hi, everyone." Garrett heard Skylar addressing the small group on the dock. "Welcome, and come aboard. Hello again, Mr. Gibbons!"

"Please call me Mike. And after the second session today, I have some papers for you. I also know someone else that is interested in renting your boat for snorkeling trips."

"That sounds great, and thanks, Mike." Skylar's smile must have covered her entire face as she watched the group settle in for their ride out to the reef. She looked over at Garrett, who almost seemed to be laughing at her but gave her a thumbs-up.

The boat ride this morning was a bit choppy with a little more wind than usual, but everyone seemed to enjoy the ride. Once anchored, all the divers got into their gear while listening to Mike's instructions. Then one by one, they fell into the sea below. Suddenly, it was just Skylar and Max on board. As usual, they double-checked everything and then settled in to wait—Skylar with her tablet, drawing, and Max playing some game on his iPhone.

"You really like him, don't you?" Max said.

"That's none of your business," Skylar answered, a little shy, knowing where this conversation was heading and trying to stop it before it began.

"Skylar, it is so obvious," Max said, looking at her and just rolling his eyes.

Skylar sighed. "I will say that we are going out to dinner this Friday in Islamorada. We will see how things go from there. Is that enough for now to satisfy your curiosity?"

"Way to go, boss! Now, do you think you could help me persuade Casey to at least give me a try?" Max looked at her as though Skylar would have the magic solution to his problem.

"Max, I'm not sure about Casey. It's obvious she has a thing for Garrett. I know that you have to have seen the way she clings to him like a piece of seaweed wrapped around his feet. And I can't say anything because it's very clear she doesn't care for me at all. But if I think of something that might help, I'll let you know."

"You're right, but I can't help but try. I'm a sucker for a beautiful redhead!" Max said as he went back to the game he was playing on his phone. Skylar loved his ever-present positive attitude. Even though the pretty intern had rebuffed him several times, he still remained optimistic.

Suddenly, they both heard water splashing and voices coming from the side of the boat. A few sounded distressed, sending Skylar and Max running to the side. It seemed everyone had surfaced, and one girl was completely hysterical. Garrett and Mike were trying to calm her down.

"Come on, Tricia," Mike said in a soothing voice as he helped the young girl climb aboard the boat, with Garrett close behind.

"What happened?" Skylar said quietly to Garrett as everyone else got into the boat.

"We had a close encounter with a very large shark. His fin actually grazed Tricia's arm, and she panicked, but we got to her quickly so she wouldn't shoot up to the surface too fast," Garrett said calmly. "The shark's skin was rough enough to scrape her arm and draw blood. We figured we'd better get everyone back into the boat safely." Skylar could see the fear in the girl's eyes, but she was calming down.

The shark had cause quite a bit of excitement, and it was all anyone talked about as they made their way back to the dock. They would be getting back a bit earlier than planned, so

Skylar didn't have to rush. They would have two hours before they took out Mike's afternoon scuba class. She was so lost in thought that she didn't realize that Garrett was standing right beside her until his arm touched hers.

"I'm glad you were here today. I know Mike and his assistants could have handled the situation, but having two experts aboard is better than one," Skylar said, looking up at him admiringly.

"Sharks can really catch you off guard. Though you have to be careful, most of the time, they will leave you alone as long as you don't do anything to provoke them. I've had my own close encounters—a few that really scared me, honestly, but not enough to stay out of the water. What about you?" Garrett said, watching Skylar steer the boat so masterfully back to the marina.

"I've seen them while diving but only had two close calls. One was with a tiger shark that really had me scared, but he passed by uneventfully, thank goodness. I did get a little bite on my arm from a baby barracuda when I was snorkeling once. There was no damage, except a small scar." Skylar continued to look ahead as the marina came into view, but all she could think about was the man standing beside her.

"We will have to exchange battle stories this Friday. It could prove to be quite interesting," he said, with a grin, as the boat slowed down and made its way to the dock.

Before Skylar knew it, they were back at sea, anchored in a different spot this time. All the students dived with Mike and Garrett, while Skylar and Max stayed on board. But this time, the wind was picking up, with dark clouds developing in the distance. Skylar checked the radar on the boat—it showed only small showers scattered around them, nothing that looked worrisome. But what she saw developing in front of her was no light rain shower, more like a dark storm.

"Max, I don't like the way the sky looks. Use that tank to hit the hull underwater to signal everyone below. I know they haven't been down as long as they wanted, but I don't want this storm to put us in danger." Skylar continued to watch the clouds thicken as Max signaled the group below. Then she saw it—the first streak of lightning.

Garrett was the first one to pop his head above water. "What's wrong?"

"There's a storm brewing fast and I need everyone to come up as quickly as possible," Skylar said anxiously. She watched as Garret quickly looked at the darkening sky and dove back underwater without saying a word.

"Max, get the life jackets out. Have each person put one on, just in case."

Everyone was coming aboard the boat, but they weren't fast enough for Skylar. They were now beginning to hear small rumbles of thunder, which were unnerving her. Stay calm, she told herself. You have been out in storms before—you know what to do.

"Is everyone here?" she called out to the group behind her. The boat was starting to rock from the bigger swells the wind was stirring up. "Please find a seat, and stay put. It could be a bumpy ride back, but we will be fine. The storm just came up faster than anticipated. Ready?" Everyone sat down, chatting away as though nothing was going on.

"Are you okay?" Garrett said as he came to stand beside her again.

"Yeah, this storm just seems odd. It came out of the blue, literally. It didn't even show up on radar till just a few minutes ago, even though I have been watching it form on the horizon. I wish I had gotten your attention sooner. I have a feeling it is going to catch up with us."

"You've got this, and I've been in plenty of these squalls. We will be fine. We'll do this together, okay?" Garrett put his hand on hers, noticing how tightly she was grasping the wheel.

"I've been in storms before, but not with complete strangers on my boat when I'm responsible for their safety."

"Skylar, look at me." She looked at him as if obeying a parent. "You have the skills—the know-how—to navigate these waters. We are all going to be fine." Just seeing that he had confidence in her helped Skylar get her thoughts organized.

She met each ocean swell, going as quickly as she safely could and secretly wishing her passengers had seatbelts. The rain started as a light drizzle but grew so heavy it was hard to see in front of her. Lightning flashed all around them; thunder boomed loudly. She heard a few screams behind her but didn't turn around. Skylar had to stay focused on what was in front of her. She knew the marina was close, and that was her goal. Garrett stood beside her, helping navigate the huge swells, calming her with his reassuring voice. She could hear Mike behind her, talking to the passengers, acting as though this was a common occurrence. She did glance back once to see Max sitting on the deck of the boat, trying to talk to everyone to keep things as lighthearted as he could. He had been through storms like this too, and to look at him, it was as though nothing was going on around them.

As she saw the markers for the marina through the torrent of rain, a small bit of relief flooded through her, but she wasn't home free yet. She looked up at Garrett with a slight smile as she noticed he saw them too.

"You know what to do from here. There is another boat there." He pointed to her right, just a little way in front of them. "Be careful." Skylar slowed the boat down just a bit, but not too much, because she didn't want to stall the boat over a swell. The other boater pulled into the marina, and then she guided her boat into the entrance. Though the rain was still quite heavy, the lightning had seemed to move a little farther away which was a good sign. The storm was moving fast.

Soon, they moored the boat to the dock. Everyone quickly gathered their stuff and hurriedly headed to their vehicles. Apparently, Mike had given them instructions before they docked. But Skylar didn't see any of what was happening behind her. It wasn't till Garrett slowly put his hands on hers that she realized she was still gripping the wheel. He gently touched each finger to help her remember that she could move.

"Thanks so much," Skylar said, looking at him with so much appreciation that very slight tears began to form in her eyes, but she pushed them aside. "I'm not sure whether I could have done that without you."

"Of course you could have. I didn't really do anything except stand here in case you needed help." Garrett was trying to sound nonchalant, but for Skylar, he had helped her more than he knew.

"I've been in storms before, but that one was probably the worst. And I'm frustrated with myself for not getting everyone out of the water a little sooner." Just then, she noticed Mike and Max had joined them.

"Skylar, you did do a good job out there. Don't cut yourself short. Storms creep up like that all the time, and we are back here safely. That's what counts," Mike said, giving her shoulder a reassuring pat. "We just know better for next time."

"You're not canceling your contract are you?" Skylar asked nervously, knowing that this mistake would probably cost her some future work.

"Should I cancel over a storm? I don't know one boat captain out here that hasn't gone through something like that. That was normal."

"I've been through storms before, but never with people's lives in my hands. Thanks, Mike, for your confidence in me. Really, thanks to all of you. I might have been concentrating on what was in front of me, but I heard your stories, Max. Thanks for keeping everyone distracted. You too, Mike. And thanks, Garrett, for helping me navigate."

"No problem, boss," Max said, before he continued securing the boat for the evening.

"So, I'll see you Saturday around one o'clock. Remember, this time it is a snorkeling trip. Let's go to the shallow part of the reef. It seems the perfect place to snorkel and I have quite a few first timers booked," Mike said, before walking down the dock, waving to those still on board.

"Skylar, are you sure you are okay? You still look a bit pale." Garrett gazed at her, concerned. It had been a rough trip in, no doubt about that, but Skylar had done as well as any captain he had known.

"I'm fine. I think I'm just ready to make sure this boat is secure and go home to relax a bit."

"That sounds like a good idea," he said, giving her a quick hug, which she didn't pull out of. It felt good to be in his arms—so reassuring and so right—she just fit against his chest, and his arms felt like a warm blanket around her.

Garrett was having similar thoughts as he held Skylar against himself. There was a sensation that passed between them. He could feel her trembling start to ease, and her body molded to his. He realized he didn't want to let her go. He wished that he could take her home to be with her after this rough afternoon, but they were still just getting to know each other. But each day they spent together, he was feeling closer to her and strangely protective of her, also. Feelings he had denied himself for years were coming back to the surface, making him feel out of sorts, but in such a good way.

"Um...I'm leaving," Max said as he walked up to the pair, who were still embracing. But as soon as Max uttered those words, both Skylar and Garrett quickly parted, as if they had been caught doing something very wrong.

"Thanks again, Max, for everything. See you bright and early tomorrow, okay? Then we'll have Friday and Sunday off, just like last week."

"See ya!" the young man said, as he hopped to the dock and went quickly to his car.

"He is a great guy. And his attitude is amazing. Is he always that cheerful?" Garrett said, as he watched the boy run down the dock.

"Yep, ever since I've known him. He just seems to look at everything in a optimistic way. He even wants me to help him with Casey. He wants to ask her out, even though I told him she has the hots for you." Skylar laughed, watching Garrett's tortured expression.

"Well, I hope it works!"

"Garrett, I meant what I said earlier. Thanks for your help. I couldn't have navigated that storm alone. I almost panicked, and as a boat captain, I can't do that. But you also helped Mike with the students. They love you! I really need to pay you for helping out."

"Are you kidding? I love this! These are the times I can talk about fish and the ocean all day, and no one starts yawning in my face," he said, with a laugh.

"Anyway, thanks." Skylar hugged him once more. "I appreciate it more than you know." When she looked up at him, they were mere inches from each other's faces. It would be so easy to give him a kiss, Skylar thought, wondering what it would feel like to touch the lips of the man that had been occupying her mind nonstop.

"You are very welcome," Garrett said in a husky voice, also noticing how close they were and how she felt against him.

As they walked toward their vehicles, there was silence, but each could feel the bond that was forming between them. Neither knew what it was, but they both secretly couldn't wait till Friday night.

12

The next two days proved difficult for Skylar in more ways than one. She was still nervous after Wednesday's storm. She had gone over every detail in her mind, making sure she had done everything correctly. And she had. But for her, things had to be perfect, especially with passengers on board, whose lives were literally in her hands. She even talked about the experience with a friend of hers—an old sea captain who was like a father to her. After she recounted the story, he told her that she was on point. That helped calm her anxiety, but when she stepped on the boat the next day, a feeling of anxiety swept through her. But it wasn't long until everyone—her, Garrett, Max, and, of course, Casey—fell into their normal routine.

Casey continued to cling to Garrett, flirting with him while they worked. Skylar watched from afar, laughing to herself at times as she could see Garrett's irritation from being the center of the girl's attention., Skylar had to give him credit because he continued to be so polite and kept their conversations completely about the work at hand. Casey was trying her best to break through to her boss but having no luck. Skylar almost felt as if she was watching a TV show. But whenever Casey saw her watching them, her glances toward Skylar were nothing but icy stares. This had to be due to the upcoming date she was having with Garrett which, unfortunately the intern was fully aware of.

When she woke up on Friday, Skylar was looking forward to her evening with Garrett more than she had realized. She was up early and for once didn't do a quick run to the dock to check on the boat. Instead, she quickly finished up her paper work and errands in the morning so she could actually try to relax that afternoon before Garrett picked her up for the drive to Islamorada. She chose a tropical-looking dress and gold sandals. A light summer sweater would accompany her outfit, in case it was cool after sunset. She loved this type of bohemian clothing, but in the real estate world, her family frowned upon this attire. But for Skylar, this was truly her style, and she was glad to be able to wear this dress for the first time. It had been hanging in her closet for a while now, waiting for a special occasion. What better time than this evening, she thought to herself with a smile on her face.

For Garrett, the nerves had set in the moment he opened his eyes this morning. Normally, he would get out of bed, grab a cup of coffee, and find something to eat. Then he would go over paper work or go out on the boat. But this morning was definitely out of character for him. He lay in bed, thinking of the coming evening. Was his truck clean enough? He would have to check. What was he going to wear? He thought he had one pair of jeans without a hole. What about a shirt? All he had were T-shirts, so he would have to go somewhere today to find something that would be suitable. It had been too long since he had allowed himself to feel something for someone. And while it was just him, he never owned anything fancy—his vehicle, his living space, or his clothes. How should he dress for his date with Skylar tonight? She was so used to high-society events that she would probably dress nicely. Crap! He wondered whether he could buy a suit today somewhere on the island. Now, he definitely felt he couldn't wear jeans. Skylar just wasn't that kind of girl. And what about the restaurant? She said she loved the Lorelei, but would she wear something real nice to eat outdoors? So many questions bombarded his mind at once that he could feel the tension building up in his shoulders and neck. You can do this, Garrett. Suddenly, he knew the answer to his many questions. He would call his friend, Abbey in Key West, for advice.

"Hi there, Garrett! It's a little out of character for you to be calling this late on a Friday morning. Aren't you out on a boat or something? Is everything okay?" asked the sweet-sounding woman on the other end of the line. He loved Abbey and felt so blessed that she had become his neighbor in Key West.

"I need some female advice," Garrett said hesitantly.

"Oh boy, this sounds good. What's up?" said Abbey enthusiastically.

"I have a date tonight, and I'm not sure what to wear."

"Are you kidding?" Garrett heard a small snicker on the other end of the line.

"This is serious, Abbey. I kinda like this girl, and I want to make sure I make a good impression." Garrett proceeded to tell Abbey the abbreviated version of how he had met Skylar, who she was, and why he was so nervous about making sure everything was perfect.

"First of all, way to go! You never dated anyone here, so I was convinced you were a committed bachelor. It sounds like Skylar is a pretty nice lady. And it seems you know how to pick them too. A Miami socialite! Wow! And she isn't married."

"That's another thing. She's only twenty-nine. I'm ten years older than she is."

"You are full of surprises today, Garrett, but I'm happy for you. Age doesn't matter, so that is the least of your worries. Now as for clothes, I'm not sure what to tell you. I would think a nice pair of pants and a pullover shirt would be fine. I never saw you dressed in anything other than T-shirts, shorts, and flip-flops. If you get dressed up, send me a picture!" Abbey said excitedly.

"We'll see. I was just thinking I might need to wear a suit."

"You are eating outside. I think a suit would be overkill. You are going to be fine, Garrett. Just make sure to talk about something other than fish and turtles, okay?"

"Will do! Thanks, Abbey. Tell Zach I said hi." And with that, Garrett hung up and grabbed his keys. It was time to clean his truck and do a bit of clothes shopping.

Skylar looked in the mirror one more time and then glanced around her house to make sure everything looked present-able. She had never been this nervous about a date. For some reason, Garrett felt important to her, and she wanted this to be a wonderful evening. She had texted him earlier with the address to her little house on the canal, which was becoming more like a real home each and every day. Suddenly, she heard a vehicle outside and then a door shutting. He was here.

Her house is nice, Garrett thought to himself. And so close to the water. But surely, she could have afforded something grander than this. As he walked to the door, he took a deep breath to calm the jittery feeling he had inside. He felt like a teenager going on a first date all over again.

When Skylar opened the door, Garrett felt as if someone had taken his breath away. Her beautiful chestnut-colored hair was down and hanging across one shoulder. She had on a hint of makeup that made her eyes shine a more brilliant green than he had ever seen. Her skin seemed to glow, and she was in a tropical dress that showed off her curves. She was stunning. Not that she wasn't before, but tonight it was as if she was a different woman.

"Hi," Skylar said as she attempted to take in the scene before her. Garrett was as good looking as before, but he was now in street clothes, with his hair combed and his chin shaved. But he looked as sexy as ever. She could still see the ripple of his muscles through his shirt; the color of it accentuated his tan, and his jeans fit perfectly. Skylar couldn't help but stare at the man at her door. "Come in," she finally said, opening the door wider, feeling that current once again running between them as he walked through the door.

"I love your house. And you are so close to the water. But for some reason, I imagined something bigger," Garrett said.

"Well, it's just me, so I really didn't need anything that big. This is a house I was renting out, but when I started the business here in the Keys, I decided to make it my permanent home. Usually I have my dog with me, but since I'm gone all day, she is staying with my little brother back at his place. I really miss her, so I'm hoping one day she can come down here and start going out on the boat with me." Skylar felt as if she was rambling; her nerves were getting the best of her.

"Are you ready to go?"

"Definitely!" she said, and she locked the door and closed it behind them.

Garrett walked her to his truck. "This is my only transportation. She might not look too great, but I love her just the same. She's very reliable and great for toting all my gear."

"I think she is perfect. I kinda have a thing for my truck too. Especially in this business, I need lots of room for hauling things. You should have seen my friend when she found out I was looking for a used truck. She, like my father, wanted me to buy a new one, but that would be just another expense I don't need. I think I did pretty well finding the one I got."

They were both nervous. It had been so easy to talk on the boat, but going out on a date was a completely different story. They shared various stories about their time so far in Key Largo as they drove to the Lorelei. Skylar loved it there because they could dine on the beach, and it looked as if they had timed it just right to hopefully watch an amazing sunset. They arrived and chose a table right along the water's edge. After the waiter took their drink orders, they both sat staring at the water and the sunset that was getting ready to take place.

"Our timing was just right. With that clear sky, the sunset is going to be nice," Garrett said. "But it won't be as beautiful as the woman I'm sitting with." His voice sounded husky, low, and sweet. Skylar couldn't help but smile while she melted a little inside.

"I have to admit I feel like a pretty lucky girl to be sitting beside the best-looking man here," Skylar said sweetly. After she looked around the outdoor restaurant, her eyes finally landed on Garrett.

"How opposed are you to selfies?"

"Not at all, but let's see if we can get the sunset in the background," Garrett said, taking Skylar's phone. They stood up and snapped a couple of photos just as the sun was making its final descent. As they reviewed the pictures together, they started laughing at some of the faces they had made and at the angle Garrett had used when trying to get just the right shot. But there were a few pictures that Skylar couldn't wait to see on her computer.

"I love taking photos. But I have to say, my brother Chase is the photographer in the family. I think if he wasn't dealing in real estate, he would do photography on a professional level or be a chef. Now, how is that for diversity?" Skylar laughed.

"If you and your siblings love doing other things, why do you stay with the family's business?" Garrett said, realizing that it probably wasn't the best question to ask at the start of their first official evening together.

"You know, that's a good question. I guess part of the reason is that we are the third generation to work in the business, and it feels like there is an obligation to make sure it continues.

My grandparents started it, my dad and uncles followed in their footsteps, and it's like the grandchildren should take over so the parents can retire. In truth, it's a bit complicated. But out of my siblings and cousins, it seems I'm the most rebellious. I'm the first one to completely step away. The whole family has tried to keep it hush-hush because they don't want it to look like there is any discord in the family, but frankly, I don't understand what all the fuss is about. I have a friend whose family is in the auto business. He is around all kinds of vehicles all the time and likes his career, but he loves boats like I do. When I told him my idea, he was the one who helped me find the *Sea Gypsy*. I didn't want to pay for something new, so he found just what I needed. He texts me every now and then, asking how everything is going.

"But I think my parents see it as a blemish on our family. Don't get me wrong—I love my parents dearly. They are wonderful, but they just don't see the world like I do. They were raised in a time when how you looked, what you did, and who you knew were so important—more important than is necessary. Not that it hurts to know the right people, but I truly feel if you follow your heart and throw in some hard work, you will be successful. If it doesn't work, then maybe there is a different path for you, but at least you know in your heart that you tried. I don't see it as a failure but as a learning experience." Skylar paused and laughed. "Wow, I sound like I'm giving a motivational speech. Sorry!"

"No, I love it. It is just hard for me to imagine being—what's the word—confined. Not being able to do what I wanted to. I can't imagine if I wasn't able to work as researcher. I've always had this obsession with and passion for the ocean. My mom thought I was a bit over the top, but she supported me nonetheless. Then, most of my friends would tell me I talked too much about my work. As a matter of fact, I called my friend Abbey earlier today and told her I was going out with someone special tonight. First of all, I think she was shocked I had a date but she told me I wasn't allowed to talk about fish or turtles."

"I don't mind if you talk about either. But who is Abbey?" It wasn't that Skylar was jealous, but Garrett had never mentioned her before.

"She was my next-door neighbor in Key West. We became good friends when I was living there. She's really sweet, and she's getting ready to marry a guy she met at work when she moved to Key West last year."

Just then, the waiter brought their dinner entrées—baby back ribs for Garrett and grilled chicken with lemon caper sauce for Skylar. They were hungry, and they both agreed they had picked the best spot for dinner.

"Tell me more about your family," Garrett asked as they continued eating.

"Well, there is my mom, Sadie, and my dad, Jonathan. I have two brothers: Harris is the oldest and is engaged to a wonderful girl, Tracey. And Chase, my younger brother, is dating a girl named Blair. My older sister, Mara, is married to Paul, and they have a daughter, my adorable niece named Lyla. My parents still live in the house where I grew up on Key Biscayne, and we all have our own houses or condos nearby. We used to joke about separating the house into individual units and having a family compound," Skylar laughed. "But I think at this age, we all need our own privacy. But the house is big enough for it."

"How big is big?" Garrett asked, fascinated.

"About eighty-eight hundred square feet."

Garrett choked on a bite of coleslaw. "Wow, that is big. I'm not sure if I have ever seen a house that size!"

"I guess since I grew up there, it doesn't seem huge. But when I started selling real estate, I realized that I was pretty lucky growing up where I did."

"I hope you don't take this the wrong way, but you don't seem like you are from a family that wealthy." Garrett realized what he said and tried to correct his mistake. "I didn't mean it that way. You are just so normal. Okay, that sounded a bit wrong too."

Skylar just smiled. "Don't worry. I know what you meant. I think it was my grandma. She lives with my parents now, and she is so…what is the word…grounded. She likes simple things. She still insists on growing her own food in a little garden beside the house. My grandpa might have gotten wealthy with his real estate empire, but grandma has told me about their humble beginnings. They didn't have much, and she says she almost liked those times better. People were closer. They talked more. They had more family time. She is the main reason we have family dinners every Sunday. She is determined that as long as she is here, we will have family time.

"I think I get my spunk from her. When I wasn't at the beach, I was with her, usually in the garden or listening to her stories. And then there is our cook, Maggie. She was just a little girl when her family moved from Cuba in the late 1960s, bringing nothing with them. She would tell me fascinating stories, so I would hang out in the kitchen. That's how I learned to cook!" Skylar said proudly.

"You know how to cook. Do you mean I could have had a home-cooked dinner instead of coming here?" Garrett said teasingly.

"Well, play your cards right, and I might just invite you over for some lasagna!"

"You learned to cook from a Cuban woman, and you would make me lasagna."

"I make the best. I love Italian food!" Skylar said, with a huge smile.

"We could have eaten somewhere else," Garrett said quietly.

"No way! I love this place, and we would have missed that wonderful sunset. Tonight has actually been perfect." Skylar took the last bite of her chicken and glanced up to see Garrett looking at her with a sweet smile on his face.

"This really has been so—" Garrett started before a very familiar voice found its way to his ears.

"Oh my gosh! What are you two doing here?" It was Casey. Of all the places in Islamorada, how had she found the two of them? Garrett wondered as he nicely tried to give her a hint of a smile.

"We're just having a lovely dinner by the water. What are you doing here?" Skylar said, not giving Garrett a chance to answer the girl, even though she had been looking directly at him when talking.

"Oh, we just decided we would have a girls' night out. This is my friend Mindy. Mindy, this is Skylar Cartwright, the owner of the boat I work on with my boss, Garrett Holmes," she said, looking over at him.

"It's nice to meet you, Mindy. Hi, Casey," Garrett said nicely but in a flat tone of voice. Skylar knew right away that he wasn't happy, but he was doing his best to be civil.

"We are waiting on a table at the moment, but I just happened to see ya'll sitting here and had to come by."

I bet, Skylar thought to herself. Then, she had a different idea.

"Well, instead of waiting, why don't you two join us?" Skylar said sweetly to the two young women standing at their table. Then she looked over at Garrett, whose eyes asked what she was doing.

"That would be terrific!" Both girls sat down quickly, with Casey sitting right beside Garrett.

"Let me get our waiter." Skylar motioned to the young man, who quickly came over.

"We have had a few people join us. Do you have menus, please?"

"Here you go. I'll be back in just a few minutes to take your order," he said, but before he could leave the table, Skylar had one more thing to say. "And if you would, we would like our check."

"No problem!"

When Skylar looked at the group assembled before her, Casey's face looked shocked. There had to be some way that Casey had found out about where they were going, but there was no way she was going to spoil their evening.

"This worked out perfectly. You can have our table, since we are done. Now we're going to go listen to some live music down the street. Maybe we can even have some key lime pie for dessert there," Skylar continued as she looked at Garrett, who had yet to say one word. He just smiled and followed Skylar's lead.

"That sounds like a great idea. Casey, how are you coming on that paper I needed? Were you able to finish it?" Garrett said in an authoritative voice.

"Uh...yes. It was rather straightforward." Casey's body language told Skylar that Casey knew she had been defeated at her own little game. But Skylar also sensed that this girl's obsession with Garrett wasn't over.

Within a few minutes, Garrett and Skylar were saying their good-byes, telling the two girls that they hoped they enjoyed their meals. Skylar looped her arm through Garrett's, and they walked to the truck.

"I can't believe you just did that!" Garrett said. "When you asked them to sit down, I thought you had lost your mind. But the look on Casey's face when you said we were leaving was priceless. I don't mean to sound heartless, but she just won't let up."

"And she won't till you are more firm with her. Apparently, your talk the other day didn't dissuade her at all. Unless you are interested in her." She knew this wasn't true, but she said it to watch his reaction. What she got instead was much more.

"Let's take a drive back to your boat," Garrett said.

It felt different walking down the dock to the boat at night. It was a beautiful evening, with a moon that was almost full.

The marina was quiet, as if all the boats were sleeping before tomorrow morning's activities. Garrett climbed on board first and then helped Skylar, even though she could have done it herself. He was being the perfect gentleman tonight, and she loved every second of it.

"Now, here we can talk. No one is around. We are on the water we both love, under a beautiful moon. I doubt 'you know who' has even finished dinner, and if she is trying to find us, she will be checking every bar that has live music to see whether we are there. I'm finding you are a bit devious, Miss Cartwright," Garrett said as he took her hand, and they sat on the cushioned seats, close enough to feel the heat coming from each other's bodies but not touching.

"Well, I didn't want her to ruin one of the best nights I've had in a long time," Skylar said softly as she gave Garrett a sideways glance.

"I have to admit—tonight has been pretty nice. I've learned so much about you."

"And I didn't get a chance to ask you a thing about yourself before our uninvited guests showed up." She laughed.

"Do you mind if I play some music?" Garrett said.

"Sounds good," Skylar responded.

Garrett went to the radio on the console, found a soft rock station, and turned the music on just softly enough for some background music. But then he took Skylar by complete surprise with his next question.

"I know it's not live music, but would you dance with me?" Garrett asked in a soft, deep voice, looking at her so tenderly that she got up and went into his arms without even answering.

At first, he had his arm around her waist, holding her hand up in a normal slow-dance position. But as Garrett looked at Skylar, he couldn't help but encircle her with both arms, bringing her closer. And she didn't fight it. He could tell she wanted to be closer too, which brought him a happiness he hadn't felt in so long. When she looked at him, their faces were mere inches apart. And Garrett had waited long enough for this moment.

Garrett gently brushed his lips against hers in a light kiss, as they both swayed to the music in the background. It felt like magic to him—something he had dreamed about for what now seemed to be forever. This boat captain was stealing his heart, and one light kiss wasn't enough. So he kissed her again, more hungrily, to which she responded the same. Their bodies pressed closer together, if that was even possible.

For Skylar, the feeling that overcame her was one of pure joy. She could honestly say that the way she felt being in Garrett's embrace was like nothing she had experienced before. No other man she had dated had ever had this effect on her. His kisses were like a decadent lotion that soothed her entire body. To be so close to him, dancing under the moonlight, pressing her lips to his, was making her heart beat faster and faster.

"Maybe we can talk about your family later," Skylar said as their lips parted for only mere seconds before she reached up for another kiss from his inviting lips. The tension that had been building between them was being released as they finally realized that there was more to their relationship than boat captain and marine researcher. The chemistry between them was too hard to deny. And Skylar wasn't going to fight it anymore.

"I hope that wasn't too forward," Garrett said, still holding her close. Now her head rested on his chest as they continued dancing on the deck of the boat.

"Definitely not," Skylar said, kissing him yet again. It was as if she couldn't get enough of this new drug that brought her such happiness.

"Skylar."

She recognized the voice immediately but knew it couldn't be. But Skylar suddenly dropped her arms from around Garrett, quickly stepping back. They both turned around to see a man standing on the dock.

"Dad?"

13

Garrett stood stunned when he realized that the man now coming aboard the boat was Skylar's father. All he had wanted was an evening to spend time alone with Skylar, and now they were facing a second obstacle. A big obstacle that was making Garrett very uncomfortable.

"It seems like I've caught you at an awkward time," Jonathan Cartwright said as he looked at both his daughter and the man standing before him.

"We…ah…Garrett and I were just spending some quiet time on the boat after dinner. Dad, this is Garrett Holmes, the marine biologist I told you about, who is renting the boat for the next few months for research purposes. Garrett, this is my father, Jonathan Cartwright." Skylar watched as the two men shook hands, but she could read body language well. Her dad was not happy at all, and Garrett seemed to act as if he was under a microscope but his easy going manner served him well.

"It's nice to meet you, sir. Skylar has told me a lot about you and your family."

"She hasn't told us much about you though," Mr. Cartwright said in a monotone voice.

"Dad, what are you doing down here? And why are you here so late?"

"I just thought I would take a drive and see the boat."

"That's fine, but why at night? You could come anytime during the day. You can even go out with us on a boat trip."

"Like I said, I was just taking a drive. But since it seems I've interrupted your evening, I'll be going now. Mr. Holmes, it's nice to meet you. Skylar, I'll see you on Sunday. Have a nice evening." With that, Skylar's father exited the boat and slowly walked down the dock, with Skylar watching, feeling anxious. What was he thinking now after seeing her and Garrett together? She slowly turned around to see Garrett standing there like a statue, afraid to move.

"I'm really sorry. I had no idea he would come here. Or that he even knew where the boat was, for that matter. Every time I talk to him about the business, it is like he shrugs it off, like he's not interested in the least. He has never been down here, as far as I know, and why did he come tonight? This all seems a bit crazy." Skylar sat down, trying to make sense of the last few moments.

"Well, this evening might not have turned out like either one of us planned or wanted, but I have to admit that I have had a wonderful time. Except for the unnerving part of meeting your father. He is quite intimidating," Garrett said, with a smile.

"Aren't you upset?"

"Why would I be? I got to go to dinner with the most gorgeous girl on the island, then dance under the moonlight on a boat. But the best part was giving her the kiss that I've been thinking about for quite some time," Garrett said, pulling Skylar to her feet to give her another soul searching kiss, which helped release some of the anxiety she was feeling from her father's visit.

"Do you think there will be repercussions from your family for what happened tonight? If so, Skylar, I don't want to get in the way. I have to tell you—I really like you. I have since the first day I saw you. But we both live very different lives, and I am older than you. It would be hard, but if we could only be friends, I could live with that."

Skylar was so focused on the fact that he had said "I really like you" that she could have cared less about the rest of his speech. "Garrett, I feel the same way about you. Right now, I really don't care what my family thinks. Maybe we can just concentrate on spending more time together. I'm hoping that if you feel like I do, maybe we can go on another date. I still have lots of questions about your family, remember?"

Garrett smiled. "I think I could manage a second date. Maybe next time, we will have more time to ourselves without being interrupted."

"That sounds wonderful to me. How about I make that lasagna I mentioned. Does Sunday night sound okay?" Skylar said.

"What about your family dinner?" Garrett asked.

"I'll get home in plenty of time. How does seven o'clock sound to you?"

"Sounds great," Garrett said in almost a whisper as he wrapped himself around her once more, his lips meeting hers again in a kiss he hoped she wouldn't forget. And one that would hold him over till they could be alone again.

On Sunday morning, Skylar was feeling happiness such as she hadn't experienced in a long time as she drove along US Hwy 1 toward Miami. Her date with Garrett had been unusual, to say the least, but she replayed every second over in her mind, except for the parts where Casey crashed their dinner and her dad showed up at the boat. The best part was the kisses Garrett had showered her with while they were dancing under the stars. It had to be one of the most romantic dates she had ever been on. No, she determined, it was the most romantic. Even Casey and her father couldn't dampen the excitement that coursed through her body.

And yesterday's snorkeling trip had been so different from any other outing on the boat since Garrett showed up. She had smiled all day as she watched him interact with the group, especially the kids, teaching them so many things about the different living organisms they saw in the water. He had even brought a few of them to the surface to show, including lobster, a very nimble starfish, and a sea anemone that he needed gloves to handle. As she had observed Garrett, he had been totally in his element, and adults and children alike had gravitated to him. Every now and then, he had sought her out, given her a smile or a wink, and gone back to teaching. And now tonight, he was coming over for dinner, and Skylar could hardly wait.

Before she left for Key Biscayne, Skylar cleaned up the house and fixed the lasagna, along with a salad. All she had to do was pop it in the oven when she got home, set the table, and make sure the key lime pie had thawed for dessert. Maybe they could even take a little walk down her street to a sandy spot dotted with rocks that looked out over the Atlantic ocean where someone had placed an old swing. The forecast looked promising for a nice evening, so she kept her fingers crossed. Also, she hoped to have Garrett all to herself this time, unlike what had occurred on their first date.

As she pulled up to her childhood home, the usual cars were parked neatly along the circular driveway. After the run-in with her father the other night, she was preparing herself for a barrage of questions from the whole family. So as she got out of her truck and headed for the front door, she took a deep breath, giving herself a pep talk as she walked along the way.

Everyone was in the family room, talking. Lyla was playing on Chase's shoulders, and some of her family were watching the very large flat-screen TV. Skylar quickly looked for her father, whom she found sitting in a lounge chair with his feet propped up. He and Harris seemed to be in some kind of deep conversation. No one appeared to notice that she had walked into the room, so she quickly went to the kitchen.

"Hey, Maggie! It smells good, as always. What is for dinner today, and can I please help?" Skylar asked quickly and with some anxiety in her voice.

"What's wrong?" Maggie said as she pulled out two beautifully roasted chickens from the oven.

"Why would anything be wrong?" Skylar said as cheerfully as she could.

"Because I can tell. You have to remember I've known you since you were a very little girl. Could it have something to do with a gentleman?"

"Does everybody know?"

"Does everybody know what? I only overheard your parents because it sounded like they were having a very, shall I say, heated discussion. Your name happened to come up."

"That's what I'm afraid of." Skylar hung her head, coming to rest her forehead on her crossed arms on the counter.

"Hey, Sky! When did you get here?" Chase said, coming into the kitchen, with Lyla now firmly attached to his back.

"Just a few minutes ago. I had to see what was for dinner; it smells so good," she said apprehensively.

"Well, it's time for my rider to go back to the barn. Tell Aunt Skylar bye," he said, and off the pair went. He didn't ask or say anything, Skylar thought as she watch her little brother and niece exit the room.

"I thought for sure he would have said something," Skylar said to Maggie as she helped her stir the creamy peas that were simmering on the stovetop.

"Sweetheart, you are confusing this old lady. Would you please tell me what is going on."

"My dad came by the boat on Friday night."

"And why is that a bad thing?" the older woman said as she began to put food in serving dishes.

"Well, I was on a date. He kinda caught us in a compromising position."

Maggie's eyes flew open, her head swiftly turning to look Skylar straight in the face.

"Oh, nothing like that!" Skylar was quick to add. "Just a… uh…passionate kiss."

"I'm so happy for you!" Maggie said, giving Skylar a big hug. "Who is he?"

"I bet I know who it is," someone said suddenly. She and Maggie turned to see Mara and Tracey standing side by side, with big grins on their faces.

"It was the guy from the picture, wasn't it?" said Tracey. The smiles on both of their faces reminded Skylar of two kids that were going to Disney World for the first time.

"I didn't know you two liked to eavesdrop on other people's conversations," Skylar said quickly to the two women, who by this time had grabbed her arms and sat her on a barstool, each of them pulling one up on either side of her as quickly as they could.

"We came to see if Maggie needed any help and couldn't help but overhear. So…" Mara's eyes were about to bug out of her head.

"So, what?"

"Damn it, Skylar," Tracey said. "You know what—details please."

Skylar sighed, knowing that she had no choice. "Yes, I had a date with Garrett."

"His name is Garrett. That makes him even more handsome," Mara said, with a dreamy look in her eyes.

"What did you do? Where did you go? And please tell me he is a good kisser. It's all about the kiss," Tracey said, while Mara and Maggie, to Skylar's surprise, nodded in agreement.

Skylar told them an abbreviated version of her date—dinner, Casey's interruption, dancing on the boat, and her dad's visit. With that last bit of information revealed, all the women in the room went silent, their eyes as wide as possible, their hands over their mouths.

"It can't be that bad. I'm a grown woman, and I can choose whom I want to date. Mom and Dad will just have to accept that."

"You are right on all counts, but things tend to get a bit rocky when us kids take that approach," Mara said. "Look what happened when I met and married Paul."

Skylar did remember. Mara and Paul had met in college. They were both from wealthy families, but Jonathan wasn't happy with the fact that Paul wanted to be a high school teacher. He felt that Mara deserved better and couldn't believe that Paul's parents supported their son's decision. Plus, Mara let it be known that neither of her parents would stop their marriage, even if the pair would have to elope.

"But you didn't let that stop you. And besides, I've only had one date with Garrett."

"He also looks older than you."

Skylar took another deep breath. "He is thirty-nine." Another look of shock crossed each woman's face.

"Is everything okay in here?" asked Sadie Cartwright as she came into the kitchen, looking as regal as ever.

"Yes, we were just getting ready to bring everything to the table," Skylar said as she grabbed two dishes. She quickly gave her mom a kiss on the cheek and headed toward the dining room. Her sister and future sister-in-law followed suit. Soon, the table was full of food, with the family surrounding it, passing food to one another and talking lively. Her father had given her a quick hug before sitting down, acting as though his visit to the boat had never happened. Skylar was glad, but something wasn't quite right. That, combined with what Maggie had said earlier about her parent's argument, told Skylar that before she left today, she would have to talk to him about what had happened, preferably in private.

"Skylar, could we go upstairs to talk? I want to discuss something with you about your charter business," her dad said once everyone was finished eating and the dishes were put away. No one seemed to think anything was out of the norm except Mara and Tracey, who looked at her with concerned eyes.

"Sure," Skylar said as cheerfully as she could and followed her dad to his study on the second floor.

It was a beautiful room that overlooked the aqua-colored lagoon where the family yacht was moored. Skylar remembered that as a young girl, she would sneak in here especially on rainy days and pretend she was out at sea. As she got older, this was her place to steal away and draw or write when no one else was around. But now, it was a place for family discussions, mostly about business.

"Dad, if this is about the other night—" Skylar said before she was cut off by a look and a raised hand from her father.

"Skylar, I know you are a grown woman. You are very capable of making your own decisions as far as your love life is concerned, but I have to say that I think that man is not suitable for you. I don't know his age, but he looks to be significantly older. Plus, he is just a marine biologist renting your boat. The probability of him just using you till he moves on to the next town and the next young lady is very high. I don't want you to get hurt in the process. You deserve much better than that."

"Dad, I don't mean to be disrespectful, but don't you mean he is not good enough since he doesn't come from money?" Skylar regretted saying the words but knew that was what he really wanted to say.

"That's not what I said."

"But that's what you think. Dad, you know I love you with all my heart. I love this family too. I've been blessed beyond measure to have grown up in this wonderful house with family I adore. But I've always been your wayward child. I've tried to be a good Cartwright and follow in the family tradition. But it's just not me. My date with Garrett felt so ideal, for the first time in my life. It wasn't like being with the other guys I have dated that are acceptable because they are in your social circle. Some of my friends might like that, but it's just not me.

"For once in my life, I feel like I'm on the right path for myself. The boat feels like a new home, one where I'm supposed to be. Each day, I can't wait to get to work."

"Is it the boat or the man?" This time the question came not from her father but from her mother, who had walked into the office.

"Your father told me about what happened. But only after I badgered him into telling me where he had been most of the night." Her mother's speech was a little bold; she was not her usual self.

"Sadie, that's enough. This is about Skylar and her business." Her dad was now looking distressed, but Skylar had the distinct feeling this conversation wasn't all about her anymore.

"Why don't you tell her why you were really down at her boat? The boat that you didn't want to get involved in. The one that you were hoping you could spend the night on and leave early enough that Skylar would never know that you were even there."

Suddenly, Skylar realized that her mom had been drinking, something they didn't do on Sundays with Lyla around. And why would her dad want to sleep on the boat? What was truly going on?

"But I agree with your father. This man you are seeing is not for you. You have several men here in town that would love to date you, and they are much more appropriate than a mere marine biologist." With that, Sadie Cartwright took another big sip of the drink in her hand.

"I don't know what is going on between the two of you, but I know that I can make my own decisions. And that is because I was raised by two of the best parents. You should be happy about that. As for Garrett—he is one of the most genuine men I've ever met in my life. He may not be in your social circle, and yes, he is older than I am. But he is passionate about his work, like I am about mine. Being around him, with him, I feel like I finally belong somewhere. I've always been out of step in this family, and that used to bother me, but it doesn't anymore. I'm sorry if I have disappointed you by not wanting to be in the family's business. You have three other children that are there. You don't need me too. Can't both of you just be happy for me?"

With that, Skylar walked out of the room and quickly down the stairs. Tears were threatening the corners of her eyes, but she wouldn't allow them to fall till she was in her truck and heading back to Key Largo.

"Hey, where are you going so fast?" Harris said as his little sister walked by quickly.

"I have to get back home. I have a busy day tomorrow." But then Skylar stopped and turned. "Harris, is something going on between Mom and Dad?"

"Not that I know of, but I only see Dad at work and Mom when she stops by. Why?"

"I was just wondering. I don't think the conversation I just had with them was just about me. Keep an eye on them, okay?" Skylar said to him with concern.

"Okay, but I don't know what I'm looking for."

"You can't leave yet!" Mara said as she came around the corner to see her sister and brother standing at the front door. "Did the talk with Dad go that badly?"

"What is going on?" Harris said, looking at his two sisters in exasperation.

"Skylar is dating an older man," Mara said, with a smile.

"Then that is what is wrong. You know how they are about keeping up appearances in this town," Harris said. "They will be okay. Just give them time, but be careful about those older men, Sky."

Skylar wanted to scream. She felt as if she was in a whirlwind, and just when things seem to be at a climax, Chase joined the group to find out what was going on. After they filled him in, he just smiled, gave his sister a friendly punch in the arm, and held his hand up for a "high five", which Skylar returned weakly.

"I can't do this right now. I have to go. Just watch Mom and Dad. I don't know what is happening, but I have a feeling that something is going on between the two of them that we aren't aware of," Skylar said softly.

"They will be fine," her sister said. "They are just being normal, as far as I can see."

Skylar gave everyone a hug and quickly got in her truck. It wasn't till she was on Hwy 1 back to the Keys that she let the tears fall. She had known that today would be stressful. She had expected a talk from her dad but the way her mother had acted was so strange.

In the back of Skylar's mind, the only conclusion she could come to was that her parents were having problems. She didn't have a clue what the problems might be, because they always seemed so refined and in agreement with everything they did. During her childhood, she could only remember a few times that they had even raised their voices to each other in front of her and her siblings. They would give each other a hug now and then, but there were never overt displays of affection. Skylar always wondered whether they really loved each other because their relationship seemed more like one of politeness instead of affection but they never really gave her reason to think otherwise. Mara always called her a hopeless romantic when Skylar talked about her dreams of a knight in shining armor swooping in to pick her up and give her a fairy tale ending. Recalling her childhood suddenly made her feel even more out of sync with the rest of her family. Maybe she was meant to be a loner. Today had shaken her confidence in everything around her. But as she pulled up to her little house, she suddenly remembered—Garrett would be here in a few hours. Skylar had to pull herself together. Even with the stressful events of the morning and afternoon, she was truly looking forward to spending the evening with the man that was honestly stealing her heart.

14

As Garrett made his way to the little house, he couldn't believe how excited he was to see Skylar. It seemed as if he thought of her day and night, so much so that his work was suffering. He had found himself replaying the romantic scene on the boat, especially as he had watched her the next day during the snorkeling trip. It had been hard for him to concentrate, even though he loved all the questions the tourists were asking him. He had found himself stealing every chance he could to watch for her and smile if she happened to be looking his way. Skylar was so stunning, and he couldn't wait to spend more time alone with her so that they could talk and relax.

He walked to the door with a small bouquet of flowers. He felt so awkward because he had never given flowers to a girl that he could remember. But he wanted to do something for her and wasn't sure what to bring. He had called Abbey again, listening to her laugh as he asked for dating advice. Abbey wasn't making fun of him, but it wasn't long before Zach, her fiancé, was on the speakerphone, helping him out with lots of ideas.

"Stick with flowers right now, Garrett." And that is what he did, holding them right in front of himself as he knocked at the entrance to her home.

"Hi there," Skylar said as she opened the door. Garrett was once again captivated by the woman standing before him. She looked as stunning as she had the other night, even though this time, she was dressed in shorts, a dressy T-shirt, and flip-flops. He was glad that he hadn't dressed up again, wearing his normal clothes but at least choosing items without holes in them.

"Come on in. The lasagna is about done."

The small house had a family room with an open kitchen. He could see other rooms down a hallway and a screened-in porch through the doors in the kitchen. It was very much a Florida house, with a beach vibe throughout.

"I really do like your house. Oh, these are for you," Garrett said, handing her the small bouquet of flowers. Even though this was their second date, he had those first time jitters all over again.

"Thanks! They are beautiful. Like I was telling you the other night, I actually purchased this as a rental several years ago when it came on the market. I didn't think back then I would be living here one day. But I love it. I'm renting out my apartment in Key Biscayne, and it is a tad bigger than this one. Now that I have lived here for a while, I really like the coziness of a smaller home. It's much simpler. Come sit down."

"So, how was your dinner today? I have been wondering all day if your dad said anything." Garrett looked at her as she sat down on the couch a short distance away, tucking her leg underneath as she sat. It seemed that her facial expression went from happy to worried, and Garrett wished he hadn't asked the question so soon after arriving.

"Let's just say it was interesting. It seems my dad had a discussion with my mom about me, the boat, and you. But he didn't say anything to anyone else. But my nosey sister and Harris's fiancé overheard me talking to Maggie, and from there, it was a chain reaction. After we ate, my father had a talk with me," Skylar said, shaking her head.

"Was it that bad?" Garrett asked apprehensively.

"It was just a little out of character. My parents are acting a little strange. Something is up, and I can't quite put my finger on it. My mom made a remark that my dad had been at the boat the other night to find a place to sleep. That sounds to me like they are fighting. And I've never seen my parents hardly disagree about anything." Skylar left out the details about her dad's disapproval of Garrett. She didn't want anything to ruin this evening and was determined to put today's roller coaster family dinner out of her mind.

"So, what have you been doing all day?" Skylar asked, giving him a smile that immediately made him want to pull her into his arms and touch her lips once again. The urge was strong, but he resisted.

"Well, I was supposed to be working on some papers, but for some reason, I couldn't concentrate." He reached over and intertwined his fingers with hers where she had rested her arm on the back of the couch. "You are a hard woman not to think about, especially after our last time together."

The compliment left Skylar speechless, and when she finally put her thoughts together, the only thing that came out was, "I think our dinner is just about ready." She jumped up quickly to check, took the bubbling dish out of the oven, and set it on the stove, with Garrett standing right behind her.

"Well, I must say that does look awfully good. But then, so do you." Skylar turned around, finding Garrett standing so close that she slowly put one arm around his waist just as he gently cupped her face in his hand, bringing her lips to his. It was a slow, enticing kiss that left Skylar wanting much more.

"What do I need to do to help?" Garrett said softly as he pulled away from the kiss, now wrapping his arm around her waist. He was still staring at her, not once looking at the food prepared on the counter.

"It just needs to be moved to the table. Everything else is ready." Skylar's words were slow and soft; she was still focused on him, totally taken in by the man standing so close to her. They only had eyes for each other, and Skylar felt as if food was secondary to what they both wanted.

"Let me grab the rolls out of the oven," she said, quickly catching her breath. Man, he looks amazing tonight, she thought as she began to breathe normally again..

Soon they were sitting at her small table, with a tiny candle lit for some ambience sitting next to the flowers Garrett had brought. Though the thought of watching another sunset with him by the water was appealing, their dinner and a very lively conversation took place instead.

"Did you really do that?" Skylar asked incredulously.

"Yes, I did. I had to try it at least once, and I would do it again anytime. I will have to admit—they were some big-ass great white sharks, but by being in the cage, I was protected. Plus, I see sharks most of the time when I'm doing research. I've gotten used to it, and I just steer clear of them. I've only had a few times when they have made me just a bit nervous. And there've been no bites to date." Garrett took another sip of the wine with which Skylar had completed their Italian dinner. To be able to sit with someone and talk about his adventures was like a breath of fresh air. Skylar was so easy to talk to, and her beauty reeled him in like a fish on a hook. Though he couldn't say it out loud yet, this wonderful woman had captured his heart, and it felt so good. But he wouldn't allow himself just yet to think forward to what the future could possibly be. That had been his mistake before, and he never wanted to feel that way again. Skylar's next question was as though she had read his mind.

"I want to ask you a personal question," she said softly. "Why aren't you in a relationship or married?"

"Wow, you get right to the point," Garrett said, taking a bigger sip of wine this time. "Well, as far as marriage goes, I came close once, but things just didn't work out at the last minute. Even though she said yes when I asked her to marry me, I could feel that she was hesitant. But we made plans and such. A couple of weeks before the big day, she told me she couldn't do it and wished that she had never said 'yes' to my proposal. And since that time, I've never really met anyone I wanted to get to know better than a first or second date. I'll admit that I have had a hard time trusting women since then. I guess I'm really married to my work."

"Do you think I would lie to you?" Skylar asked.

Garrett couldn't hold back what he had been wanting to tell her for a while now. "Honestly, I don't feel that way about you. That is what has me thinking about you constantly. Skylar, you are so different from the other women I've known in my life. You have a genuine enthusiasm for everything you do. You are kind and compassionate, and I can see how much you love your family. You're the type of woman every man dreams of. And you're stunningly beautiful, to add to that sweet personality." Garrett looked into her eyes, wanting to gauge her reaction to what he had said.

"You sure know how to make a girl feel good," Skylar said as she smiled back at him. "Garrett, I don't lie. I tell people how I feel, being as tactful as possible. I promise, no matter where this leads between you and me, I will always be honest. I am sorry you have been hurt in the past. There are some devious women out there, and men too, I might add! But you are different for me too. I love watching you get so involved in your work. Your commitment to what you do is amazing. I think I'm so drawn to you because we are like kindred spirits. You're giving, kind, and sweet. I love the way I feel when I'm around you. Plus, it's kinda hard not to stare at those tanned muscles when we are on the boat," Skylar said, with a laugh. "Hey, how about a walk down the street to sit in the swing by the water," she asked, finding herself and Garrett once again in her kitchen, with just inches separating them as they put away the dinner dishes.

"Only if you tell me about those devious men in your life. I spilled my story, so you're up next." He smiled at her and then gave her a quick kiss on the nose.

"I already told you my sordid tale," she said, with a smile.

As they walked down the little road, he reached for her hand, and they intertwined fingers. The skin of her hands was so soft, making him wonder about the rest of her body. But he quickly tucked that thought away, knowing that if he wanted to see how this relationship would work, he wanted it to be a slow process, not rushed like the times he had experienced before. They were just getting to know each other, but seeing her as she was tonight made it difficult not to want to carry things further, and fast.

The swing that Skylar had talked about was an old wooden porch swing that someone had fixed up and placed on a sandy ledge where the water lapped gently against the rocks. Even though the sun had set, the sky was beautifully clear, and they were able to see the stars above since the swing was hidden from streetlamps.

"So," Garrett said.

"What?" Skylar asked.

"Tell me about these terrible men in your past."

"It's not really terrible, just different. It's that the Miami society I grew up in was very rigid. As teenagers, we were all encouraged to date within our own private little groups. I dated but not much. Remember I'm the oddball here," Skylar said, laughing a little bit at herself.

"You don't look like an oddball to me," Garrett said, giving her a sideways glance.

"Anyway, in college, I met my best friend, Kimberly. While my parents paid my tuition in full, Kim had to get scholarships and work to be able to even go to school. And though we grew up so differently, we instantly became best friends. We did everything together, even against some very heavy objections from my parents."

"What did you do that was so bad?" Garrett asked.

"Nothing really. I loved going to her home in Orlando. Her parents were wonderful, and the atmosphere at her home was completely the opposite of mine. Their family dinners were big, loud, and full of fun. No one cared whether you dressed in the latest fashion or drove the best car. You could just feel the love the minute you walked through the door." Skylar was looking off into the black inkiness in front of them.

"So, what does this have to do with boyfriends?" Garrett asked.

"In college, I dated a guy my parents didn't approve of at all. I thought we were really in love, but when I brought him home to meet my family, let's just say the weekend was so horrible that on Monday, he told me he wanted to break things off. I was so hurt. I just thought that once my parents met him, everything would be fine. I was so naïve.

"After college, I just threw myself into work. At least I got to sell waterfront property. It helped that I was usually by the water. But I just didn't want to be there. Then one night at a charity fund raiser, I met Andrew. And I already told you that story. There is really not much to tell," she said.

"I know you must have dated more guys than two. But as far as Andrew is concerned, he sounds like a jerk to me. He probably did you a favor."

"I think you are right. He was only interested in my family's money. It seems that most of the people my family runs around with are so superficial, and money means you are somebody. Having money is nice, and I'm grateful to my parents, but it can bring out the bad in people so easily. That's why I love living down here," Skylar said as she brought both her feet up onto the swing and wrapped her arms around her legs. It felt so good to be talking to someone about her true feelings—she was always afraid to express them because she felt as if she was weird or sounded ungrateful.

"Are you saying the people that live in the Keys are poor?" Garrett said sarcastically.

"No, I don't mean that at all! I'm sorry if it sounded like that!" Skylar said quickly and apologetically.

"I'm just kidding with you," Garrett said, leaning into her.

"Actually, some of the wealthiest people in Florida live here. They have just moved away from being in the social elite. They don't need it in their lives to be complete, and I love that."

"I know. I've talked to a few of those people, and they seem pretty genuine to me. It is hard for me to grasp this society thing you have lived with all your life," Garrett said.

"It was just how I grew up, and had I not met Kimberly, I'm not sure how I would be today."

"I think you would still be right where you are because it sounds like you have had a different mind-set since you were a little girl. You are passionate, kind, and caring. You love what you do, and it shows in how you treat people, run your business, and live your life. You don't have to have a huge house, even though you could. You are living like us normal people," Garrett said laughingly.

"Well, I like this 'normal' living. I can be myself. And I like that I can be myself around you, that I don't have to have money, fancy clothes, and all that stuff."

"I definitely like you just the way you are. I'm also glad that you are very single, but I'm sorry that you had to go through that pain. I don't wish heartbreak on anyone." Garrett looked over to see her staring at him. "What?"

"You are such a sweet man."

The way Skylar was looking at him, he couldn't help himself. He leaned into her and gently kissed her lips yet again. But Skylar turned to face him because she wanted more. The passionate kiss that came next left both of them breathless, feeling that they could not get enough of each other.

Though he didn't want to leave this spot, Garrett knew it was getting late, and they both would have to be at the boat early in the morning. "Are you ready to walk back?"

"Not really, but I know we should." They both got up, but Garrett pulled her into a loving embrace under the canopy of stars above. For Skylar, once again, it had to be one of the most romantic moments of her life. And she didn't want to let him go. So they walked hand in hand back to her house. But it wasn't till after they had shared one more sizzling kiss that Garrett left. As she watched his truck drive down her little street, she couldn't wait for the next morning. Being with Garrett had nearly erased all the drama of the family dinner.

15

Being on the boat together so often felt like the best dream to her. Every morning, she looked forward to Garrett's smile, and if they happened to be alone, they would steal a quick kiss to start the morning. During the day, especially if Casey or Max was nearby, they kept everything completely professional, but there were those times when they were able to be together for a quick chat or touch as they brushed by each other that seemed to solidify their growing feelings for each other.

Most evenings, Garrett and Skylar were now spending together. Whether it was at the local bar and grill, at a nicer restaurant on the weekends, or spending time at one of their homes, they were learning so much about each other, yearning to spend more and more time together.

Garrett was teaching her more about the sea life for future boat charters, and he also helped her add yet another client to her ever-growing list. Skylar was beginning to think about adding another boat, something she was now discussing with Garrett, but she knew that the money was not quite there yet. One thing was for sure: her business was growing and becoming more successful, and if her projections were correct, she would meet her father's demands. Skylar might be the wayward child in the family, but she would be a successful one, of that she was determined.

"The heat is a little brutal today," Max said as they all sat under the canopy of the boat, eating their lunches. Skylar and Garrett were sitting side by side, much to Casey's consternation. Skylar was grateful that Casey had never brought up the incident at the restaurant, though she was sure that she was still steaming at their deception that night. Casey continued to be ever so attentive to Garrett, while ignoring Max most of the time. As for Skylar, Casey avoided her, and if they happened to look each other, the icy intern gave Skylar a stone-cold stare.

"I think we lost that ocean wind," Garrett said as he looked across the water. "Why don't we all go for a swim before Casey and I take another dive? That way, you guys can cool off too."

"That sounds awesome to me," Max said, already taking his T-shirt off, ready to dive into the ocean.

"I would love to swim without all the dive gear," Casey said in the sickeningly sweet voice as she walked toward Garrett. Skylar could only watch and shake her head. "Skylar——you coming?," Garrett said, turning to her with eyebrows raised and a wink.

"The boat is anchored safely, but it feels funny not to have someone on it," Skylar said, voicing her concerns out loud.

"It will be fine," Garrett said, reaching out to touch her arm for reassurance. When she turned, Casey was looking right at her, and a frown was showing prominently on the girl's face.

"Okay. I haven't been swimming for a while."

"Then I'll make sure to keep an eye on you and protect you, if needed," Garrett whispered in her ear as he moved a bit closer to her. Skylar couldn't contain the smile that came across her face, and she didn't care whether Casey saw her or not.

Max dived into the water, followed by Garrett. Just as Skylar was taking off her T-shirt and shorts, Casey came up beside her.

"Have you been on any more dates?" Casey asked sarcastically.

"It really isn't any of your business," Skylar answered, trying to keep her cool.

"If I were you, I wouldn't get too attached to him. From what I've heard, he doesn't stick around in one place too long. And it seems as if trouble follows him everywhere. You just might want to be careful." Casey was just about to walk away, but Skylar stepped in front of her.

"Casey, don't you think you are being a bit pathetic, trying to ruin our date, flirting with him every chance you get—so openly that it is disgusting—and throwing yourself at him? He shared with me that he told you that you are only an intern and assistant to him. Why do you keep persisting when it's clear he is only your boss for a few more weeks?" Skylar kept her tone as even as she could, choosing her words so as to avoid antagonizing the girl, but it was taking every ounce of willpower she possessed.

"I'm not really sure, except that he is exceptionally good-looking. And maybe just one date with me would show him there are much better women out there. Besides, he probably only likes you for your money, or shall I say, your family's money." Casey raised her eyebrows and smirked, which made Skylar want to smack her.

"Or maybe he wants to be with someone who doesn't act like a slut!" Great! Skylar thought. Now I've lost my cool.

"I was wondering how long it would take for you to lose that little-girl simplicity. You are just like every other society girl I've met. It seems I just finally got under your skin. Now, if only Garrett could see the real you."

Before Skylar could say another word, Casey dived into the water not far from Garrett, coming up and splashing him and Max. Skylar only looked over the side of the boat, her interest in swimming now disappearing.

"Are you coming in?" Garrett asked, waving toward her.

Skylar decided that she didn't really want to go in now, but seeing Casey trying to dunk and splash both guys bothered her. She was not going to get away with her words, so Skylar jumped into the water, coming up beside Garrett. She swam to him, put her arms around him, and gave him a quick peck on the cheek. Garrett was so stunned at the open display of affection that he quickly turned to see whether Casey was watching them.

"Do you want to tell me what is going on?" Garrett said quietly.

"Casey and I had a girl talk, didn't we?" Skylar said loudly enough for Casey to join in the conversation. "She was giving me a bit of dating advice, which I really appreciated. She also let me know that she knew that we were dating, so I guess we don't have to be so secretive."

"Okay," Garrett said slowly, trying to comprehend what was happening between the two women.

"Dang, it's about time!" yelled Max. "I've been watching you guys, and it was so obvious. I'm happy for ya!"

By the look on Casey's face, she certainly didn't share Max's sentiments. And Garrett was looking very uncomfortable.

"Maybe it's time to go back aboard. We have one more dive to do, and then I need to head in to do some work on the reports due next week." Garrett quickly swam to the boat, with Skylar close behind. Before Casey was on the boat, he quickly turned to Skylar.

"What the hell was that?"

"I'm sorry. I overreacted to Casey's remarks."

"What are you talking about?" Garrett asked, but Casey was just coming on board, and Skylar turned away.

"That girl drives me crazy! I can't believe I just did that and probably ruined any chance I had with Garrett!" Skylar practically screamed once researcher and intern were back down beneath the clear blue waters.

"What are you talking about?" Max said, looking at her as if she was going crazy.

"There were just some things Casey said before we all went swimming. Max, for your own sake, stay away from her. She is up to no good."

"No problem there. She has already informed me that I'm not her type. It's no big deal," Max said cheerfully. Skylar looked at him and suddenly wished she could adopt the carefree attitude that he had. Max never let other's opinions bother him. He was true to himself, something that she was doing, but it just seemed to come easier to him. Skylar only wished she could duplicate that for her own life.

"Well, she said some very derogatory things about Garrett, and I would hate for her to take advantage of you. So, I'm sorry that things didn't work out for you with her, but then again, I'm glad you aren't pursuing her after her spiteful remarks today."

"She's that bad, huh?"

"She's that bad," said Skylar, defeated. For some reason, she felt that this wasn't over with Casey. She would tell Garrett everything that had happened, and then he could decide what to do from there. Skylar felt that Casey was now a ticking time bomb. And she and Garrett both needed to be on guard. She would tell Garrett that she wouldn't antagonize Casey as she had today, but it would be hard not to. And not because she wanted to make the younger girl jealous, but because today, swimming in the water with Garrett had been such a rush. Even with the heat of the stressful situation, Skylar couldn't get the feeling of Garrett's body next to hers in the water out of her mind.

Beneath the boat, Garrett and Casey were collecting more data for the report that was due next week. But Garrett's mind wasn't on the task before them. He added the memory of Skylar's body next to his in the water to the ever-growing proof in his mind that she was meant to be his. Even though the increasing feelings for this special woman still caused him a slight bit of anxiety, there was an overwhelming feeling of happiness that surpassed the little fear. And it wasn't as if he was just attracted to her physically, which he definitely was, but Skylar was basically the woman he never knew he wanted.

Skylar heard the pair surface and felt a knot in her stomach. She just wanted to head to the marina and then home. This tug-of-war with Casey was playing on her nerves, and she just needed to get away from her as quickly as possible.

Soon they were pulling into the marina, which was a very welcome sight for Skylar. The way she felt about her confrontation with Casey earlier had led to a feeling of just wanting to be alone tonight, even though she was torn because the thought of spending time with Garrett felt like the medicine she needed to calm the uneasiness of the day.

"What a day," Garrett said, securing their gear as usual and putting away the notes he had made on their way back to the marina. "Casey, I have so much information that I'm not sure if we will be diving next week. I'll let you know on Monday." Garrett was staring at a paper, and as he got ready to put it in his bag, Casey reached up, gave him a quick kiss on the cheek, casually grabbed her stuff, and jumped off the boat.

"That sounds good, Garrett. I'll see you on Monday, if not before." As Casey walked down the dock, Skylar looked at her in disbelief and then turned to see Garrett just standing there, as if he didn't know what had just happened.

"I promise I don't know what that was," Garrett said quickly, looking at Skylar, seeing frustration in her eyes. But then, he didn't know what else to say. He was dumbfounded.

Skylar picked up her stuff, locked everything, and jumped down to the dock. She just wanted to leave the scene. Maybe this relationship had been just too good to be true. She needed time to think.

16

"Please answer your door," Garrett said for what seemed like the fiftieth time. Skylar wasn't answering, but he could hear the TV playing. She had to be home. Skylar had to know that he had no feelings for Casey. He had told her how he felt at their very first dinner at her house.. Then suddenly, he knew where she was.

"I thought I might find you here," Garrett said as he stood quietly beside the swing. She was just where he had thought—in the small swing at the end of her street, staring out at the waters of the ocean.

"I really just want to be alone tonight," Skylar said, not even looking over at him. She knew if she did, her resolve to be by herself would crumble into little pieces.

"Sorry, but I'm not going anywhere. Do you mind if I sit? I can continue to stand, or even sit on the ground beside the swing, but sitting beside you is where I would rather be."

"Garrett," Skylar said. "This thing with Casey. I know you have talked to her. But she is still hell-bent on getting to you, one way or another. When you and Max were swimming, she basically said so, and more."

"What did she say? Skylar, I spend my time with you. I've never even been out with the girl! And why the hell she kissed me—I'm as shocked as you. I didn't even know what to say!"

"That was very obvious." Skylar continued to stare out at the water while Garrett took the seat beside her, but this time, he didn't sit as close as he would have liked to.

Garrett took a deep breath, closed his eyes for a brief moment, and then began. "Skylar, you're truly the only woman in my life right now. You're beautiful, sexy, smart, caring—hell, I could go on and on. But the one thing I want you to know is that I want to be with you, not anyone else. And don't take this the wrong way, but the way I feel about you seems foreign to me because I haven't felt like this in such a long time. But its is not a bad thing. Actually, you make me feel crazy good. I love the way you make me feel like I'm the only person in your world. You get me. You let me talk about my crazy job, laugh at my stupid jokes, and more." He noticed that Skylar was finally looking at him; her eyes were so soft that it was melting his heart.

"I only want you. I only want to date you. I only want to see you. I only want to be with you, no one else. Sometimes, things start out one way and end up another. I want us to be more than just friends. I know I'm not exactly what you are looking for, but I hope like hell that you feel the same way."

These were words that Skylar needed to hear to heal the way she was feeling. She felt the same way for him, but she was scared to voice it out loud because she had never been in a relationship like this. Everything before Garrett seemed to be manufactured, like something that she was made to do or had to do to please those around her, unlike what was happening now. Her feelings were organic. If he was having feelings he didn't understand, then so was she. But they felt so good that she didn't want them to stop or go away.

Instead of saying anything, Skylar scooted closer to Garrett, as close as she could. She reached up to touch his face, feeling a rush of excitement course through her hand and travel through her body at the simple gesture.

"You are what I have been looking for. And I feel the same way about you too. I'm sorry about my behavior today. Between Casey's snide remarks, her icy glares my way and watching her kiss you, I let my emotions get the best of me." She reached over, leaning into him, and gently let her lips touch his. It was as if they were in a world all their own, only the two of them, being consumed by each other.

"I've wanted to tell you that for days but was just so scared to. I'm not the kind of man you are used to. I'm definitely not the kind of man your parents or family will approve of. I even thought that it might be better for us to just be friends, but I can't. The thought of being without you is more than I can bare to think about."

"Garrett, you are the best man I've ever met. I thank God that you decided to take a chance on me and my boat, because I don't know if we would have ever met otherwise.

You have changed my life for the better. Thank you. And I only want to be with you." This time, she pulled him to his feet so she could circle her arms around his neck, pulling him even closer to her. They stood there for a minute, hugging each other tightly.

"What about your family?" Garrett asked.

"I don't care. But personally, I think they will love you," she said, smiling at him as he continued to hold her in his strong embrace.

"As a matter of fact, why don't you come to family dinner with me on Sunday?"

"I don't think that will be such a good idea."

"Why not? If we are going to be together, I don't want to hide from anyone, including my family or Casey."

"Ugh, Casey. I think after I get this next paper written, I'm going to have to let her go. I know she only has a few more weeks, but she is making everyone miserable."

Skylar took his hand as they began to walk back toward her house. "Let her continue to work. If we have to, we will both talk to her. But I think if you tell her we are dating, maybe she will back down. If not, we can handle whatever she throws our way."

Garrett sighed at Skylar's words, knowing that she was right. As much as he wanted to let the girl go, he had made a commitment to his friend, and he could stick it out for a couple more weeks. He kissed the top of Skylar's head. "You're right. Together we can do anything, right?"

"Definitely!" Skylar said as they opened the door to her house.

The feeling on the boat the next morning was completely different. It was like an atmosphere of fun, excitement, and joy all wrapped up into one. It was Saturday and time for the snorkeling tours for the tourists, which Skylar loved, especially when Garrett was there. After their evening last night, she wanted him with her every moment. His infectious attitude was one that everyone gravitated toward. To watch him talk and teach about the very things he loved—the ocean and all its creatures—filled her with happiness. She had found someone who had embraced what he loved to do despite what others thought, and she was starting to feel like she belonged in this world.

"Now, the captain here can tell you all about the boats," Garrett said, coming up to Skylar with a little boy, who appeared to be about seven or eight years old. "This young man wants to drive the boat home." Garrett looked at her with a smile and then blew her a little kiss.

"Do you? Have you ever piloted a boat before?" Skylar asked, kneeling down to his level.

"No," the little boy said in a low voice.

"What is your name?"

"Joey."

"Well, let me see. Where are your mom and dad?" The boy turned and pointed to a couple that were watching her.

"Is it okay if Joey is my co-captain on our ride back to shore?" Skylar looked over at the boy, whose eyes were as big as saucers at her words. Then he quickly turned to see his parents shaking their heads yes.

"Okay. The first thing we have to do is make sure everyone is safely on board and ready for the ride back. Let's check." Skylar took Joey's hand, and she let the little boy ask whether everyone was ready. It was as if the child had grown a foot in confidence as Skylar let him ask the questions. Then she shared the seat with him, and they began their journey back to the dock. He was full of questions. Skylar never once tired of talking, while at the same time piloting the boat over the ocean waters.

Garrett sat with Max near the rear of the boat, watching Skylar, his heart swelling with pride. He had found someone like him. She was his other half, something he hadn't felt as if he would ever find, and frankly, it hadn't mattered to him anymore. But apparently, as he had told Skylar the night before, things don't always start out as it seems they will. He had to admit—he had fallen in love with this beautiful boat captain. He hadn't told her yet because of fear, but he knew even more as he watched her with the child that this woman was part of his heart that he had found in the Keys.

"That was a good day," Skylar said just as Max left the boat, leaving only her and Garrett aboard. He quickly put his arms around her waist, kissing her before she could say another word.

"Man, I've wanted to do that all day!" Garrett said once they came up for air.

"I'm not complaining." Skylar said as she continued to stare into Garrett's deep blue eyes.

"So, are we still on for dinner with my family tomorrow?" she asked, with a slight hesitation in her voice.

"Yes, but I have to admit I'm apprehensive. I'm different. I don't usually fit in with—" But Garrett didn't finish his sentence.

"You fit with me. And my family isn't at all uppity. Well, maybe my parents are, but they are still great people."

"I didn't mean anything bad," Garrett said quickly.

"I didn't take it that way," Skylar said, looking up into his eyes, which seemed worried that maybe he had said the wrong thing. "Just come with me tomorrow. If things don't go as I think they will, we don't have to go back."

"Skylar, you don't understand. I can't make you choose between myself and your family. That's wrong."

"I'm a grown woman. I'm not being disrespectful, but they will have to honor my decisions, in all areas of my life. I'm learning that now, especially with the boat business. I have more charters and more calls each day, which is such a blessing. I really need to look for another boat and a captain. I wasn't ready to take that step, but I think I am now. You have given me the confidence to step out even more boldly than I have before. I'm still the same me my family has always seen. It's just that now, I'm Skylar 2.0," she said, with a happy smile.

"Well, honestly, I don't know about the '2.0' part because I only know the person I met when I came aboard the boat. And you completely changed my life." Garrett sighed, looked at her, and smiled. "So, let's meet the family then," he said as he wrapped his arm around her shoulder, and they walked toward their trucks.

17

The ride to Key Biscayne the following morning was beautiful—a blue sky overhead, a temperature just right for enjoying a ride with the windows down, and the girl of his dreams sitting close beside him. Garrett was feeling happy, but an undercurrent of apprehension simultaneously ran through him. He had read about Skylar's family once before when he found out who she was. Now that he was going to see them in person, he had researched more information last night, praying that he would have something in common with this family. Skylar was so important to him, and he didn't want this visit to cause a rift in their budding relationship. But he could imagine the questions already, with the first one being, "How old are you?"

When they first met, Skylar had seemed to be too young to be a competent boat captain, much less someone with whom he could see himself spending time. But when Garrett's feelings for her developed, he only saw an alluring woman. Age was never an issue in his growing feelings for her. And her interest in him couldn't be founded in money because he certainly didn't have any; he basically lived from one research project to another, but he loved his life. Garrett did sometimes wonder what she saw in him, but that question quickly disappeared every time he saw Skylar, or even thought about her, for that matter.

"Don't be so nervous," she said, looking at Garrett and seeing him grip the steering wheel very tightly.

"I'm fine," he said, quickly giving her a smile.

"It looks like you are about to rip that wheel out of the column." Skylar looked toward Garrett's hands and grinned. She patted his leg, saying, "I promise everything is going to be fine today."

"Do they even know I'm coming?"

"No, but that is the beauty of it. They will be able to see us together just being ourselves. And, Garrett, that is what we need to do. Please don't let the surroundings or my family intimidate you at all. Just be yourself. I know two people who will be your biggest fans, other than me."

"What are you talking about?" Garrett said, giving her a very puzzled look.

"My sister, Mara, and my future sister-in-law, Tracey, saw your picture already. In truth, my entire family saw your picture when they asked to see photos of the boat. But Mara and Tracey were whispering in my ear about the gorgeous hunk on my boat, wondering why I didn't ask you out."

"Really. Okay, I like them already. So, why didn't you ask me out?" Garrett now had a smirk on his face.

"Because I felt it was more ladylike to let the gentleman ask instead. Plus, I didn't think you really liked me."

"Are you kidding? I liked you from the moment I laid eyes on you." Skylar couldn't resist leaning over to give him a quick kiss on the cheek.

"We will follow that up with something better later." She smiled. "Take this exit."

Before Garrett knew it, he was parking in front of the most magnificent home he had seen in southern Florida. It was a beautiful tropical mansion that seemed to be the size of a very exclusive hotel. Garrett was speechless.

"You grew up here," he said, looking at Skylar.

"Yep. It's a little too much, huh?"

"It's beautiful. And big! Did you need a GPS to navigate the house?" Garrett said as he started to laugh.

"Ha, ha." Skylar grinned back at him as they both got out of the truck, and it only took a moment for Garrett to be standing beside her.

"Are you ready?" she said, looking up at him eagerly. She couldn't wait to introduce him to everyone, even if there was a slight bit of anxiety. Skylar felt in her heart, deep down, that they would find that he was perfect for her, just as she had found out over time.

But before they reached the front door, it swung open wide to reveal Mara and Tracey. Here we go, Skylar thought as she looked at the two women.

"Well, hello, you guys. Skylar, we didn't know you were bringing a guest today. I'm Mara, Skylar's most wonderful older sister. It's nice to meet you..." she said, waiting for Garrett to finish the sentence. But he seemed to be like a deer stuck in the headlights.

"Mara, Tracey, this is my friend Garrett. Garrett, my sister, Mara, who has already so graciously introduced herself. Tracey is my older brother's fiancé."

Garrett shook both women's hands, and each had a look on her face of sheer adoration, making Skylar cringe just slightly.

Suddenly, Mara grabbed him and gave him a big hug. "We girls don't shake hands. We give hugs!" Before Skylar knew it, Tracey had hugged Garrett too, both women still smiling as though they were at some male strip club.

"Come on. Let's go inside," Skylar said, holding Garrett's hand, guiding him into the entrance of the house. "I always go to the kitchen first to say hello to Maggie, our cook. She is the sweetest woman and taught me that lasagna recipe—remember?"

"I have to go check on Lyla. We will be back shortly." Skylar shook her head as she watched Mara and Tracey walk off like two high school girls who had just met the most popular guy in school for the first time.

"They both seem nice and normal," Garrett said.

"What were you expecting?" Skylar looked at him as they came into the kitchen. "Maggie!" she said, hugging the older lady. "I want you to meet my friend Garrett Holmes. Garrett, this is Maggie, who makes the best food in the whole state of Florida."

"It's nice to meet you, Maggie," Garrett said, once again extending his hand. But instead of shaking it, Maggie took his hand in both of her hands.

"Now I see why you like to spend your time with your precious boat, my little Skylar," Maggie said, with a twinkle in her eye. "You be good to her. She is most precious."

Garrett instantly liked the woman. She wore her heart on her sleeve, and it was evident that Skylar was like a daughter to her. "I will tell you a secret. I think she is pretty special too," Garrett said and Maggie looked at him with such a sweet smile before going back to preparing the meal.

"Can we help?" Skylar asked nervously, knowing that the next introductions would produce more stress.

"I think everything is ready and that you are putting off the inevitable. Go!" Maggie said, motioning with her hands for the couple to leave the kitchen. With that, Skylar turned to Garrett.

"Let's meet the rest of the family." She slid her hand into Garrett's, gave it a squeeze, and walked into the family room.

When they entered the spacious room, Garrett was amazed at how it was partly elaborate and partly relaxed. He wasn't sure what he had expected to find, only that he had never been to a home such as this, except for a few during fund-raising events. The room was very large, with comfortable chairs and couches placed in just the right spots so that everyone could sit and talk or watch the extremely large TV that practically covered the entire wall. Garrett couldn't even begin to figure out how large it was, but the size of the room could certainly handle it. Over to the left, he saw a big, open dining room with a long table, like something he had seen in movies but never in someone's home. The large room definitely had an upscale, tropical look, perfect for Florida. Suddenly, he felt a slight squeeze of his hand. As he looked around once more, all eyes were on him and Skylar.

"Hi, everyone! I decided to bring a friend with me today. I would like you to meet Garrett Holmes. He is a marine biologist and researcher who is currently doing some work at the reef off Key Largo." Skylar slowly walked from person to person, introducing him to her brothers and then Paul. But suddenly, Garrett felt two little arms wrap around his legs.

"This little munchkin is my niece, Lyla. Hello, little one!" Skylar said as she untangled Lyla from around Garrett, picked her up, and planted a kiss on the little girl's cheek.

"Aunt Sky, is he your boyfriend?" Out of the mouth of babes, Skylar thought.

"Hi, we've met before but not formally. I'm Jonathan Cartwright, Skylar's father." He only stood there, staring at Garrett and making him more nervous with each second that ticked by. Seeing Skylar's father once more brought back memories of that night on the boat and the nerves it had produced.

"It's nice to see you again," he said as he stuck his hand out to greet her father, but instead of shaking his hand, Jonathan turned his back on Garrett, who looked at Skylar. She quietly shook her head and mouthed, "It's okay." She might have thought so, but for Garrett, things felt as if they were beginning to go downhill, and he and Skylar had only just arrived.

"Well, my goodness. It looks like I got here just in time," said a sweet southern voice. Skylar recognized her mother immediately, even though the tone of her voice sounded a bit sarcastic and maybe even as though she had had a drink or two again.

And Skylar was right. As they turned around, Sadie stood before them, with a drink in her hand once again. Why was she drinking so much? And why today?

"Mom, I would like you to meet Garrett Holmes. He is—" But her mother cut her off quickly.

"Yes, yes—I heard your little introduction as I was walking downstairs. So, you are the one my husband found with Skylar on the boat that night. It looks like you did pretty good, Sky," her mother said, eyeing Garrett up and down like a specimen of meat. She walked by them, not once acknowledging Garrett, who just stood watching her.

"Everything is ready," Maggie said to the suddenly very quiet room.

"We will help bring everything to the table," Skylar said, grabbing Garrett's hand and walking toward the kitchen.

"That went over well," Garrett said tensely, whispering in Skylar's ear.

"Actually, it went better than I thought."

"You have got to be kidding me. Next time, prep me a little bit, okay?"

"You were awesome, and you don't need prepping. You are just fine the way you are." And she gave his hand a quick squeeze. "And thank you. Thank you for just being you and being by my side. You don't know how much that means to me."

"This looks a bit more serious than I thought," said Chase as he and Blair came around the corner, with a big grin on his face.

"Enough, everyone! Let's get the food to the table before it gets cold," Maggie said.

Garrett helped with the food and took a seat beside Skylar. The large table accommodated the entire family—eleven people in all. Garrett thought he remembered people's names but wished they were wearing name tags to be on the safe side. After little Lyla said a prayer for their meal, the food was passed from person to person. Though everything looked and smelled fantastic, Garrett's appetite was all but gone because of how he and Skylar had been received. He couldn't remember the last time he had been at a woman's house to meet her family. He thought he had been ready for this dinner, wanting to do this for Skylar, but now that he was here, Garrett wanted to run. This was not the type of family he was used to, and Skylar seemed so different from the rest of the people seated with him at the table. But in all fairness, they hadn't talked—at least, not yet.

"So, Garrett, Skylar says that you are a marine biologist. What type of work are you doing in Key Largo?" Mara asked, unable to wipe the grin off her face as she looked from Garrett to Skylar and back again.

"Right now, I'm studying the coral reef off the coast. Parts of it are dying, so we are doing some research to study the causes. Soon, I will be working with a coral reef restoration project. Plus, I tag and monitor sea turtles in the area."

"He has also been accompanying some of the scuba and snorkeling trips I've booked, giving the tourists more information on the fish and other creatures along the reef," Skylar said, for good measure.

"How long have you been in Key Largo?" Chase asked, before taking a big bite of roasted chicken.

"Almost a couple of months. The study lasts for a year." Garrett was handling himself well, Skylar thought as she looked at him, feeling so happy.

"Then where will you go? Or do you just wander around from job to job?" Her mother had suddenly chimed in from the end of the table.

"I think what my wife is trying to ask is, do you own a house here in Florida? Do you have a steady job with the university here? Are you planning to say in the Keys?" said Skylar's father almost in the same condescending voice her mother had just used. Why were they doing this, Skylar thought to herself while the rest of the table was quiet.

"I own a piece of property in the outskirts of Savannah, Georgia. Right now, since I don't usually stay in one place longer than a year or so, I rent. Being a marine biologist isn't a very glamorous job, and you certainly don't do it for the money. But I love what I do and I always have." Garrett was feeling defensive but made sure to choose his words wisely. He didn't want to ruin anything for Skylar, but he was beginning to feel he didn't belong here.

"Yes, that is what we tried to tell Skylar when she insisted on studying biology in college. There's no money there, unless you are a doctor. But did she listen to her parents? No." Her mother's words stung, but Skylar kept her mouth shut. Everyone else at the table, including little Lyla, stayed silent.

"If only she would give up this ridiculous business of hers and come back to her senses, she could retain her portion of the family's business and find a suitable husband."

"Sadie!" Jonathan said furiously.

"Jonathan, you know I'm right. You have said yourself that all you had to do was bide your time. You said that Skylar would fail, and then everything would go back to being like it should be. Maybe she could even get Andrew back into her life, but we all know that boat has sailed." Sadie sat back in her chair and reached for her wineglass, instead of eating anything.

If the room seemed silent before, now it was suddenly void of all sound. No forks clinked against plates, nor could a breath be heard. Everyone was staring at the table or at each other. Skylar was horrified. She had expected some uncomfortable moments, as occurred in any normal situation of introducing someone new to loved ones, but this was beyond anything she could have imagined.

Skylar looked at her father, who sat motionless, staring at his glass. Her mother took another swig of her drink, her eyes now looking glassy, with a slight grin on her face.

"I guess I know how to silence a room, now, don't I," Sadie said, with a laugh.

"Mom, how could you? And, Dad, do you really have no faith in me? Do you both want me to fail that badly just because I'm not falling in line with my brothers and sister?" Skylar felt badly for bringing her siblings into this argument, but it was time she stood up for herself.

"Harris, Mara, and Chase have always wanted to work with you. I've always been the one who wanted something different in my life, besides selling houses. I'm sorry I've disappointed you, but can't you please be happy for me? Please? One of the things I wanted to share with you today, besides bringing Garrett here to meet everyone, was to let you know that business is going so well that I'm ready to bring on another boat and hire a captain. I'm finally finding my place in this crazy world of ours. It might not include huge mansions, expensive cars, and society dinners, but I love my life."

"But you deserve someone other than a mere marine biologist," her father said quietly. "I'm sorry, Garrett, but I've always wanted what is best for my children. Plus, you are much older than Skylar."

"Now your father is finally being honest," her mother said.

"At least I know what honesty is," Jonathan said to his wife, who suddenly went pale, while everyone at the table quickly looked at both parents.

Now, Garrett was at his breaking point. He had nothing to lose by speaking what he felt. "Mr. and Mrs. Cartwright—first of all, I want to thank you for your hospitality. The dinner was wonderful. Meeting all of Skylar's family has been nice. But honestly, I'm just a simple man living a simple lifestyle. I don't have the kind of money you have. I never have, and I'm not sure I ever will. But I love my life. I love what I do—teaching people about the ocean, learning, and helping others. And one of the most amazing things I've done lately was meeting your daughter. I'll be the first to admit that when I found out that she was the boat captain, I didn't think she was capable. But that first day, she proved me wrong." Garrett looked over at Skylar, reaching over to take her hand.

"What started out as a friendship has grown. Is there an age difference? Yes, but I don't think that matters. Mr. and Mrs. Cartwright, I love your daughter. Skylar is the best thing to happen to me in such a long time." Skylar looked over at him slowly as it sunk in that he had just made a declaration of love for her in front of her entire family. The warmth that flooded her body washed away some of the stress she was feeling from the heated conversation.

"Love." Sadie laughed. "Love doesn't exist. You might think you love someone for a while, but it will fade. But one thing that doesn't is money, right, Jonathan?"

Skylar stood up and looked at her siblings. "I'm sorry if I said anything that might have hurt your feelings. I love each of you; you know that." Then she turned to her parents.

"I love you both very much, but your comments have let me know once and for all how you truly feel. And it hurts me more than I can say. I have tried my best to be a good daughter. I've followed along, playing the high society game the best I could. I've been respectful and never given you any trouble. All I wanted was a chance to prove myself by doing something I love. And today, I wanted to share that success with you! I wanted to let you know that everything you taught me over the years led to helping me succeed, not just in the real estate business. And I also wanted to share with you someone who has become very special to me. But you both have ruined it. Mom, I don't know what is going on or why you are drinking so much, but you shouldn't drink in front of your granddaughter. And, Dad, I've never known you to look down on people so much, or have I just been blind all these years?

"I know that there is something going on between the two of you, and if you don't want us to know, that is your business. But for future reference, it does affect all of us in this family."

She then turned to look at Garrett, with tears threatening to spill forth. "Are you ready to go?"

"I'm ready whenever you are," he said, wishing he could scoop her up in his arms and cradle her to help with the hurt that was showing on her face.

Skylar and Garrett both walked out of the room, and no one said a word. Skylar felt as if she wasn't even breathing till they were out the front door and down the steps. Suddenly she bent over, trying to keep the tears from flowing. But Garrett quickly caught her, holding Skylar in a hug that gave her more comfort than she could have imagined.

"I'm so, so sorry, Garrett. I had no idea that any of that would happen. My parents are good people, they truly are. It is as if the man and woman you met today are people I've never met before." Now the tears did start to flow down her cheeks as they made their way to the truck.

"Hey!" They both heard a voice coming from behind them. They turned around to see Harris and Chase walking quickly toward them.

"Garrett, I'm sorry about what happened back there. I promise things aren't usually that crazy," Harris said.

"Or that snobby!" Chase quickly chimed in.

"I have to admit, we were all a bit skeptical about Skylar's adventure, but she has always beat to her own drum while also keeping Mom and Dad happy at her own expense. I love what I do, but I was glad that she finally stepped out on her own, because we all knew she wasn't happy working at the office," Harris said, suddenly hugging his little sister.

"I thought you guys thought I was crazy!"

"We do, or should I say we did. None of us has ever done anything other than work for Dad. You were the first one to have the balls to do something entirely different."

"But you were right when you said something was going on with Mom and Dad," Chase said. "When we know more, we'll let you know."

"What do you mean?" Skylar said, looking up at Garrett, who had remained quiet the whole time.

"Mom is drinking, all the time it seems. Dad is really quiet. We just haven't been able to figure out why they are acting so out of character all of a sudden. I'm sure we will find out soon enough."

"I'm not coming back for a while. I need some time. You know where I am, and you are welcome to come down anytime." Skylar turned to Harris. "Please tell Mara and Paul to bring Lyla down, and we will go out in the boat. Maybe Garrett could even show her the different little sea creatures he shows others when we go snorkeling," Skylar said as she looked up at Garrett. "You too, Chase," she said, hugging both her brothers. "Promise me you will tell Mara what I said."

"I will," Harris said then turned to Garrett. "Thank you for taking care of our little sister. Personally, I don't think she could have chosen a better man."

"I totally agree," Chase said, shaking Garrett's hand.

"Well, I keep my promises. She is pretty special to me." Garrett helped Skylar get in the truck, and then they headed back to Key Largo.

18

During the ride back to Skylar's house, she and Garrett sat close together on the seat of the old truck, with Skylar resting her head on his shoulder. They said nothing during the hour-long ride back to the Key while Garrett let Skylar process everything that had just happened with her family. He himself was ruminating over everything that had been said. He was in love with a girl that came from a completely different world that he wasn't part of. She had grown up differently than he had. She had money, privilege, and a large family. And she was younger—by almost ten years. Maybe he had gotten himself into a situation he wasn't prepared for.

But then he remembered what he had told Skylar's father: "I love your daughter." And he had meant it, every single word. He loved this girl sitting beside him whose tears were creating a huge damp area on his shoulder.

It wasn't long before they were sitting in the driveway of Skylar's house. Garrett slowly parked the truck, shutting down the engine. "Do you still feel the same way now that you have met my family?" Skylar said, slowly lifting her head off his shoulder, looking at him with red-rimmed eyes. "Do you really love me?"

Garrett looked at her lovely face, wiped at the tears on her cheeks and cupped her chin in his hand. "I do. I've known for some time and just hadn't found the best time to tell you. I guess I should have told you first, but when your parents said what they did, I couldn't help myself. I felt like I needed to protect you. I do love you, Skylar." He leaned over and kissed her lips ever so softly, then gently, lovingly kissed each tearstained cheek.

"I love you too," Skylar said, happiness flooding over the heartache caused by her family. "I didn't think you could love me. I'm so different. I have a weird family, as you now know, and I'm so not normal, at least in the world I come from."

"I think that is what makes me love you more. And now that we have broken all the rules, I'm more than willing to fight for what we have."

"Me too," she said, smiling back at him. "Want to come in for a bit and maybe watch a movie or something? Since we didn't get to eat, maybe we could even order a pizza," she laughed.

"Pizza sounds good but I have to admit—that food Maggie cooked looked and smelled really good." Garrett laughed lightly, trying to help them forget for just a bit what had happened. "As for the movie, no mushy chick movie. I get to pick!"

"No!" Skylar said, laughing as they walked into the house. But before Skylar could say another word, Garrett had her in his arms, caressing her waist and back, suddenly kissing her so passionately that time seemed to stand still for both of them. Skylar found her hand wandering up to the nape of his neck, suddenly running her hands through his hair, which felt so soft and silky in her hands. She could feel his heartbeat, or was it hers, beating harder with each touch and kiss.

"I love you, Garrett. You mean more to me than I can express. And right now, I want you in ways that I shouldn't. It's too soon, and too much is happening. I'm sorry!"

"Don't you apologize. I agree with you, but taking you in my arms and carrying you to the bed in the other room sounds like the best idea I have had all day. But we will know when the time is right. And that time isn't right now. But we can still spend every minute possible together. And I can still kiss you like this." Garrett's mouth was on hers, once again giving her a kiss that sent her senses reeling. "And I can touch you like this." Suddenly his hand was running down the length of her arm, up to her neck, caressing her face and tracing her back down to her waist and hips. Every sensation was pleasurable and she didn't want him to stop. But if this went much further, neither would be able to stop the tension that was growing between them.

"I think I'll order the pizza now, while you find something to watch on TV," Skylar said, her breath coming out heavily.

"If you insist," Garrett said, releasing her from his embrace ever so slowly.

She watched him sit on her sofa as she reached for her cell phone. Skylar had forgotten that she had silenced it during the ride home and was shocked to see almost twenty messages. But she was in no mood to listen to them now. After the afternoon they had, tonight was a time to celebrate that she was really in love for the first time in her life. And even if the rest of the day hadn't turned out so well, she was definitely going to do her best to make sure the evening was wonderful.

It wasn't long after they finished eating that Skylar looked down to see Garrett sleeping, with his head in her lap. He had stretched out on the couch to watch a favorite fishing show, but she heard slight snores within a few minutes. And even though she was tired, she didn't want to move. Skylar loved watching him sleep, using her fingers to gently move the hair from his forehead. He looked so peaceful, especially after the crazy day they had.

At that thought, Skylar began to replay the day's events in her mind. She had expected some resistance, but something was really wrong with the whole scenario. It was so frustrating that she couldn't figure it out. She was usually such a good judge of what was going on with people, so this bothered her badly. Her mother wasn't a drinker, but it was clear that she was drinking now. And her father—his whole demeanor seemed to have changed from the self-assured, confident man she had known her whole life. Even though he might seem snobby to some, he was usually gracious to everyone. Was it the fact that he felt he was protecting his daughter? Or was he acting strangely because of something else he was going through? Right now though she wanted to stay away as much as possible, and she would have to take time to talk to Mara and Harris to check on everyone, since they worked most closely with her parents. Hopefully, they would be able to get some clarity on what was going on.

But she couldn't do anything about it right now, and Skylar was tired. She really didn't want to wake Garrett up, so she slowly grabbed a pillow from behind her head, and as she gently slipped off the couch, she quickly put the pillow under his head. Then she got the blanket from the chair, unfolded it, and put it over him. He was so tired that he didn't even notice that she was no longer his pillow.

"I love you, Garrett," she said, kissing his forehead before walking to her bedroom and closing the door.

"Good morning, sleepyhead." Skylar woke to the sound of a man's voice. She knew it was familiar, but in her sleepy state, she couldn't comprehend what was going on. Then suddenly, she remembered last night. Her eyes opened to see a very sexy man sitting on the edge of her bed.

"Hi there," Skylar said sleepily, reaching over to touch his arm. "I hope you were able to get some rest on the couch. You were so tired I didn't want to wake you."

"I slept fine, but sitting here on the edge of the bed makes me think I might have had a better night in here," he said, playfully leaning over to give her a quick kiss. "Right now, though, I think we are running a bit late. Thank goodness I'm your client."

Skylar saw she had overslept by an hour. Max would be at the boat shortly, and so would Casey.

"Crap! I've got to hurry."

"I'm going to go by my place to get my gear, and then I'll meet you at the boat. See you there, my love." And with that, he dashed out the door.

It didn't take Skylar long to get ready. Though she liked to take her time in the mornings, today would have to be the exception. She was determined to get there before Max or Casey, but at this rate, she wasn't sure that was going to happen. She grabbed some cereal and a few snacks for the day and headed out the door.

Sure enough, as she pulled into the parking lot at the marina, Max's and Casey's cars were already there. And just as she parked, Garrett pulled up beside her.

"I guess we are officially late," Garrett said, grabbing his tote bag and slinging it over his shoulder.

"This isn't like me, but I guess there is a first time for everything," she said. "Do you think I can get another kiss before we walk down the dock? Not that we need to hide from Casey, but we should probably keep things as proper as possible on the boat." Garrett's answer to her question was to let his tote fall to the ground and playfully pull Skylar into another mind-blowing kiss; his hands felt like electricity on her body.

"How was that?" he asked, smiling at her mischievously.

"Perfect!" Skylar said almost in a whisper, using the only word that came to her mind as she looked at her new boyfriend.

"Well, maybe if you could keep your hands off each other, we might get some work done. People should show up on time so those of us that are trying to accomplish something can actually work." Casey's voice sounded hard and mean. They both turned to see her staring at them, with both arms folded across her chest.

That was it. Garrett had had enough. "Casey, we are a bit late this morning, but please remember this. You are working for me, not the other way around. I will not tolerate outbursts like that anymore. We will work together, but I need you to remember that I'm the researcher and you are my assistant for school purposes only. I will be the one signing off on your papers to let the school know you have finished your internship, and I can also make recommendations. Please remember that next time you think about talking to anyone like that." Skylar noticed that Garrett was being very authoritative for once, and she almost felt sorry for Casey. Almost being the operative word.

"Are you threatening me?" Casey said, hatred clearly showing on her face.

"No. I'm just stating facts. When this internship is over, I just want things to be on good terms. So, let's keep things professional, okay?"

"You mean just like you two are." Casey was now staring at Skylar.

"Anything between me and Skylar is none of your business. Now, if we can get to the dock, we have work to do. I also need that paper I asked you to write."

"I wasn't able to finish it, but I will have it for you tomorrow," Casey said in a monotone voice.

"Thanks," Garrett answered while he and Skylar followed the girl down the dock to the boat, where Max was waiting.

It wasn't long before they were back at the reef. The day fell into their usual routine, but Casey wasn't her normal clingy self. Apparently, Garrett's talk before leaving shore had finally gotten through to her.

But today was very different for Skylar—she watched every little thing Garrett did, knowing now that he loved her. And though they couldn't show their affection openly during the workday, they would share a smile, a wink, or an occasional blown kiss to let each other know they were thinking the same thoughts. But they were always careful not to let Max or Casey see them. Though Max would be perfectly fine with the couple's relationship, Casey had made it clear that she wasn't happy at all. But her internship would be over very soon, Skylar thought happily.

The rest of the week was normal—more scuba trips, more snorkeling for the tourists, with Garrett by her side. It felt as if they fit together as they worked alongside each other on the boat. They usually spent the evenings at her house, cooking, taking walks, and sometimes just sitting in the swing at the end of the street.

"Are you really not going to the family dinner tomorrow?" Garrett asked her tentatively as they sat side by side looking out over the water.

"I'm sure. I finally talked to Harris and told him I wasn't coming back for a little while. He told me he understood but that he needed to talk to me in person. He, Mara, and Chase are coming here after dinner tomorrow. Apparently, they have some news that they didn't want to discuss over the phone. It's made me a bit anxious." Skylar took a deep breath and just sank into Garrett's arm, which he had wrapped around her shoulder.

"When did you find out about this?" he asked her quickly.

"A little while ago actually. They have been calling all week and leaving messages, but I never returned them until today. Harris was a bit perturbed, but he reluctantly said he understood but that it was important that we talk. I think something must have happened after we left last week."

"I promise I will leave when they get here. I think you guys should talk as a family," Garrett said quietly.

"I don't have anything to hide from you. You are a part of my life now. And if you want to be in mine, this comes along with the territory. At least, I hope you still want me."

Garrett looked at the girl snuggled up in his arms. Even if he had wanted to say no, he wouldn't be able to. For every time he looked at her, he was falling in love just a little more. It seemed that all he had to do was just look at her and hold her, and she breathed life into him. It was a feeling so surreal and delicious that he never wanted to let her go, no matter the circumstances.

"Skylar, I want you in my life more than I will ever be able to tell you. I just don't want to complicate things for you with your family. I've never had what you have with your brothers and sister. And the things you have at your disposal—goodness, you already own two homes, and I'm still renting a little apartment with just a small piece of land back home. I wonder if I'm really good enough for you."

With those words, Skylar sat up quickly, turned to him, and stared into his eyes.

Slowly, she took both of his hands in hers.

"Garrett, you have completely stolen my heart just by being who you are. I don't care about material things. They are just that—things! What matters to me is what is in here," Skylar said, placing her hand on his chest, over his heart. "You inspire me, and I feel incredible when I'm with you. To me, it's amazing that you came along, and you have rearranged my life for the better. The best thing is that you love me for me, not for what I have or for my family. Any woman would be blessed to have you in her life. I'm only glad that the woman you have chosen is me."

Garrett didn't know what to say as he let the words sink in. Skylar was real, honest, and wise beyond her years. Her kindness and sincerity were amazing. He thought to himself how lucky he was that the only boat available for his time in Key Largo happened to be the *Sea Gypsy*. He didn't believe in coincidences, so he knew that they were meant to be together.

"Come here," he said, pulling Skylar onto his lap; she giggled like a schoolgirl as they sat wrapped up in each other, while the swing moved back and forth so gently. They watched the sunset before walking back to her house.

"I know it's kinda early, and I definitely don't want to leave, but I need to finish up some paper work and check some e-mails. I have to admit, I haven't been as attentive to my work this week because someone has kept me pretty occupied in the evenings," Garrett said as they reached her door. He enveloped Skylar in his arms.

"Are you complaining? If so, I'll change things. I've got things I need to do too, but you are just so irresistible it makes it hard for me to concentrate." While saying these words, Skylar was on her tiptoes, softly kissing Garrett's cheeks and then lips; she even nibbled on his earlobe, which sent a shiver down his spine.

"You do make it very difficult to leave you!"

"Do I?" Skylar said, with an impish grin.

"Very much so. But let's make plans for breakfast in the morning. Why don't we go back to the Lorelei and have a relaxing outdoor breakfast. What time is everyone coming here?"

"Well, it won't be till after the family dinner, so I'm guessing around four or five o'clock. Harris said he would call."

"Then we have all day. Maybe we can even take a stroll on the Seven-Mile Bridge."

"That sounds excellent, as long as I'm with you," Skylar said, wrapping her arms tighter around him, as though he might slip away. This woman had him in a wonderful daze, and he loved every minute of it.

"Then tomorrow it is. I'll pick you up around eight o'clock. Is that too early?"

"Not at all. So, I guess I should go get my beauty sleep."

"You are already beautiful, my dear. I love you just the way you are," Garrett said breathlessly.

"And I love you too, Garrett." After one more enticing kiss, she turned to walk into the house.

Her phone started beeping at seven o'clock the next morning. Skylar rolled over in bed, and a smile suddenly came to her face as she thought about having breakfast with her favorite guy and walking along the famous old bridge. A quick look out the window showed partly cloudy skies, but that didn't matter to her. If it started raining, as long as they were together, the day would be divine. And thinking of their time together even helped her cope with the unsettled feelings she was starting to have about talking to her siblings later.

She hurried to get dressed, wanting to make sure that she was ready on time, but the appointed time for their date came and went. Skylar tried to reach Garrett on his phone, but it went straight to voice mail. After forty-five minutes of worrying and wondering, Skylar heard his truck pull into the driveway. As she opened to the door to make sure everything was okay, the look on Garrett's face was one of anger and frustration.

"What happened?" she asked as Garrett came racing into the house, looking as if he might hit something. This was definitely not the morning greeting she had reviewed in her mind.

"Casey!"

"What about her?"

"She ruined my paper. She possibly lost my grant money!"

"Slow down! Come over here, and sit." Skylar took him by the hand and led him to the kitchen table, where they pulled out chairs.

"Let's start again. What happened?" Skylar said as Garrett seemed to stare out into space as if she wasn't even there.

"Last night when I got home, I checked my e-mails. I had several from the university and another research team. Two reports that Casey sent in were missing vital information. And another had data that was completely wrong. These e-mails were two days old, and I was supposed to respond immediately. I've got the missing information to send, and I spent last night writing the corrected report. I don't know what I was thinking. I checked the reports she gave me, and everything was fine. She must have switched the information and sabotaged the reports before sending them in. I can't believe she could be this vile!" Garrett stood quickly, unable to stay still. He paced around the kitchen, running his fingers through his hair. Skylar wanted to comfort him, but she was trying to choose her words carefully.

"Casey was pretty upset the other day when she saw us in the parking lot. Plus, you let her know just how things stood, as far as her being your intern. I guess she is used to getting her way. Believe me, I saw a lot of girls like her while growing up. When they don't get what they want, they find a way to make everyone miserable. Will you be able to fix things?"

"I've already sent in the corrected documents. It was my fault, so I couldn't explain what happened, except to say there was a misunderstanding with my assistant. Ultimately, it was my responsibility." Garrett sighed, sitting back down at the table and putting his head in his hands. "I do know this. As of tomorrow, she will be finished working with me. And I will not be giving her any recommendations, but apparently, she doesn't need any. I did a little Internet research on my intern. It seems that she comes from a very privileged family in Connecticut. I don't understand why people think they don't have to work for what they want! They are handed everything under the sun and don't appreciate it at all. They're spoiled little rich kids!" Garrett stood up again, both hands on his hips, and suddenly, what he had said hit him. He turned to see Skylar standing up, with a slight look of hurt on her face.

"Honey, I wasn't talking about you. I promise," he said, coming around the table and reaching out for her, but Skylar backed away.

"Are you sure?"

"Skylar, I've already told you how much you mean to me. You are so different—genuine. You are working your ass off to get what you want, even though if you wanted to, you could sit in the lap of luxury. You even have enough guts to go against your family's wishes to achieve your dream. Again, sweetheart, you are so different. I'm sorry! The words just came out because I'm so frustrated with that girl! She has been nothing but a pain in the ass since she started working with me."

Skylar knew in her heart that he was just angry, but his words did sting just a little. She was a rich girl and privileged. What if he was voicing his true opinion? Suddenly, she felt as if she needed to guard her heart, just when she had been willing to give it all to him. But then again she knew his frustration for Casey because she had felt it too.

"Everything has been corrected and resubmitted. Now, I'll find out tomorrow if they will accept the new documents. Skylar, I'm really sorry about that comment. Are you sure you're okay?"

"Yeah." And Skylar truly was now that she had a minute to think about it.

"I promise I was just venting. You are in a class of your own. I could never see you in a group of women such as Casey. You have more integrity and passion in your little finger than that girl has in her whole body!"

Slowly, Skylar's sudden fear was subsiding. It had started out as a beautiful day but it felt clouded now as it seemed people and circumstances were trying to tear them apart—first this spiteful younger woman and then her own family. Skylar suddenly wondered whether they were fighting an uphill battle for their relationship.

"Let's head to the restaurant. We still can have that relaxing breakfast, and I promise there will be no more talk of Casey or your family. Let's just concentrate on you and me," Garrett said, giving her a hug for reassurance.

"Okay," she said softly, putting on her flip-flops, grabbing her handbag, and heading to Garrett's truck.

The ride to the restaurant was quiet. Skylar was lost in thought. "Are you worried about today? Oh, crap, I'm sorry. I said we wouldn't talk about that. So, let's see. Have you made any more progress on the purchase of the second boat?"

Skylar smiled weakly at Garrett's attempt to change the tone of the day. "I turned in the papers to the bank and have talked to two men who are potential captains." Garrett noticed her voice was flat and monotone; he was not used to this Skylar.

After they sat down at the table by the water, they both ordered breakfast and sat quietly. But Skylar couldn't help it. She had to say something.

"Garrett, have you noticed that since the day we got together, there has been one thing after another? You didn't like a female boat captain. Then Casey came along to make both of us miserable. My dad caught us on the boat that night. There was the disastrous family dinner. Today, Casey is purposefully sabotaging your research because of our relationship, and who knows what my siblings have in store for me this afternoon. It's like a roller coaster, with tremendous highs," she said, reaching for his hand. "And then suddenly, it is like we are dropping so fast that I'm not sure how we are going to land." Skylar stopped and looked at him. She thought that he would feel the same way, but instead, he had a smile on his face.

"What are you smiling for? Is this funny to you?"

"You make me smile. Every time I look at you, I can't help but smile." Garrett scooted closer to her seat. "First of all, I apologize. I shouldn't have stormed into your house this morning, raving about that lunatic intern of mine. Now that things have settled down and I've got it out of my system, I'm sure things will be okay. I just have some explaining to do tomorrow, which should be fine. And we won't have to worry about that redhead after tomorrow either." Just then, the waitress set two steaming plates of scrambled eggs, hash browns, and toast in front of them, even though Skylar's appetite was all but gone due to the craziness of the morning and worrying about what would happen later.

"As for your family, you will be able to talk to them today, and I don't know much about having brothers or sisters, but I have a feeling you guys will be able to work something out, whatever is going on. I really liked Harris, Mara, and Chase. And they seem to have your back. When it comes to family, that's a gift to be treasured.

"Now for me and you—I'm not an expert on relationships, but I think they all have their ups and downs. Yes, ours has been quite a ride so far, but even with the stress, I wouldn't trade meeting you for anything in the world. You are the first woman that gets me, so I'm letting go. If it means a roller coaster ride with you, then strap on the seat belt, and let's go for a ride. Because in my book, Skylar Cartwright, you are so worth it."

As Skylar looked at Garrett, she could tell he was not just saying what she wanted to hear. No, he genuinely meant every word he said.

"You really mean that, don't you?"

"You bet! I've never told you anything I didn't mean, and I don't intend to start now. You mean that much to me, and I want this to work. I've had some really crappy relationships before. I pretty much swore off ever being with someone. But you, Skylar, are changing my mind. I keep telling you the same thing. You are different, like me. We have passion, and we love what we do. For us to find each other is a gift. Don't be scared. But if you are, just hold my hand, okay?"

Skylar didn't have to think twice. She squeezed his hand, which she was already holding, and leaned over, placing her forehead onto his.

"I'm going to hang on to you and your words. Just please don't break my heart. I'm putting all my trust in you, letting my intuition guide me."

Garrett didn't care that there were other people surrounding them. He pulled her closer for a steamy kiss. "I hope that lets you know how serious I am and, once again, how much you mean to me."

"It does; it truly does," Skylar said softly, finally feeling a peacefulness settle over her.

"Do I need to take your food back and warm it up?" said the waitress playfully as she came to their table. Both Garrett and Skylar grinned, with Skylar's cheeks turning a bit red from embarrassment.

"I think we are okay," Garrett said, looking at the beautiful girl sitting beside him..

"I think we are more than okay," Skylar said, looking back at the love of her life.

19

The rest of the breakfast was more relaxed, as they discussed things they wanted to do, such as travel. Then suddenly, they were trading childhood stories that had both of them laughing so hard that at one point, Skylar had tears in her eyes. But these were happy tears, and she loved it. It was just the medicine she needed with all the turmoil that was surrounding her.

The next stop on their Sunday morning date was a beautiful walk on the Seven-Mile Bridge. It didn't matter how many times Skylar went there, it was as if she was seeing the bridge and the surrounding scenery for the first time.

"I love it here," Garrett said as they both leaned against the old rusted railing, shoulder to shoulder, looking out over the aqua blue waters and surrounding small islands.

"Me too. I feel like when I'm walking here, I'm stepping back in history," Skylar said. As they began walking down the old bridge, her hand traced the edges of the rusted rail. There were people doing their daily runs or walks, and also tourists were taking pictures but to Skylar, it felt as if it were only the two of them walking along the bridge.

"Have you ever thought about where you want to be in ten years?" she suddenly said, looking up at Garrett as they continued walking slowly, hand in hand.

"Well, for one thing, I'll be an old man!" Garrett said playfully.

"An old man! You are only going to be forty-nine. That's not old," she said. "Really, what do you see in your future?"

Garrett stopped, glancing up for a minute into the sky and then looking back at the wonderful woman beside him. "I would love to have my own home, by the water, of course. And to be married to the love of my life and have a couple of kids, so I can teach them everything about the ocean."

"Is that it? Is there anything else?" Skylar asked again.

"No, not really. Why?"

"Because I love it. You have a plan, although it would be too simple for many people, especially those I grew up with—not grand enough. But that is how I felt my whole life."

"I don't understand," Garrett said, stopping her for a moment to look at her to make sure everything was okay.

"Garrett, my family—or should I say, my parents—always had this plan mapped out for each of their children. We would go to the right schools, from elementary through college. They even chose our classes for us. Then we were to report to the family's business as soon as we received our diplomas. When we were growing up, we had money. We traveled; we were able to buy the latest and greatest thing that hit the market. But to me, it wasn't a big deal. Getting the newest clothing or gadgets, or anything really, wasn't a big deal to me. I was much more in tune with my grandma." Skylar looked into the distance, as if she was stepping back in time.

"Are we talking about the grandmother I've heard so much about?"

"Yeah. I wish I could spend more time with her now. When I was growing up, I think I spent more time with her than with my parents. My grandpa started the real estate business with his two brothers. My grandma took care of the kids and house. They didn't have much in the beginning, and they lived a much simpler life. They liked gardening, reading and just spending time together. Then as the business grew, they began making a little money, and they were able to afford nicer things, but my grandma said she still liked her old life, especially her garden. She loved nature and still does to this day. She has her own garden in the side yard, with all kinds of veggies and herbs. She tends to it every day, much to the consternation of my mom. She says it's an embarrassment, but my dad was adamant that Grandma have her own space. And I have always loved the wonderful stories she can tell about her life. Anyway, I always felt like I was in tune with her, rather than with my own parents or, for that matter, any other members of my family. My grandma and I have a special bond. When I told her what I wanted to do, she actually had tears in her eyes because she was so happy for me. She said it was about time someone in this family had enough gumption to do what they were put on this earth for and not follow some ridiculous plan that someone else had come up with. She even offered to buy the boat for me!"

"Are you kidding?" Garrett said, stunned.

"It seems Grandma had been stashing away money all these years, listening and learning from my grandpa. Plus, when he passed away, she acquired his fortune. When I was old enough, she put me in charge of her money, much to my father's disapproval. But she is one tough lady, and there was no changing her mind. I think my dad still resents that to this day, but my grandma is as stubborn as it gets while also being the sweetest woman on the earth." Skylar paused, continuing to look out at the passing boats heading out to the Atlantic for the day. "I'm sorry; I'm rattling on and on. I just feel so happy one minute, and the next, all this anxiety creeps up. In the past, when I felt like this, I would go and visit my grandma. I miss that."

Garrett tenderly hugged Skylar, gently stroking her hair to reassure her that things would be all right. He could feel the tightness in her body loosen the longer they stayed in the calming embrace.

"Skylar, you have to believe that everything will work out. There may be a lot of irons in the fire right now, but we—you and I—will tackle them together. Okay?" he said, lifting her chin up to pass his positivity on to her.

"Okay," she said, and he gave her a reassuring kiss as they stood in the middle of the old bridge.

"Are you sure you will be okay?" Garrett said one more time as they stood at the door of his truck. "I know I said it should probably be just your family for this talk but if you need me, I'll stay."

"I'll be okay. They should be here shortly, and I think you were right earlier. It might be better for it to be a sibling talk. I don't know what they have to tell me that is so important, and part of me doesn't want to hear it. I just wish I could stay away from that world altogether. But even with all the craziness, they still are my family, and I do care." Skylar wrapped her arms around Garrett's waist once more, needing one more reassuring hug before he left.

"If you need anything, you call me, all right?" he said while nodding.

"I promise," Skylar said, planting a kiss on his soft lips, which sent that tingle through her that she just could not get enough of. "I'll call you later and give you the scoop."

She watched as Garrett's truck drove down the road and out of view. Now she had to wait till they showed up, but it wasn't very long. Only fifteen minutes passed before Harris, Mara, and Chase were standing at her front door.

"We need to talk," was all the greeting Skylar got as she opened the door.

Soon, all four Cartwright children were sitting around Skylar's kitchen table. The tension was thick. No one wanted to be the first one to say a word.

"Since each of you look scared to say anything, I'll just ask. What is going on? What happened after I left that afternoon with Garrett?"

"We found out a few things about our parents, because you can probably imagine the conversation that took place after you guys left," Harris said in a quiet tone. "To begin with, Dad had an affair a few years ago, which supposedly led to Mom's secret drinking habit ever since. I'm not sure if we can say she is an alcoholic or not, but that's not all. Dad just found out that Mom was having an affair, which, according to Mom, has now ended."

"And now, all they can think about is how they will be cast out of their precious social circles. They don't seem too concerned about their own family." Mara said the words so fast that Skylar had a hard time comprehending them at first.

"Damn, Mara. We don't know that!" Harris said quickly.

"Are you kidding? They want to keep up appearances and make sure no one finds out their dirty little secrets, or their precious reputations will be ruined, taking the business with them."

"Well, even though I've had time to sit with it for a while, I'm still in a bit of shock. It's just crazy. And I have to admit that Mom and Dad are quite the actors," Chase said.

Skylar finally came out of her shock to ask a few questions. "Okay, so let me get this right. Dad had an affair. When, and with whom?"

"He said it was a few years ago, but he won't tell us who it was," Chase said.

"You mean he told you all this." Skylar was taken aback again.

Harris got up and started pacing the floor. "That day after you left, things got a bit crazy. Dad told Mom that she should have been nicer. She yelled back he wasn't very pleasant either and that she didn't have to listen to him anymore because they were even, but she was slurring her words. That's when he called her an alcoholic and said that she needed help. Then she proceeded to tell him that it was his fault, since he slept with that whore. Dad told her that if she hadn't been so uptight and focused on trying to please her high-society friends, things would have been different. And he said that now that she had her little tryst, she was just as guilty."

As Skylar listened to all that Harris had to say, she looked around at her siblings' faces to see how they were responding. They seemed much calmer than she was, but they had also had more time to deal with the information.

"I'm so sorry," Skylar said suddenly.

"Why are you apologizing?" Mara said.

"I shouldn't have brought Garrett that day. I just thought things would be fine, and I wanted everyone to meet him. We had been dating, and things were going so well."

"You guys are still together, right? We all liked him a lot, especially since he had enough guts to stand up to Dad. He surprised me! And when he said he loved you—wow! That was so romantic!" Mara said sweetly, looking into Skylar's eyes, with her eyebrows going up and down.

"We are fine. Actually, we're more than fine, even though he has his own crap that he is going through. It's just some work stuff. But what is going to happen with Mom and Dad? Are they talking about divorce? What will happen to the business? And who else knows? Does Mom need help with her drinking?" These questions were flooding Skylar's brain; her whole being was still reeling from the news. Her family was not perfect, but she would never have thought that it was in this kind of condition.

"Mom says that she doesn't have a drinking problem, even though we found liquor stashed all throughout the house. Dad seems to be in a weird depressed mood, but at work, he is his normal self. Mom still attends her charity functions. They're both acting as though nothing happened that day. And if we ask about it, they either act as though we haven't said a word, or they coolly change the subject. So, as far as what to do, we don't know. But we did think you should know what is going on. And right now, personally, I wish I was like you—in my own little place, away from everyone, doing my own thing," Harris said. "Tracey was beside herself that day, and now she is acting a little weird about getting married. It makes me wonder if she loves me or the money."

"I was just glad that Paul grabbed Lyla and took her out to the pool before Dad and Mom went on that rant about their secret lives," Mara said.

"So far, Blair has been very encouraging, but we really haven't talked about it much," Chase said, looking at his siblings. "As far as the business goes, I don't want it to be affected, but I really don't want to work in real estate. I was just afraid to do something else till I saw Skylar do it."

"I didn't know that," Skylar said. "I thought you loved it, like Harris and Mara."

"I don't really, but I just thought it was the right thing to do. I haven't decided what I want to do just yet, but I have a few things in mind." Chase sat there, looking at his hands and wondering whether there would be any repercussions.

"Well, right now, the priority is Mom and Dad. Let's not change anything just yet, Chase, until we can get this straightened out with our parents," Harris said authoritatively, as the eldest. "I think that is great though."

"The one problem I see is the upcoming charity event for the Children's Resource Fund. The company—along with Mom and Dad—hosts every year, and I just hope they can keep it together to get through the event. So, whatever we can do to survive should be our first priority. Then we will take it a step at a time. Hopefully, we can keep their little secrets in the family and not spread them throughout Miami. Reputation is everything around here, but I know for sure that we can't be the first family to go through something like this," Harris said, still pacing the floor.

"Are you worried about our parents or the business, Harris?" Skylar said very defensively. "Don't you think we should be helping them? Maybe they need a therapist, or maybe we should get Mom to Alcoholics Anonymous, or whatever she needs to help her with the drinking. Do we really care what others think at a time like this?"

"I'm not being unfeeling, Sky, but we have to look at the big picture. Something like this could take down a three-generation family business in the blink of an eye. Do you really think that would benefit Mom and Dad, or would it make things worse? I really don't care what people think or say, but we have to take everything into consideration, and this is a pretty big problem."

Skylar realized that Harris was right. Mara and Chase must have agreed because they sat at the table, not uttering a single word.

"Okay, so what needs to be done for the charity function?" Skylar asked.

"I'm going to take care of that tomorrow. I'm making a list and checking to see what has been done and what we still need to do. I'm going to try to talk to Mom, if she's willing. She has been pretty tight-lipped about everything, barely saying anything to any of us. But since this is not related to the problem, she might actually have a conversation," Mara said.

"Then let me know what I can do."

"Blair and I will help too, but I'm also working on the ocean condos renovation right now," Chase said.

"You have to take care of that property first. But if Blair doesn't mind helping once Mara knows what to do, that would be great." Harris finally chimed in. "Oh, and, Sky, I just thought you should know that Andrew is back in town and has been asking about you. He contacted me about a week ago. I didn't give him any specific information except that you are chartering boats now. Not sure why he was asking, but you never know with Andrew Danforth."

And this day just keeps getting better and better, Skylar thought to herself. Her ex-boyfriend, who is supposedly engaged, was asking about her. She could tell that there had to be another story here, but what it was, she had no idea.

"Wow, Harris, you could have shared that before now," Mara said sarcastically. "And don't worry about Tracey. I think she is just still shocked from the outburst between Mom and Dad that day. I'll talk to her. She will be fine."

"Thanks," Harris said, sounding very tired.

They all finally stood up and began walking to Skylar's door. She noticed that they all seemed to have the weight of huge rocks on their shoulders.

"We'll get through this little situation and we can help our parents. The crucial thing is whether they want the help," Harris said as the three of them got in the car. Skylar stood in her doorway, watching as her brothers and sister left to head back to Miami. She was still trying to process all the information. And though she was worried about her parents, the news about Andrew made her a bit disconcerted. He could be a snake, and Skylar had no idea why he had asked about her; she could care less. She just wanted him to leave her alone, which should be easy since she lived in the Keys now.

This day had been full since the moment she had woken up. It was already eight o'clock, and Skylar didn't know whether she wanted to call Garrett or not, but she had promised. But to help her relax, she took a nice hot shower, grabbed a quick sandwich, and then crawled under her covers before she dialed his number.

"Hey there," said the sweet-sounding voice on the other end of the line. "I was wondering how things were going." Skylar sighed deeply and told Garrett the news, from start to finish.

"Whoa. Are you okay? Do you want me to come over? I'm so sorry, Skylar," Garrett said sincerely.

"I'm okay. I'm already in bed, just lying here, thinking. But I had to talk to you. I feel like I'm burdening you with so much. You have all your work problems, the situation with Casey, and now, a girlfriend who has put you in the middle of her crazy family's circumstances. I promise if you want to bail out, I don't blame you one bit!"

"Hey, we already talked about that earlier today. We are here for each other, no matter what. We made a promise, and I for one keep my promises," Garrett said, reassuring her.

"I do too. I was just giving you an out. So much going on: my parents, Casey, my ex-boyfriend."

"Ex-boyfriend..."

"Oh, I forgot. For some reason, Andrew is back in Miami and has been asking about me. Not that it really matters. You are my one and only, Garrett. Always."

"Okay, now I feel better," he said in a voice that told Skylar he was smiling. "But he better not mess with my girl!"

20

Garrett and Skylar met at the boat early the next morning. Skylar knew that the coming confrontation between Garrett and Casey would not be pretty, so she decided to go onto the boat while Garrett talked to Casey in the parking lot. But then, Garrett asked Skylar and Max, who had just joined them, whether they would stay to be his witnesses, in case Casey decided to pull something new on him, which Garrett knew by now that she was more than capable of doing.

The three of them were standing by Garrett's truck when the young woman pulled into the marina's parking lot. She hesitated when she saw them all standing there. She had to know that she would be caught, Skylar thought. But as Casey exited the car, her body language said that she didn't care. It was as if she was proud of the fact that she might have ruined something for Garrett.

"Wow, there's a welcoming committee this morning. How thoughtful!" Casey said sarcastically.

"I think we need to talk," Garrett said as the young woman walked toward the group.

"Really. What for?"

"Casey, I think you know what I'm referring to," Garrett said, doing his best to stay calm and keep his thoughts collected. "And I have asked Skylar and Max to be here while we talk, as witnesses."

"Why in the world would you need witnesses?" Casey asked defensively.

"Casey, I know that you sent in reports that were altered to leave out vital information for my grant. I had approved the written documents before I gave them to you to send. When I received e-mails back from the committee, I rechecked the reports, and you had changed them. I have the e-mail with your address as proof that you sent them."

As Garrett talked, Casey stood there defiantly, not saying one word, trying to look confident as though she had done nothing wrong.

"What I don't understand is why. Why cause a problem for me, and now for you? Jerry told me that you were the best in his class and that you would be more than helpful and willing to learn."

Casey looked at all three people standing before her. "First of all, I am the best in the class. Secondly, I don't have to explain my actions, and I really don't care. It won't cause me any problems that I can't get fixed. I've already met a few people in

Miami that will help me once I move there. My dad has already seen to all the arrangements."

Suddenly, it was as if a light bulb turned on for Skylar. "I know you. Now I know where I've seen you," Skylar said, stepping up to the girl. "Your father is Mr. George Powell, a real estate broker in New England. Our families went to a few events at Cape Cod and in New York City. That's where I met you!"

"As soon as I stepped onto your boat, I knew who you were. I was completely surprised to find you here. I never would have thought you would lower yourself to be a boat captain, but the gossip was that you were always strange." Casey had a smirk on her face as she continued. "I can see your father bought you this nice little boat to keep you happy. You always seem to get your way with everything."

"Why would you say something like that? I barely know you!" Skylar was getting angrier by the second.

"My boyfriend, now my ex-boyfriend, sure couldn't keep his eyes off of you, especially after you sweet-talked him in New York City."

Suddenly, it hit her—Andrew. Skylar stepped back.

Casey's laugh broke the silence. "I think she has put it all together now. Yes, Andrew moved here to be with you after he broke up with me. You didn't know that about him, did you?"

"Is that why you are in Miami—for Andrew?"

"I guess that is none of your business, seeing that he dropped you too. I heard he didn't like the little adventure you have here. But it didn't take you long to find his replacement,"

Casey said, looking over at Garrett. "And to think I thought we would make a great couple."

"Why would you be an intern for a marine researcher?" Garrett asked.

"I have my reasons, none of which I have to explain to you."

"Casey, I think it's time for you to leave. I don't know what you plan to do, and frankly, I don't give a shit, but I will report what has occurred during your internship. If you can get your precious money or your daddy to fix this, I don't really care. But I will say this: You and Skylar might have run around in the same circles, but Skylar is nothing like you! She has worked her ass off to get this charter business going by herself! She didn't need her parent's money, she doesn't use people, and she hasn't played petty games." Garrett was angry but kept his voice in check. Right now, he felt as if he could strangle Casey, mainly because of the hateful remarks she had made to Skylar.

"You don't have to tell me twice. But I think Skylar and I will be seeing each other again. Maybe at the charity function for the children that your family does every year." She turned to get into her car, but then she suddenly looked back at Garrett. "And by the way—you might be good-looking, but she would be crazy to give up everything for someone like you."

At that remark, Skylar started toward the girl, but Garrett grabbed her arm before she could even take a step. "She's not worth it, Sky. Just let her go," he whispered.

They all stood there, not knowing what to say as they watched Casey peel out of the parking lot.

"Wow, what a way to start a Monday morning," Max's cheery voice said. But he looked over to see Garrett and Skylar looking at him as though he was crazy. "You've got to admit that she is one fiery redhead."

"Only you, Max, could see the good in that whole situation," Skylar said, suddenly laughing, relieving the stress from the confrontation. It wasn't long before Garrett and Max found themselves laughing too.

"I knew that I had seen her before, that I'd met her or something. But I could never quite figure it out. The whole time I was growing up, I never played the social games. My sister, Mara, did, but she was never mean. I definitely have to give my parents credit for that, even if they are driving us kids crazy at the moment." As soon as the words came out of her mouth, Skylar wished that she could erase what she said.

"What's going on with your parents?" Max said.

"It's just the usual parental stuff," Skylar said so casually that Max didn't ask again, to her relief. Garrett looked at her with raised eyebrows to let her know she had dodged a bullet.

"I say we get on the boat and go to the reef. Do you think you could be my partner today?" Garrett asked, looking at Skylar.

Skylar wanted to, but she wasn't sure about leaving the boat. As the captain, it didn't feel right, but she would love to dive with him. This whole time they had been together, she had never gone with him, and they had only swum briefly that one time.

"I can handle the boat, Sky," Max said quickly. "And maybe I could dive with you too sometime."

"Definitely," Garrett said to Max, but he was still looking at Skylar. "Actually, I only need to go out today and tomorrow. Then I'm finished for about a month. Now comes the paper work time, which is not my favorite part."

"But you rented the boat for six months. I thought that meant you would go out every week," Skylar said weakly.

"I always pay for the time so I can go out if needed, but I've collected enough information to keep me busy for quite a while. I'll need to go back to check on my work in a month or so. This is just how it works. But think of this: it gives you more time to book other dive and snorkel trips. And I will come whenever I can," he said, giving her a hug. They didn't have to worry about showing their affection for each other now. Max could care less, and Casey was out of the picture. But all Skylar could think about were the future boat trips without Garrett aboard. She had gotten so used to him being there.

"Hey," he said to her. "I'm not going anywhere. We are still in this together, right?" She nodded, but the sadness was still there. It just seemed as if everything from yesterday and this morning was falling on her like heavy bricks. But she had to act as though everything was okay. She could do this.

"Let's go diving!" Garrett said as he looked at his new as-sistant who just happened to be his wonderful girlfriend.

Being above the water was nice, but their time below the surface was amazing. Garrett showed Skylar all kinds of crea-tures, including sea anemones, crawling starfish, moray eels, lobsters, octopus and more. A huge stingray graced them with its presence, along with a big shark. Even though she had encountered sharks before, this one was quite large, and she froze for a minute, but Garrett's gentle hand reassured her as the shark moved along without noticing them. But before long, he had checked what he needed to, and he gave her the thumbs-up to return to the surface.

"That was amazing," Skylar said as soon as her face mask was off. Max helped her take the tank off her back, and Garrett released himself from his gear. Skylar didn't notice that he was watching practically every move she made. She was beautiful in her one-piece coral bathing suit, which had beautiful netting across the stomach area. If Max hadn't been on board, there was no telling what might have happened between the two of them.

As they headed back to shore, Max sat at the rear of the boat. Garrett came up and put his arms around Skylar's waist as she steered the boat. "Let's take tomorrow off," he said into her ear.

"I thought you said you had to dive again, but what do you have in mind?" she asked, looking at him playfully.

"Let's take the boat out, just me and you. We can take a picnic lunch and just go. We can do a little island exploring, maybe even anchor on a sandbar. We won't plan the day, except for what time I pick you up in the morning."

Skylar only had to think for a second. It would be great to get away from all the craziness that had surrounded them during the last few days. "That sounds perfect!"

21

It felt odd to be on the open water on this gorgeous day with only Garrett, but Skylar loved every minute of it. They had pulled out of the marina without an itinerary except that they wanted to explore the waters around John Pennekamp State Park. They were making a whole day of it, just the two of them. She felt as if she was playing hooky, and watching Garrett steer the boat while she wrapped her arms around his waist was different, but it felt so good.

The last few days had been so full of stress that a break for both of them was definitely in order. Even Max didn't mind taking the day off, saying he was meeting some friends for their own boat trip down in Marathon Key. Though the business side of her mind said, "You can't take a break," Skylar ignored it.

Garrett had picked her up promptly at eight o'clock that morning, and before she knew it, they were already out of the marina, following other boats heading out for a beautiful day on the crystal-blue waters. They had a huge cooler full of food and drinks. Another bag was devoted to those items that didn't need to stay cold, along with swimsuits, towels, the iPad for music, and Skylar's camera, of course––they were set for the day. Even though they were together almost every day, this time together seemed like another wonderful date. And Skylar couldn't wipe the silly grin she had on her face even if she wanted to.

As they got to the waters around the state park, the boats were more numerous, with snorkeling trips and dive flags in several spots. Garrett slowed the boat down, looking around.

"So, what would you like to do? We could anchor and swim or snorkel. My one request is let's not dive today."

"Or we could just stay on the boat," Skylar said, and she turned his face to hers very slowly, with a smug smile that Garrett was finding hard to resist. When she reached up to give him a kiss that was so delectable that he couldn't get enough, he thought it was probably a good thing they were out in public, even if the other boats weren't that close.

"Miss Cartwright, I thought we were having a proper date. You are making it very difficult to keep my gentlemanly manners," Garrett said, with a slight laugh in his voice.

"Then I'm doing just what I was hoping to," she said as she reached up to kiss him once more, more deeply than the first time.

Garrett felt as if he was on fire from the tip of his head to the ends of his toes. This woman had him wrapped so tightly around her finger, and she didn't realize it.

"Have I told you how much I love you?" Garrett said softly as he looked at her glowing face.

"Not today, but I can see it in your eyes. You don't know how glad I am to know that. You didn't run away from all the downright stupidity that is going on in my family. And thanks for believing in me and sticking up for me yesterday. I'm really not like Casey, but so many people think I am because of my family's money. I know this sounds weird and ungrateful, but growing up with money isn't all everyone thinks it is. Did it afford me luxuries? Yes, and I feel blessed. But it also brought a stigma that I can never run away from. People just assumed the worst instead of getting to know me." By now, Skylar's head was on Garrett's chest as he held her in his arms.

"I have to admit that during the first week, I wasn't sure what to think about you. You came from the type of family that I just assumed was snobby, but you seemed so different. Now I know you are different. Money didn't make you, and you didn't let it affect you. You are willing to get dirty and work, to take chances and do things on your own, when it would be so easy to let someone do things for you. You are kind and caring. You have a passion for life, not for other people's approval. That's a gift, Sky, a true gift, no matter what your station is in life. I feel blessed that you want to be with me." When she looked up at him, he felt as if he had struck pure gold. She was priceless to him.

"I say that since there are so many boats here, let's head toward Islamorada and find a sandbar. Maybe we can anchor, swim, and picnic," Garrett said and started the boat once more.

"I think that sounds great," Skylar said, once again putting her arm on his waist has they moved through the ocean channel.

It wasn't long before they were at the Holiday Isle Sandbar off Islamorada, where at least twenty boats were anchored. Everyone was swimming, grilling food on what the locals considered "the beach", and playing music. Since it was the middle of the week, there weren't as many people as were sometimes there, but there were enough that everyone was having a party. The couple anchored nearby, and soon Skylar and Garrett were swimming in the shallow waters, cooling off from the warm sun. Just by floating in the calm waters, Skylar felt all the stress leaving her body and mind, especially with Garrett so close by. If only things could be like this every day—no conniving interns, no arguing parents, no people hoping she would fail, no ex-boyfriends—just her and Garrett, in their own little world. It would be so nice, and in her mind—perfection. But the world didn't work that way, so she would take the calmness wherever and whenever she could.

Instead of taking their picnic to the sandbar, they decided to eat on the boat so they could people watch. There were quite a few colorful characters that provided much entertainment for Garrett and Skylar, to the point that at times, they were laughing so hard they almost choked on their food. But they both loved how everyone was just having fun, enjoying the day and each other. The island vibe of the Florida Keys was very much alive and well on the little sandbar that was surrounded by crystal-clear water; it was so pretty that a picture couldn't do it justice.

"Are you ready to head back?" Garrett said as he popped up in the water next to Skylar, who continued to just float, staring up at the clear blue sky.

"Not really, but I guess we should," she said, putting her arms around his neck while wrapping her legs around his waist. "I think I would rather stay here in this little slice of paradise with you instead."

"Damn, you are so beautiful, Sky," Garrett said, looking at her so adoringly. "You make it very tough to get back in the boat to go home. You know we could just take the boat on to Key West, get jobs down there selling T-shirts or something, and never go back home. It would just be me and you. What do you say?" Garrett looked at her with his eyebrows going up and down and a big grin on his face.

"If only it could be that easy!"

"Hey, are you Skylar Cartwright?"

Garrett and Skylar both turned around to see someone on the sandbar, not too far away.

"Yes," Skylar said hesitantly. "Who is asking?"

"It's Ben, Andrew's friend."

You have to be kidding, Skylar thought to herself. I'm out on a sandbar in the ocean, and I run into someone I know. Ugh!

"Do you know him?" Garrett whispered in her ear.

"Barely! If I remember right, he and Andrew went to college together. I met him a few times at a couple of functions. I'm trying to figure out how he recognized me," Skylar said quietly so only Garrett could hear her.

The two of them walked to the man standing on the little shoreline. "I haven't seen you in a very long time," Skylar said to the tall blond-haired guy as they approached him. "Are you on vacation?"

"I'm down here for the month for a combination of work and vacation. Andrew told us about this sandbar, and we thought we would check it out. I'm staying with my wife at a house we rented in Marathon. How have you been doing? Andrew said you started your own business chartering boats."

"Well, if you can call one boat a charter business, then he is right. I'm working on adding a second boat soon. This is Garrett Holmes, my boyfriend," Skylar said, introducing the two men.

"It's nice to meet you, Garrett," Ben said, extending his hand.

"I guess we will see you at the Children's Resource Fund charity event next weekend. Stella, my wife, and I are really looking forward to it. I still think it's great what your family does for those kids. Actually, I think Stella wants to talk to your parents about forming a nonprofit in Atlanta using the same techniques you guys did to make yours so successful in Miami." The more she talked to Ben, the more she remembered the sweet guy who was Andrew's best friend. He had seemed so different from Andrew that it had been hard to believe that the two men were close friends.

"We'll see you there," Skylar said as she turned with Garrett to wade into the water and go back to the boat.

"We…" Garrett asked.

Skylar sighed. "Yes—you and I. Unless you don't want to go. I guess I should have asked you. Garrett, please go with me to the event. I promise I've been meaning to talk to you about it. I don't even want to go, but if I have to, I certainly want you by my side."

"I'm not good at those kinds of things. Rich people and I don't mix very well. You should have seen me stumble my way through the last event I went to where I was talking to people about applying for a grant. I just didn't fit in."

"I don't seem to have the rich-girl gene, but I can play nicely just to get by. I really would like you to be there. Please." The look Skylar gave him when he glanced over at her after pulling up the anchor was one that he couldn't resist. She had a very exaggerated pout on her face, but it was too cute at the same time.

"I don't even own a decent suit!"

"You need a tuxedo for this party."

"A tuxedo! No way! It's too much money!" Garrett said.

As Garrett steered the boat back to the marina, Skylar was full of excitement. "The tuxedo is going to be my treat! And we need to go shopping soon so it will be ready in time. The party is next Saturday night at seven o'clock. I have no bookings on Thursday. We can ride to Miami and get you fitted," Skylar said enthusiastically. The dread that was filling Garrett was hard to contain, but he did it. He couldn't let Skylar know how much he didn't want to go. He especially didn't want to face her family again. And her ex-boyfriend and even Casey could be there. When had things gotten so complicated in his life? That answer was so simple—when he met Skylar. And even though Garrett didn't like all the twists and turns that had taken place lately, he honestly wouldn't trade them, because those bumps in the road had led him to a wonderful woman, who was everything he wanted and needed in his life.

"I'm not sure how I'm going to look in one of those get-ups," Garrett said. "And please don't ask me to cut my hair!"

"Why would I do that? Your hair is just fine. I know one thing is for sure––you are going to be the sexiest man at the event. I will be the envy of every woman there, even though that is not my intent. I just want to share this with you. You will love the kids. They get to dress up and come for a small party before the larger fund raiser, which is a silent auction and dance. It is the one society event I enjoy each year. The rest I try to duck out of, if I can. Living here in Key Largo makes that a lot easier."

After tying the boat to the dock and making sure everything was secure, they made their way to the truck, just as the sun was getting ready to set. On the way to Skylar's house, they sat in silence, as close as they could get on the bench seat of the old pickup truck. After he helped her put everything away from the day's excursion, they cuddled up on the couch.

"I really wish you could stay for a while. I have loved playing hooky from work with you. I kinda felt like I did when I skipped school as a teenager," Skylar said, with a smile.

"I can't imagine you doing something like that. You're the perfect girl!" Garrett said, caressing her back while gazing down at her.

"I did a few things that were out of the norm, but compared to everyone else, I was pretty boring. As long as I had a boat, the beach, and a sketch pad, I was happy."

"Now, that's my kind of girl. I love you." Garrett whispered, but it was loud and clear to Skylar.

"I love you back," she said just as Garrett's lips graced hers, softly at first, then hungrily, as if he couldn't get enough of her. She responded at the same fever pitch that was making their senses reel. Suddenly, they found themselves laying side by side on the couch, their legs and arms intertwined. The kiss resumed, and they were in their own world.

"I'd better go," Garrett said, his breath coming in ragged gulps. Skylar sounded almost as breathless. The way they were laying brought other things to mind that they weren't ready for. "I have a day of heavy-duty paper work tomorrow, and you have a bunch of tourists that are looking for the best snorkeling experience. I wish I could go with you."

"I wish you could too. I don't want to be apart from you, Garrett. You are such a big part of me now." They slowly sat up, not wanting to let each other go.

"So, shall we have dinner tomorrow night?" she said in a smooth, sexy voice that made him groan.

"I was going to work, but I can't resist. How about dinner at my place. No cooking for you since you have two boat groups."

"That sounds perfect to me." Skylar reached up and touched his face so softly and gently. "You really do make me so happy."

22

Even though Skylar and Garrett saw each other every day, it wasn't the same without him on the boat. The day after they played hooky was the hardest, as Skylar couldn't help but look for him when the tourists gathered for their snorkeling adventure. Of course, she and Max knew what to do, but Garrett's presence was the puzzle piece Skylar felt she had been missing all her life. But the best thing was that she knew he wasn't going anywhere. She could feel it even when he wasn't with her. It was as if they were becoming one. They might be different people, but they shared an excitement for the simpler things in life, and as corny as it sounded, they were like two magnets, completely drawn to each other.

Their trip to Miami to buy a tuxedo for Garrett proved to be more than fun for both of them. Garrett said he felt weird and out of his comfort zone while they were taking his measurements, but Skylar couldn't help but stare at him. Garrett was handsome to begin with, but he looked completely different all dressed up. She couldn't wait to have him by her side at the charity gala—she knew that she would definitely be the envy of every woman there, and probably the talk of the town. He might feel odd wearing the tux, but he looked beyond sexy.

"What are you staring at? Do I look as ridiculous as I feel?" Garrett said, seeming annoyed. "Do I really have to wear this? Do I even have to go?"

Skylar put on her best pout once again. "Just remember it is for the children, Garrett—those poor little souls you so dearly love to teach about the ocean. Remember?"

Garrett rolled his eyes as the man continued to take measurements, and Skylar knew she had won the discussion, but there really wasn't anything to discuss. She knew he would come with her. He just had to show his manliness by voicing a few complaints. But Skylar felt as if he might actually be looking forward to going, except for seeing her parents again. Actually, Skylar was not looking forward to that moment either.

On the days that Garrett wasn't able to break away from work and accompany her on the boat trips, Skylar would tell him all the latest news while they ate dinner at his apartment. She had even navigated another small storm, relying on Garrett's belief in her abilities to get her through. When Skylar had a day off, they would spend those evenings at her house, unable to be without each other. They laughed, they talked, and they shared their lives. To Skylar, this was what a true relationship was all about.

Garrett missed not going out to snorkel and dive each day. And for the first time in as long as he could remember, he wished he wasn't on a time line for his research grant. He wanted to be with Max and Skylar, talking to the scuba students or tourists, teaching them about the world below the surface of the water, answering their questions, which at times could come one after another. Garrett never tired of it. He was in his element on the boat.

He also never tired of being with Skylar. Each day, he still was amazed at this woman who was such a positive force, even though her family was still in turmoil. Her sister kept her up-to-date on what was going on with their parents; the situation seemed to be going downhill instead of getting better. He wished there was something he could do to help Skylar navigate the feelings that would overwhelm most people, but she seemed to be handling things well. She shared her thoughts and ideas about what she could do to help her parents and family, and Garrett listened, offering advice only if asked. But his favorite times with her were when they cuddled on the couch to watch a TV show or watched the sunset from the swing at the end of her street. Sometimes they went out to eat or took a picnic dinner to any little spot they could find near the water.

At times, Garrett felt as if he was on vacation with Skylar instead of being at work. When he did go out in the boat with her and Max, they all just worked together as if they had been doing this for years. Garrett also noticed that Skylar was teaching Max more about the captain's job, so he wondered whether she was thinking of him to work on her second boat. It looked as if it wouldn't be very long before she had another one, with the number of bookings that seemed to come in daily. Skylar was even beginning to have to turn away business, which she told Garrett was so hard to do. If only she could show her dad how well she was doing, Skylar confided to Garrett one day. But with everything going on, there was no way she could even broach the subject with her father.

"So, are you ready for tomorrow night? My sister has been keeping me filled in on all the details. In the past, I've been in Miami to help, but this year has been so different. The best thing is that you are coming with me." Skylar reached around him, giving him a hug, which he quickly returned along with a sweet kiss.

"I'm ready, but I'm just being honest: I'm not looking forward to it, except to spend time with you and because it is so important to you. I've only attended these events in the past to meet the right people for research grants, and that has only been a few times. But even if I feel a little out of place, you are worth it."

Only a second after he finished his statement, his lips were on hers. In the past, Garrett had thought he had been in love, but it had felt nothing like this. What was happening between them was on a completely different plane of existence. It felt right, natural, and organic. And even though he admitted that he wasn't looking forward to a society event, it was okay because he would be with her. Hell, he thought to himself, I might even enjoy it because I'll be with her. Skylar made all the difference in the world to him.

"If we are going to be there on time, we need to leave here by four o'clock," Skylar said, still wrapped up in his arms.

"Really. Why so early?"

"I want to help if there are any last minute preparations and also see the children. I convinced Mara to give the children's party an ocean theme—like mermaids, sea captains, and pirates—especially since you will be with me. It should be lots of fun!" Skylar was talking with so much enthusiasm about the coming evening that when she looked up at him, he could see the sparkle in her eyes.

"I love you," Garrett said to her softly.

Skylar looked at him peculiarly. "Are you okay?"

"Yes—why?"

"It's just the way you are looking at me. Am I talking too much about tomorrow?"

"No. I just love seeing you this happy. And each time I look at you, I can't believe I got so lucky that you want me in your life—an old man who, I've been told, talks too much about his work."

"First of all, you are not an old man. Our age difference doesn't mean anything to me, and you need to let that go. As for talking about your love for the ocean, people probably say that about me too. I love boats and the water. I think that is why we fit together so well, in more ways than one," she said, snuggling just a little bit closer and giving him a slight, loving squeeze. "We love our lives, and I know mine feels more complete since I met you."

"I know mine is! You know, I can't wait for you to meet Abbey," Garrett said. "She always kidded me about being a workaholic, but in a sweet way. If she saw both of us together, I'm not sure how she would react. She and Zach became good friends of mine while I lived there."

"Maybe we could go visit them. I would love to meet some of your friends. You will be meeting my crowd tomorrow. But the one friend I really want you to meet is Kimberly, my college roommate. Max is her little brother. As I've told you, I was completely grateful for everything I had while growing up, but I always felt so at home when we visited Kim's family on school breaks or on the weekends. They are so close and loving to each other. I mean, I know my parents love me, and so do my brothers and sister. But there was just something different about Kim's family that I craved. Now, here in Key Largo, I have found a little slice of what I was looking for. And you have made it even better than I could imagine." Slowly, she untangled herself from him and sat on his lap, putting her hand on the nape of his neck.

"I love you, Garrett. I don't think I can say it enough in this lifetime."

"And I can't hear it enough," Garrett said as Skylar nuzzled closer to him sending a sensation through his body like he was on fire.

23

"Well, here we are," Skylar said as they pulled up to the Marriott Marquis in downtown Miami. The valet took the keys to the truck with raised eyebrows. Apparently, he was used to seeing nicer vehicles, but to Skylar, her truck was just right. "The traffic was worse than I thought it would be. I hope Mara isn't mad at me!"

"Don't worry. It will be okay," Garrett said, putting an arm around her shoulders and giving her a quick kiss on the cheek. "By the way—you look absolutely gorgeous tonight!" And Garrett meant every word. Skylar's dark hair was long and straight, with a beautiful shine that matched the glow of her skin. Her emerald eyes seemed to shimmer. And her red dress seemed to make her glow. It was formfitting, wrapping around her and showing every curve of her body. Garrett remembered when she had opened the door at the house. At first he hadn't been able to speak, and then the only word that came out was, "Damn!" Though to him she was beautiful no matter what she was wearing, tonight is was as if she was a model straight out of a magazine.

"Well, I have to say you clean up extremely well. You are looking mighty hot tonight, Mr. Holmes," she said, taking his arm. "Okay, here we go."

They walked through the hotel's lobby and found the signs for the charity event. As they walked, Skylar said hi to a few people here and there but didn't stop to talk to anyone. She wanted to get to Mara first, find out what was going on, and see whether there was anything new happening with her parents before the gala officially began.

"I promise to introduce you later," she said to Garrett. "I really need to find Mara right now."

"I'm with you," Garrett said, giving her a reassuring smile, even though inside he was feeling more and more out of his element with every step he took. But as he had told himself from the moment Skylar convinced him to go, he could do this for her. She was so worth every bit of discomfort, and it was only for one evening.

They entered the room, and much to Skylar's dismay, the children and their parents were already preparing to leave. I should have left Key Largo earlier, she thought. But she quickly walked over to say hi to a few of the kids, stooping down and talking to them about their outfits and more. Garrett was amazed at how easily she spoke to them, as if she knew the children and their parents personally. She introduced him to each person she talked to and was eager to tell the children he was the Fish Man, because he studied the creatures of the ocean. And each child seemed to have a question for him, usually about sharks. Now a part of him did wish they had gotten here earlier, especially as the children left and more adults filled the room.

The ballroom was huge, with yellow-gold lights that lent a soft ambience to the evening's affair. A grand buffet lined one side of the room, and there were large round tables throughout the room for seating. A band area was set up, with a dance floor in front. As Garrett looked around, he decided it was definitely bigger than any other fund-raising event he had ever attended. And the people that were streaming into the ballroom were dressed as if they were going to the wedding of the century. He even had to chuckle at a few of the women's outfits.

"What is funny?" Skylar asked when she heard him.

"I'm sorry, but that poor lady. I wonder if she picked that out," he said discreetly, pointing to a woman in the corner with a bright-purple dress that cinched at the waist, making her look way bigger than she actually was. But it was her hat with the bird on it that took the prize. All of a sudden, Skylar found herself giggling too.

"What is so funny, you two, and why are you here so late?" Mara said, practically running up to them.

"Cathy looks as though she was sprayed with purple paint. But the hat..." Skylar couldn't help but laugh a bit harder, and her sister looked over, joining them as soon as she saw the unusual object atop the lady's head.

"There's no telling what she was thinking. Why are you two so late? I practically had to do all the kids' activities by myself. I coerced Tracey and Blair into helping me, but it was like pulling teeth, especially with Tracey. I'm not sure if Harris is making a good decision there, but we will leave that for another time. There is already too much drama in our family."

With that statement, Skylar cringed and felt Garrett suddenly give her a reassuring squeeze around her waist. "What's the latest?"

"Dad is doing fine, and you wouldn't know that just a few hours ago, they were fighting like two mean old cats. Dad was blaming Mom; Mom was blaming Dad. Both are afraid their precious reputations are going to be hurt. If they can just keep their personal lives to themselves, it will be okay. But if Mom drinks too much, there is no telling what will happen. Skylar, she really needs help, AA or something. I've tried to talk to her, and she flies into a rage. I've asked Dad about counseling for both of them, but he only says he will think about it. I'm beginning to wonder if he might want a divorce. I just wish they would get their shit together.

"And Grandma won't talk to either of them. She told them they were both being foolish and that they needed to start fixing themselves instead of trying to be people they aren't. She even refused to come tonight, and you know this is the only event she ever goes to. Sorry, I've rattled on and on. I'm just ready for this night to be over!" Mara looked around the room nervously.

"Take some deep breaths. It will be fine. Where are Harris and Chase? You watch Mom. I'll take care of Dad. Harris and Chase can entertain the guests. When it comes time for Dad's speech, I'll give him a pep talk. And hopefully, Mom will just stand by and smile. Let's go greet everyone, okay?" As Skylar and Mara turned toward the open doors of the grand ballroom, both her parents were already there greeting guests, along with Harris and Chase.

"I'll stay here," Garrett said as Skylar started to walk away.

"No, you can stand behind me. You are part of the family now because you are with me. Do you see how Blair, Tracey, and Paul are with us? I want you there with me. Please." She quickly reached up and softly caressed his cheek for encouragement.

How could he say no? So Garrett gave her a quick smile, and he followed her toward the ballroom entrance. Once they were all in place, Garrett was amazed as he watched the beautiful woman in front of him. Skylar was gracious to everyone that walked through the door, remembering names and asking them personal questions, as if she was their best friend. She was a natural hostess, and it seemed that everyone gravitated toward her instead of the others in her family. He felt so proud that he was here by her side.

"Hello, Mr. and Mrs. Cartwright. I'm so glad I was in town and able to come." Skylar heard the voice, and her insides cringed. It was Andrew Danforth's voice and she looked over to see his fiancé with him. "This is Alicia Tanner. I believe you know her parents. They should be here shortly."

"Good to see you, Andrew. I've heard some great things about you and your parent's yacht business. Maybe we can talk later," Jonathan Cartwright said, shaking the younger man's hand.

"I would love to. Hi, Skylar," Andrew said, nodding his head toward her.

"Hi there. And hi, Alicia. It's so nice to see you," Skylar said without missing a beat, staying on point and not letting Andrew rattle her. Alicia shook her hand very delicately. She was the type of woman that was perfect for Andrew, Skylar thought. Suddenly, Andrew's friend Ben and his wife, Stella, were in front of her.

"It's nice to see you again. We had so much fun the other day on the sandbar. I wished we could have spent more time with you and…the gentleman you were with," Ben said, searching for a name.

"Garrett. He is right here with me tonight." Skylar turned around and motioned him to join her. Even though he really dreaded it, he put a smile on his face and went to stand beside her.

"Hey, Garrett! It's nice to see you again. We would love to go snorkeling with you guys before we leave the Keys. I keep hearing great things about your boat charters, Skylar," Ben said, not realizing that it was an unpopular subject with her family, or really with anyone in this social circle.

"I think we would love that too, right, Garrett?" she said, giving his hand a slight squeeze.

"Just let us know when." Garrett extended his hand to Ben, giving him a friendly shake.

"Wait a minute. Do you guys know each other?" Andrew said, listening to the conversation.

"I remembered Skylar from a long time ago. We met her and Garrett out on a sandbar off Islamorada not too long ago. It was beautiful out there." While Ben and Stella were smiling, everyone else except Alicia looked as if they had just stepped into a minefield.

"Hi, Garrett. I'm Andrew Danforth. I'm with the Danforth Yacht Brokers. This is my fiancé Alicia Tanner." Garrett reached out to shake both of their hands, but the look on Andrew's face was purely mean. Garrett could immediately sense that this guy intended something, but he couldn't be sure what. "It's nice to meet a friend of Skylar's. We have known each other since we were children, haven't we?" Andrew said, looking over at Skylar with a menacing grin.

"Yes, we have. Maybe we can get together a bit later to catch up." With that, Skylar turned and greeted the next guest in front of her, while Garrett stood beside her. She hated that he had been thrust into the limelight, something she was hoping to avoid for his sake, but at the same time, Skylar wanted everyone to know that this special man was with her and that he meant everything to her. But for her family's sake, she would play the high-society game, and as soon as this event was over, she and Garrett could go back to Key Largo, leaving this behind, except for the situation with her parents. So Skylar took a deep breath, telling herself to take it a little at a time to get through the rest of the evening. But after seeing Andrew, something in her gut left her feeling as though things were going to be anything but smooth.

As she continued to greet the guests streaming into the ballroom, Skylar would look to see Garrett still standing just behind her, close enough that she could feel the connection between them. Suddenly she felt his hand on her arm and he whispered in her ear. "Casey is about to come through the door."

This night just keeps getting better and better, Skylar thought as she cringed inside. She had hoped that Casey's threat of coming to the gala had been just an empty one but apparently not. No one in her family knew the turmoil she had caused for both Skylar and Garrett so as Casey and her date greeted each one of her family members, she was gracious and overly kind. But Skylar knew the real girl underneath that false exterior.

"Good evening Casey. Who have you brought with you tonight?" Skylar asked, not recognizing the gentleman at the girl's side.

Casey couldn't hide the contempt she held for Skylar and Garrett as she sent both of them a menacing smile. "This is Charles Denson. He is new to Miami, having moved here from Connecticut."

"Hi, Charles, I'm Skylar Cartwright and welcome to Miami. Hope you love it here as much as we do," she said as the man seemed on the surface to be totally opposite of his date.

"So far I'm loving it and Casey has been so kind to show me around. She has told me about your charter boats in Key Largo and suggested that we take one of your tours. I can't wait to go since I've never snorkeled before," Charles said enthusiastically while Casey stood beside him, smiling like a cat that just ate the canary.

"I look forward to it. Just let us know when you two want to come. Casey knows where to find us. Oh but one more thing––Casey, I thought I should let you know that your friend, Andrew, is here with his fiancé, Alicia. You might want to say 'hi'." With that the couple proceeded into the ballroom but not before Casey turned around and gave Skylar a cold stare.

"Can't believe you just said that to her but I'm sure glad you did," Garrett whispered in Skylar's ear once again.

"I've got a feeling she is up to something," Skylar whispered back. At this point, she just wanted to get through this evening and go home. What had once been an event she looked forward to was now one that was filled with dread. The only thing that made it tolerable was the fact that Garrett was with her and every time she looked at him, she couldn't help but smile and feel this deep sense of love and connection.

Soon, everyone was going through the elaborate Caribbean buffet that carried on the evening's ocean theme. Skylar was glad that two tables had been reserved for her family and that they wouldn't have to sit with others.

"Part one is done," Mara said quietly to everyone at the table—her siblings and their dates. Her parents were still making the rounds and talking to people, but Skylar was concerned.

"Mara, Dad seems to be okay, but has Mom been drinking this evening?" she asked.

Mara's eyes said it all. "I caught her about an hour ago in the back room with a drink. She's not drunk, but I don't think she is feeling any pain either. If we can just get through this whole thing without a scene" she said, taking a quick bite of the mahi-mahi on her plate.

"I'm going to go get her. Maybe if she eats, it will lessen the effects of the alcohol. All we need is for her to unravel tonight. I don't care what others think, and we can take care of our family. But I don't want the charity to suffer because of what's going on in our personal lives." Skylar quickly turned to Garrett. "I'll be right back as soon as I know mom is okay. I'm really sorry this isn't turning out like I planned."

"Skylar, it's okay. I think you are doing fabulously. You even handled your ex-boyfriend with complete finesse. Go take care of your mom. I'll sit here with Chase. We've been having a great conversation," he said, with a wink.

At that, Skylar leaned over and whispered in his ear. "Do you know how adorable you are? Love ya!" Then she was suddenly on the move, trying to find her mom.

Mara quickly took Skylar's seat. "Garrett, can I talk to you for a moment?"

"Sure. Is everything okay?" he said looking at Skylar's sister with concern.

"I just want to make sure you will please take care of Skylar. We have all been talking, and we think you are the best thing for her. She is happy in Key Largo, and she loves her boat. We always knew she would do something different, but Dad can be pretty forceful. Skylar was always one to make sure everyone was happy, often at her own expense. I especially don't want that for her now. You guys might have differences, but I've never seen her like this before—this confident and this happy—in spite of our, at the moment, dysfunctional family. Promise me." Garrett looked at Mara and could see that she meant every word.

"Like I told your dad the first time I met everyone, I love Skylar. I know I'm not the kind of man your parents wanted for their daughter, and I can't provide like some of these other guys here, but she has my heart, and I will make her happy. Always." As Garrett finished his words, he was stunned that Mara reached over and gave him a quick kiss on the cheek.

"Thank you! Just what I needed to hear. Now, since Skylar is taking care of Mom, I have to go make sure Dad is ready for his speech."

Garrett sat at the table, watching Mara walk off. Then he looked to the other side of the room, where Skylar was walking with her mom through the buffet line. He was finally beginning to realize that though Skylar's siblings had money, they weren't as showy or snobbish as he had imagined. They all loved each other in quirky ways. And yes, their parents were having problems, but every family seemed to have its share of drama. That was just life. He could feel himself starting to relax a little. Hopefully, one day, Skylar's parents would feel about him the way Skylar's siblings did about their sister's choice of the man in her life.

"Good evening," Harris said into the microphone, just as Skylar returned to the table with her mother. Just as Mara had told them earlier, Garrett could tell that Sadie had been drinking just a little. "Welcome to tonight's fund-raising dinner for the Children's Resource Fund. I don't know if you got to see the little sea captains, mermaids, and pirates that were here earlier, but they had a lot of fun. My family feels greatly honored and privileged to work with these children, and we want to thank each and every one of you for your support, not only this evening but throughout the year, in helping underprivileged children be able to have money for school, clothing, and more. And with that, I would like to introduce my father, Mr. Jonathan Cartwright." As the room broke into applause, Skylar's dad took the stage.

"Thanks again to everyone who has come tonight. I really can't add any more to what my son has already said. As a family, we look forward to this every year. So enjoy the sumptuous buffet; the bar is open in the back, and in just a few minutes, the band will be here so you can dance the night away. Have fun, everyone!"

Skylar looked at Garrett. "Part two is finished."

"Why do you and Mara keep saying that?"

"Saying what?"

Garrett shook his head. "You know what I mean—part one, part two."

Skylar laughed. "When we were younger, we, especially me, hated coming to these events. The way we got through them was counting the parts. Part one is the introductions. Part two is usually eating. Part three is dancing. Part four is getting the hell out of here. We are almost to part three, which is a good sign!"

"You really are my kind of girl," Garrett said and then kissed her, not caring who was around or watching.

"I keep telling you I was the weird one of the bunch," she said, with a wink.

"Well, I love oddballs!" he said, giving her a tight hug while his hand slowly slid down her back stopping at her waist. "If you keep that up, we might have to skip part three." She laughed.

"That's fine with me!"

Soon the band was playing. They sat there, holding hands under the table, while Skylar talked with her mom, encouraging her to eat. She could tell that the food was having the desired effect because her mom became more coherent as she sat there. She even began talking to Garrett, and this time, she was much more agreeable than at the horrible family dinner.

Skylar was so lost in thought that she didn't see Garrett stand up. He touched her shoulder, and when she turned around, he had his hand extended out to her. "I think they are playing our song. Will you dance with me?" As she looked up at him, her heart swelled with love. This handsome, sexy man was in love with her, and she felt so blessed. As she stood and they walked hand in hand to the dance floor, it was as if they were the only two people who existed in the room. The song was slow and melodic. Garrett wrapped one arm around her waist, and the other hand nestled hers against his chest. He pulled her in close to him, as though he was protecting something more precious than his life. The slow rhythm they danced to was smooth and sexy, like a fire that melted both their bodies into one. They were completely lost in each other, just like during their first dance together on the boat under the stars.

"So, you are a marine biologist." Andrew's voice brought Skylar back to reality. As she and Garrett both turned, they were suddenly dancing close to Andrew and Alicia.

"Maybe we can talk a little later," Skylar said quietly. But suddenly, the music stopped, and there was nowhere to escape to.

"Yes, I am," Garrett said to the man before him.

"Well, Skylar, when you want to change things up, you go all the way." Andrew's voice was sarcastic and condescending. Alicia stood by his side, silently, while holding Andrew's hand.

"What do you mean?"

"You could have your pick of any guy of means, if you would stick to your own kind of people. I mean you chose a marine biologist. And then you are doing boat charters. You are a Cartwright. If you played your cards right, you wouldn't want for anything for the rest of your life. That is, if your parents could get their act together too." Skylar stood there, dumbfounded. How arrogant! she thought.

"Andrew, who I date and who I want to be with is none of your business. Just because your father controls your every move with that stick up your ass, it doesn't mean the rest of us want to live like that. As for my charter business—it's mine! I'm working, and I did it on my own. I didn't have anything handed to me, like you have." At this point, several people were starting to look at them as voices began getting louder.

"Really? You think anyone would believe that? Your dad probably financed everything for you. I know he is betting on you to fail, and then you will have to work in the real estate business again. I guess he will be getting his wish real soon."

"How do you know about that?" Skylar was enraged, and so was Garrett by now. So much so that he could no longer remain quiet.

"I don't know you very well, but this is family business, and you need to stay out of it," Garrett said forcefully to Andrew.

"What is it to you? Do you really think Skylar is going to settle for someone like you? I already know her father won't let her." Suddenly, everything around Skylar began to swirl. Her dad—he had told Andrew about her business and the deal they had made. But why?

She turned to see her dad standing only twenty feet away. "Why, Dad? Why would you talk to him of all people?" she said, pointing to Andrew.

"I only was doing what I thought was best. Garrett, I'm sorry, but you aren't right for our daughter. She has such a bright future; plus, you are much older than she is. As for the boat charters, that will slow down during the off-season and prove that I was right. I knew that. I just want you back where you belong, Skylar."

"Where I belong. You want to destroy my life like you are destroying yours and Mom's right now by how you are treating each other!" Skylar said it before she thought. She was so hurt, but she never intended to air private information about their family. She suddenly looked around, and the whole ballroom was eerily quiet. People were speaking in hushed tones. She felt as if all eyes were on her.

"Personally, Mr. Cartwright, I think that if it weren't for Garrett, Skylar would have already been back here, where she belongs." That was it. The next sound that traveled across the room was of her hand slapping Andrew's cheek.

"Young lady, that is uncalled for." Skylar's dad looked at her sternly.

"I'm sorry, Dad. I know I made a deal with you, but as far as I'm concerned, it's off. I hadn't told you yet because I was going to wait till the next boat was ready, but I already paid off the loan at the bank yesterday. I don't owe you anything." With that, she looked at Andrew.

"Yes, Andrew, my dad helped me secure a loan. But he didn't just hand me money, like your parents do. I had to work to make my boating business a success, and it has become one. And don't think you can mess with it. You don't have a chance in hell to ruin it. Too many people know about your nasty reputation, and I know some good people down in the Keys. We take care of each other there, unlike some people around here."

Now she was looking back at her father. "I'm sorry that I'm such a disappointment to you and Mom. I'm sorry that I was the misfit of the family, but I finally found something—and someone—that makes me happy. Is that such a bad thing? Money can afford us a lot of luxuries, but it can't buy us true happiness—that feeling that makes you smile from the moment you wake up till you go to sleep. Money also can't buy you the perfect person to share your life with. You only find that when you are genuine and you open your heart to others. Andrew, you could learn a lesson or two about that. Ask your ex-girlfriend Casey, who is here tonight. But then again, after having to spend some time with your ex lately, you two seem to be on the same playing field. And as for me and Garrett..." But when Skylar turned around to grab Garrett's hand, he was gone.

"Looks like maybe he knows what's best for you," her dad said. But hurt and anger filled Skylar. She quickly looked at both Andrew and her dad only to see another face that brought even more pain to the situation. It was Casey standing about ten feet away with a smile on her face. Skylar couldn't take anymore and stormed out of the ballroom. "Skylar!" She heard her name being called, but she didn't turn. Chase and Mara were trying to get her attention, but she just wanted to be outside the building. The hurt she was feeling was unexplainable. Why had Garrett left? She tried to reach him on his phone, but there was no answer. Where was he?

"Skylar, wait!" Chase said just as she reached the valets' stand.

"Just leave me alone. I can't talk right now, Chase. Please."

Chase turned her around to face him just as Mara finally caught up. "It will be okay. Dad is just being Dad. As for Andrew, he has always been a jerk."

"Amen!" Mara said.

"But why would Garrett leave? And where did he go? The truck is still here," Skylar said, seeing her truck in the valet parking lot.

"Put yourself in his shoes, Skylar. Your ex-boyfriend and your father both saying he isn't good enough, he's too old for you, and more, in front of so many people. What would you do?"

Now the tears she had been holding back started falling from her eyes. "I'm so sorry. I ruined everything. I didn't mean to say what I did about Mom and Dad. It came out before I could think about what I was saying. I just want to fix things, to make everything better, to be somewhere where everyone is happy, but I can't."

"There is no such place," Mara said softly, holding her little sister in her arms. "But you have to live your own life. We will take care of things here. Don't worry about those people. They are probably glad to see a little excitement for once."

Now Mara and Chase had smiles on their faces. Just then, the valet pulled to the curb with her truck and Chase held the door open for Skylar.

"Are you sure you are okay to drive home?"

"I'm fine. I only wish I knew where Garrett was."

"I'm right here." Skylar turned to see Garrett standing at the back of the vehicle. She was speechless. She had been so worried, but now that she knew he was okay, she was mad.

"Why did you leave?" she yelled at him.

"I'm sorry. I really am. I apologize to you to, Mara and Chase. But I think Skylar and I need to talk."

"Garrett, just remember what you told me earlier tonight. Don't break your promise," Mara said before both of Skylar's siblings walked back into the hotel.

Garrett just stared at Skylar's older sister. Then he looked down at the pavement. "Let's head back the Keys."

24

The ride back to Key Largo was long and quiet. And this time, they weren't sitting side by side. Skylar was next to the passenger door, staring out the window, while Garrett drove in the darkness. It was only when they pulled up into the driveway of her house that Garrett began to speak.

"Skylar, I owe you an apology. I am really sorry I stepped away during the argument. But when your father looked at me and said I wasn't good enough for you, I started thinking he was probably right."

"How can you say that? We have talked about this so many times. I'm not like the rest of my family. I think I'm old enough to know what I want in life, and I want you. I want my boating business. I want a house here in the Keys and maybe a family. I want that simpler life my grandma has always talked about," Skylar said as tears trickled out of the corners of her eyes.

"But I watched you tonight, Skylar. You are a natural. You were amazing with those kids. They loved you. And then you greeted each guest like they were your best friends. They loved you, and you made them feel like they belonged. They were drawn to you. And the good you did with that charity tonight—from what I saw, you could probably run a nonprofit of your own with your hands tied behind your back." Garrett reached out to touch her hand, but she didn't respond.

"As hard as it is for me to say this, maybe you need someone that can give you the money and time to help others like you did tonight. Skylar, I can't give any of that to you. I don't know the right people like you do. As I said, maybe your father's assessment of me was on target. And I am ten years older than you."

"Dammit! Why do you keep saying that? How many times do I have to keep telling you I don't care about the age difference? But apparently, it bothers you." All of Skylar's emotions were at the surface. She felt like an open wound, and as Garrett said each word it was like salt being poured in, making the hurt worse and more intense.

"I'll admit that sometimes it does. I feel like I'm robbing you of a part of your life. I can't explain it any better than that. But to tell you hurts so much because I want to be with you more than I can say."

"Then let's just forget all this happened tonight. Please? I wished we had never gone, but I just felt like it would be a magical evening. Instead it has turned into a nightmare." Skylar looked at him, small tears slowly sliding down her face.

"I can't forget. Your family only wants what's best for you, and so do I," Garrett said softly, hurting so much with each word he said. It felt as if he was breaking in two, but he couldn't let her see that. He had to let her go. It was the only way she would have the opportunities that he would never be able to offer her.

"How many times have I told you I'm a grown woman! I know what I want! Why doesn't anyone listen to me? For my whole life, I feel like I've only pleased others, lived their dreams. I'm ready to live my own life, on my own terms. Is that so terrible?" Skylar turned away, hoping Garrett didn't see the tears beginning to fall more rapidly down her cheeks.

"I do love you, Sky. But I don't think we are meant for each other." As he said the words, they slammed him so hard it felt as if someone was punching him in the stomach. He felt as if he couldn't breathe, but he kept as calm as possible.

"So, you are giving up just like that, because of some rude, out of place comments tonight. You say you love me, but you certainly have no faith in me. I guess it was better for me to find out now rather than later." Skylar got out of the truck and ran to her front door.

"Please understand. This is probably better for both of us," Garrett said as he got out of the truck, running to catch up to her. He reached out and touched her shoulder, but Skylar jerked it away.

"You told me earlier we were in this together. And I believed you. I guess I have been so blinded by what I thought we had that I didn't realize you were so weak." Skylar went in the front door and proceeded to slammed it in his face.

Garrett stood on her porch, unable to move. Was he doing the right thing? Was letting her go what was best for her? Was it best for him? Every fiber of his being was screaming "no", but the logical part of his brain remembered the words her father had said earlier. So he reluctantly turned away, got in his truck, and left.

Skylar had discreetly watched through the window, hoping against hope that he would demand to come into her house and tell her that he couldn't go through with this, but as the truck went down the road, the torrent of tears came, and nothing could stop them. She had finally found the person she was meant to be with; she was so sure of it. Her boat business—her dream—was a successful reality. Why was everything going so wrong? What had she done to deserve such craziness in her life? She had always been kind, caring, and considerate, going the extra mile. She just wanted things to be as they had been before this awful night.

Skylar slowly got undressed and crawled beneath her bedcovers. Nothing she did, from trying to watch TV to listening to music, could ease the hurt that was deepening by the minute. Garrett hadn't even been gone an hour, and it already felt like days. Never in her life had she felt this way before, not even in other relationships when they had parted ways. Garrett was different because she was positive he was her other half.

Before she knew it, the pillow was soaked with tears, and she was exhausted. And finally, sleep came, even though it was fitful and full of crazy nightmares. The next morning only brought back memories of the night before, reigniting the deep pain she felt.

"Hello," said the elderly woman on the other end of the line.

"Hi, Grandma," Skylar said, trying to put up a brave front, but she knew her voice didn't sound normal.

"Hi, sweetheart. Your sister told me that last night was a bit of a mess. Are you okay?"

"Not really. I wanted to hear your voice. And I was wondering if you might want to come down to Key Largo and stay with me for a couple of days," Skylar asked.

"Will Garrett be there too? He's such a nice boy," her grandma said.

"It's such a mess, Grandma. Can we talk about it when I come and pick you up? That is, if you want to come to this little house of mine."

"Of course I want to. It will give me a chance to get out of the stuffiness around here. But you aren't coming to get me. I think it's about time I had a talk with all you kids. There are a few things I think you ought to know. I will have Harris bring me, and I'll make sure Mara and Chase are with us. We will be there in a few hours."

"They won't come, and it's okay. I'll come and get you." Skylar insisted once again.

"Oh, yes, they will. Don't you worry about that. I'll bring clothes for a few nights."

"Thanks, Grandma. Garrett and I broke up last night. I really thought he was my special one, like you always used to say about Grandpa."

"Don't you worry. We will talk." And with that, they ended the call. Skylar wondered why her grandmother would need all four of them there, but she sounded very determined to make this a family conversation, minus their parents. And she usually got her way.

25

Skylar got dressed and made her way to the grocery store to pick up a few things before her family got there. She looked around everywhere, hoping to see Garrett, to run into him or something. She wanted to drive to his apartment so badly, but she knew she couldn't. She didn't know how she was going to handle the rest of the charter agreement, but she would. And then he would leave Key Largo. At that thought, the pain deepened again, bringing tears.

Her grandma was true to her word. Only three hours later, a car pulled up to her house, and the four people Skylar knew best were at her door. Everyone came in, hugging Skylar but not saying a word. Had their grandma already talked to them? Skylar wasn't sure, but she was anxious to know what was going on.

As her grandma sat down in the most comfortable seat in the family room, her four grandchildren took seats, looking as though they were about to be scolded. Skylar was still reeling from Garrett's departure, so she was hoping that this wasn't going to make her hurt even worse.

"I think there is something that you children ought to know about your parents. Maybe it will help you understand what they are going through, and for you, Skylar, help you understand why your father said what he did. I wasn't there, but I've heard about the conversation." Mara quickly looked down at her hands, letting Skylar know that she had given their grandma all the details.

"You see, your grandpa and I had practically nothing when we came to Miami. We had just enough money to buy a piece of land, and it was big enough that we were able to sell a part of it. Your grandpa took that money, paid off our loan, and used what was left to buy another house. After that one sold, he was hooked. He liked finding cheap houses and selling them. Then his two brothers moved down here, and you kids pretty much know the rest. Your daddy wasn't even born until after the sale of the second house. And we had more money by the time he was older, so he never really experienced the times when we didn't have much. When he was finally able to go to college, he decided to help your grandpa instead. He caught that bug to sell houses too." The older woman took a sip of her sweet tea, which Skylar had placed on the side table for her.

"And God surely blessed us. We made money, but we lost some too. But your daddy and his brothers learned the business inside and out while they were young, and they built a strong, very profitable business within a few years. During this time, your daddy met your momma. She actually lived in one of the houses that the bank had foreclosed on, an event that sent her parents into the streets. But your daddy helped the family and fell in love with your momma. She had never had money. I know you think she always did, but that's just not true. So when they got married, she was determined to be the proper wife of a prominent businessman, especially since the business was growing so fast, and they were invited to almost every social event in Miami. The Cartwright name became famous in this town because of two generations of hard work, and now you and your cousins are creating a third. But your poor momma has always felt like she was never good enough for this family. Most of the wives she is friends with came from families with money. So she made up a false family history, which your daddy went along with. I told both of them it was a foolish idea, but no one ever seems to listen to their parents," she said, with a smile. She paused for a minute, causing Skylar and her siblings to try to comprehend everything she was telling them.

"Your momma's reputation became so important to her— attending social events, meeting the girls, shopping, buying the best, and so on. So much so that when your daddy met someone who reminded him of the woman he had married so long ago, he had an affair. Now I'm not saying that's right, I'm just letting you know how he felt. When your momma found out, she began drinking, and this has been going on for two years now. She even had an affair of her own! I'm surprised you kids never put the pieces together. Couldn't you tell that your parents had changed?"

As Skylar sat there with her brothers and sister, they were all trying to understand the story their grandma was telling them.

"They sure did hide it well," Harris said, suddenly standing up and pacing the floor. "Why are you telling us this now?"

"Because someone in this family needs to stop this stupid circle of lies, stop putting on an act that everything is just peachy keen. Let's be honest, even if it means airing out some dirty laundry." Grandma Cartwright sat back and took some more sips of her tea.

"Are they both still seeing other people? And how bad is Mom's drinking problem?" Chase said quietly.

"Oh, heavens, no! Your dad screwed up, and he told your momma he was sorry, but she couldn't forgive him. So she drank and drank. Then not too long ago, she had a bit too much to drink and ended up with someone after a dinner event she attended with her friends. When your dad found out, he didn't know what to do. Skylar, that was the night he came to your boat. I think he was going to spend the night there. Instead, he found you and your boyfriend." Ex-boyfriend, Skylar said to herself, and hot tears once again threatened to spill forth.

"I'm telling you all of this because we all need to be here to support each other. Your momma needs you. She may not think she needs help, but someone needs to get her to AA meetings or something. Then maybe you can encourage your parents to go to counseling. If I have my information right, they each only messed up once. And I honestly think they still really love each other. They just don't know where that love is right now. So, it's time for you kids to show them some love.

"But now that you know the real story, I'm going to bed. You can discuss what you need to do. But know this: they love you, kids. And maybe you think they are being too pushy, but it's done out of love." With those last words, she looked directly at Skylar.

"So, show me where my room is, baby girl," Grandma Cartwright said. With that, Skylar grabbed her grandmother's little suitcase and showed her to the spare bedroom. "I hope this is okay." She suddenly hugged the little woman in front of her.

"We will talk tomorrow, sweetheart." Skylar nodded her head 'yes' and slowly closed the door to her grandmother's bedroom.

"So, what are we supposed to do now?" Mara asked, looking around the room. "We can't make Mom and Dad go to counseling. And do you really think Mom would go to an AA meeting? I don't even think I would want to go."

"You wouldn't go even to help Mom," Skylar said in disbelief. "Now you sound like the snobby one."

"Hey, let's calm down," Chase said. Harris was still pacing the floor, and his two sisters were looking at each other as though they were about to fight.

"Maybe we should sit down and talk with them. Maybe it would help if they knew that we know the whole story. Then we could ask what we can do to help," Harris said in a quiet voice.

"After Dad destroyed my life last night, I have no plans to go back to Miami." Skylar was so angry at her parents, at Garrett, at her siblings—at everything. She just wished it would all magically go away so that none of this had ever happened.

"Skylar, I don't blame you. Dad was pretty harsh, but it was Andrew's fault too. Dad was just being protective. Your ex-boyfriend was being a first-class asshole," Mara said.

"Let's just see what happens during the next week, and then we can make some plans. That will give everyone time to cool down. A lot happened last night. Now all of Miami knows about Mom and Dad's problems." Chase's voice sounded angry and sad at the same time.

"What do you mean?" Skylar asked. He was pulling her attention away from her own situation.

"When you left the room after slapping Andrew, which I wish I could have given you a high five for, he made a snide comment that given the fact that Dad couldn't keep his wife in line, it was no wonder his children didn't stay in line. Dad had to ask him what he meant, and Andrew just said that we weren't the type of family he wanted to be associated with, given all of our problems. Then Dad asked him to leave. So it wasn't long before the room cleared out; there was no silent auction or anything. It was a mess."

Skylar hung her head, looking at the floor. Now she felt as if she was in the middle of a swirling category-five hurricane with no way out. One thing seemed to be piling up on top of another. She could never remember a time in her life when things had been so complicated. Even when she was in her own little world growing up and as an adult, things hadn't been this bad. She suddenly felt that she had lived such a sheltered life. Maybe that is why Garrett decided to back away, she thought. If that was it, she didn't blame him. He could step away from this chaotic situation, but Skylar couldn't. Her family was at stake, but right now, she couldn't even think straight.

"I'm sure we are the talk of the town right now. Tracey is making sure all the silent auction items are secure, and we are going to try to do an online auction in about a month. We'll let things smooth over a bit around town," Mara said. At least they had a plan, Skylar thought. For the most part, Mara and Harris always seemed so level-headed when it came to stressful situations, but something like this had never happened in their family before.

"We are going to head back home," Harris said. "I'll come pick Grandma up when she is ready. That way, Skylar, you don't have to come back till you are ready." Harris hugged his little sister tightly, and Skylar could feel the brotherly love coming from him. It was so different from when they were little kids, when he had practically tortured her and her friends. The small memory brought a tiny smile to her face.

"Thanks, guys. I'm glad we know the details of the real story. I don't understand why our parents kept so many secrets."

As their brothers walked to the car, Mara gave Skylar a hug. "Hey, don't worry about Garrett. Last night was rough but he will come around. If not, then he wasn't the man I thought he was. He promised me last night he would always take care of you."

"Mara, we broke up last night when we got home. Before he left last night, he said that stepping away was taking care of me. If so, why does it hurt so badly?" Skylar said, her face wet again.

"Because you are in love. And sometimes, it hurts," Mara said as she gave her little sister a hug.

26

Skylar woke to the smell of coffee. It was the first Monday that she wasn't required to be at the boat. Though Garrett had paid for the charter day, he was supposedly working on papers. And no reservations had come through for snorkeling or scuba trips. Maybe her dad was right. The off-season was coming, and it probably wasn't the right time to buy a second boat. She was just glad that she had paid for the first boat in full during her first season. And she did have trips scheduled during the week, so she wasn't going to worry about it. She would keep being slow and steady, as she had since she began this venture. But one thing she couldn't quit thinking about was Garrett.

"Hello, little one. I hope I made this coffee right. I'm not used to these machines," Grandma Cartwright said as her granddaughter walked into the kitchen.

"It looks and smells like you did just fine, but let me finish it for you," Skylar said as she went to stand by her grandma's side. She finished the coffee while her grandma took a seat at the kitchen table. "I'm going to fix some toast. Would you like some?"

"I want a real breakfast. Let's go get some because I already checked out your refrigerator, and you don't have anything."

"Yes, I do. I have some yogurt, cashew milk, oatmeal, and honey. There is even some cantaloupe and grapes."

"Like I said, let's go get some breakfast." Skylar couldn't help but smile at her, and it wasn't long before they were sitting at one of her favorite little restaurants—Mangrove Mike's in Islamorada.

"Now, this looks like my kind of food," her grandma said as she surveyed the place and watch as plates passed by.

"This is one of my favorite places. I used to come here with..." But Skylar couldn't finish her sentence because suddenly there was a big lump in her throat.

"You miss him. But it's only been a couple of days, sugar," the older lady said as the waitress set their food before them. "You need to give him some time."

"But why did you say yesterday that Mom and Dad's story would help me understand my now nonexistent relationship with Garrett? I don't understand."

"You and Garrett come from two different worlds. I've lived in both. Yes, money is nice and can give you luxuries, but it can't give you a sense of peace. But when you don't have money, you worry about making it from day to day, and that doesn't bring peace either. There is a fine line to walk where you need to be happy about people and experiences instead of things. If I have pegged Garrett right, and I'm pretty good at reading people, he is probably thinking he isn't good enough for you, especially after that circus the other night. You have to show him that he is."

"I don't know how to do that. I've already tried being myself and telling him how I feel. We have spent so much time together on the boat, and I live in a simple house. I just don't know. It's like my family name causes problems."

Her grandma paused before taking a bite of her food. Then she looked Skylar in the eye. "The Cartwright name is a good one; don't you forget it. You should be proud of who you are."

"I'm sorry, I didn't mean any disrespect. But I want a life like you had with Grandpa—a garden, a house, and a family."

"Sweetheart, you can have that. And you will, but you have to be patient. You keep doing what you are doing. If Garrett is meant to be in your life, he will be. If not, there is someone out there who wants the same things you do. Just have faith, and believe." Her grandma stretched out her arm and took Skylar's hand. "Just have faith, and believe."

Once again, tears were forming at the corners of Skylar's eyes, and she looked upward toward the ceiling to keep them from falling down her cheeks. There was something about her grandmother's words that seemed to sink down into her heart. The hurt from Garrett leaving was still there, but for some reason, she felt reassured. Skylar didn't know why, but she decided to grab ahold of the feeling, even if it was slight, and hang on to it for dear life.

"Now, since we are done, I want to see that boat of yours. Your dad said it was a beauty and told me how proud he is of you. He said you were following your dream."

"Really?" Her grandmother's words stunned Skylar.

"Of course! He just can't tell you to your face because you are supposed to do what everyone else in the family has done for years now. But I think a part of him, and part of your mother too, envies the fact that you had the guts to step out. Now, let's go see the boat."

Skylar helped her grandmother into the truck, and they made their way to the marina. Though she had to use a walker, her grandmother got around pretty well. They walked slowly down the dock, and Skylar was careful to watch her grandma's steps, making sure she was safe. Skylar hadn't been to the boat since before the charity event. Suddenly, it felt like years since she had been here.

"Here she is, the *Sea Gypsy*." Skylar smiled proudly, wishing she could take her grandma on the boat.

"My goodness, she is beautiful. I'm so proud of you, Skylar. You are my special little one, and always will be," Grandma Cartwright said as she gently pulled Skylar's head to hers and gave her a quick kiss on the cheek.

"I love you, Grandma."

From his truck in the distance, Garrett watched the scene before him. He had come to the marina today just in case Skylar might be here. And here she was, with her grandmother. A big part of him wanted to rush up to her and tell her how sorry he was and that he couldn't stand being apart. But he knew there would never be peace in her family with him around. It was better this way, and even though he had paid for the full six months of the boat charter, he would find another boat to make it easier on them both. But it was mostly for his own sake. Watching her smile with her grandmother tore his heart more. He had never loved a woman as he had Skylar. He had never imagined a future with someone as he had with Skylar. And now, as he watched her from a distance, he knew that there would never be another woman like Skylar. Maybe it was time for a little getaway. He needed to get out of town for a while. He could take his work with him, and he knew just where to go—Key West.

For the next few weeks, Skylar stayed busy. When her grandma went home after staying a few days, she was either out on the boat with tourists and Max, doing paper work, or talking to local hotels and shops about her charter services. Each night, she came home tired, allowing herself to simply crawl into bed. But most nights, her pillows were wet with tears and the hurt from Garrett's absence was not getting any better. She thought about him constantly, often looking at the pictures she had taken of the two of them on her phone. The last one she had was from the night of the gala. She was in the beautiful red dress, and he was in his tuxedo, looking so sexy, but comforting at the same time. Though the pictures made her sad, they also brought back happy memories of times that she never wanted to forget, even though the pain would probably always be there.

The weekends were the hardest. After her trips, usually taking tourists snorkeling, she was always reminded of the times she and Garrett had shared. They had already been in such a routine that she didn't realize it till he was gone. And she didn't understand the depth of how happy it made her till he wasn't here anymore.

Skylar had driven by his apartment a few times, even though she knew that was the wrong thing to do. She couldn't help it, but each time she had, his truck was never there. And there were so many times she almost called him, but she inevitably stopped herself.

"So, no trips tomorrow," Max said as he and Skylar finished cleaning up the boat.

"You have a Sunday free to do anything. I've been trying to book more trips on the weekends but it is slowing down just a little bit. But we are fully booked for next Saturday and Sunday. I think our midweek charters might slack off. We will just have to wait and see." Skylar was betting that she would be able to go through the season without a decrease in business. The tourists were abundant and even though the water was cooling down just a bit, people still wanted to be in the ocean. She was also talking to more scuba instructors, so the possibility of more business was there. It was now just a wait-and-see game.

When Skylar's cell phone rang, she looked down to see a number she didn't recognize. She didn't want to answer, but her instinct told her to click the button.

"Hello."

"Is this Skylar? I promise I'm not some weirdo or something."

"Yes, but who is this?" Skylar said, with hesitation in her voice.

"My name is Abbey Wallace. I'm a friend of Garrett's. He has no idea I'm calling you, but I wanted to ask you something: Are you free for a couple of days? Do you want to make a trip to Key West?"

27

Skylar put the address Abbey had given her into her phone, which gave her directions straight to the house. The closer she got to Key West, the more she wondered whether this was a good idea. She was excited to see the love of her life again, but would this go as Abbey thought? Even if it did, Skylar and Garrett would have so much to discuss if they were to move forward in their relationship.

If Abbey was at all similar in person to how she sounded on the phone, Skylar already liked her. When she told Skylar about Garrett's exodus to her fiancé's house last week, Skylar knew why the truck had never been at his apartment when she drove by. According to Abbey, Garrett was not himself—she had known him as the friendliest neighbor ever. He had helped her move into her apartment on the very first day she had come to Key West. Now, Abbey said that Garrett had been moping around, doing some work on the computer while camped out on Zach's couch. She had finally gotten out of him that he and Skylar had called off their relationship and he had needed to just get away. But Garrett was barely talking and Abbey was worried so she sneaked through his contacts on his phone and found Skylar's number. Abbey promised she only wanted to help, and she hoped her meddling didn't create problems, but Garrett was definitely not the man she remembered. And she couldn't stand to see him so unhappy. According to Abbey, Garrett was miserable, and though it sounded terrible, Skylar was happy to hear it. That meant he still had feelings for her, and maybe there was hope, as her grandma had said. Skylar was about to find out.

She pulled up to the address Abbey had given her, spotting Garrett's truck immediately. Her heart leaped at the sight, but then her anxiety started to kick in. During the entire trip to Key West, she had envisioned a wonderful, happy reunion with the man she had become so close to. But what if he was still feeling like he had? What if his feelings for her had changed? What if he truly didn't want her anymore, even after all the promises he had made? Skylar parked her truck behind his, took a deep breath, and headed to the front door. No matter what happened, Skylar needed to know.

"Hi there. Come on in," said the tall blond man that answered the door. This had to be Zach, and soon an attractive young woman with an energetic smile poked her head around him—it had to be Abbey. She said nothing, but she grabbed Skylar's hand and then put her fingers to her lips to tell Skylar to be quiet. Skylar followed Abbey into the brightly lit house, and she could see the top of Garrett's head as he sat on the couch, with his feet crossed on the table before him. Skylar could feel every nerve in her body come to life. Abbey motioned for her to walk around to the front of the couch so he could see her, but she suddenly felt paralyzed. But Skylar felt a little push on the middle of her back, and then before she knew it, she was standing in front of Garrett, looking into his sweet eyes.

"Skylar!" Garrett said, smiling and standing up so quickly he almost lost his balance.

"Hi," Skylar said, her voice cracking just a bit.

"What are you doing here?" Garrett asked, sounding surprised but not mad.

"That would be my fault," Abbey said. "I found her phone number and gave her a call. Call me nosy, but I think the two of you need to talk. Zach and I are actually going for a walk to give you two some privacy."

"Uh...yeah...uh...bye," Zach said, looking at Abbey as she practically dragged him away from the living room and out the front door.

"Do you mind if I sit?" Skylar said, still looking at Garrett's face, memorizing every detail just in case this didn't work out as she had planned so neatly in her imagination.

"Of course! I'm sorry. I'm just so surprised you are here."

"Is it a good surprise or a bad one?" Skylar asked, nervously wringing her hands.

"Skylar, it's always good to see you. How are you doing?"

"Fine. I've been busy with the usual stuff: snorkel trips, family drama—you know. Same ole, same ole." Why was the conversation sounding so stiff? "What about you?"

"I guess I could say the same thing. I just thought I would take a little trip here to work and visit friends." Garrett still couldn't believe she was here, and she was a beautiful sight. It took all his strength and willpower not to go over, pull her to her feet, and kiss her like never before. He had been dreaming of it every moment, while at the same time hoping the dream would fade because it hurt to think about it. He missed Skylar so much, but he was still convinced they weren't meant to be together. "I guess Abbey was tired of my talking." He took a minute to shake his head and then let out a little laugh. "I was hoping she would be my sounding board. I didn't know she would call you. She must have peeked at my phone."

"Abbey sounds really sweet. We had a nice conversation on the phone."

"Uh oh. What did she say?" Garrett asked, dreading the answer.

"It was just girl talk, but she is worried about you." Then Skylar spoke very carefully. "And she said that I was the only one who could fix it."

Garrett looked at her, and he knew Abbey was right. Logically, it didn't seem they were meant to be in a relationship. So many elements didn't click in the right way. Yet when they were together, his heart told him that they were like two ingredients in a magical recipe.

"Skylar, nothing has changed. I am a simple man; I don't have wealth, and I will always be a marine biologist. You will always be Skylar Cartwright, an heir to the Cartwright fortune, with so much at your disposal. The good you can do with that is amazing, and you have the heart to do it. You need someone by your side that you don't have to be ashamed of, someone who matches your status."

"Have you ever thought about what I want? Did it ever occur to you, and it should have after our many talks, that I don't want the mansions or the expensive cars or to go jet-setting around the world! I don't care about status or what the society pages say. If I wanted that, I would never have taken on the task of building a charter business. And even if I don't live like my family does, I can still contribute and make a difference to society. I don't need money for that. All that takes is heart and, preferably, someone who wants to help and share it with me."

Garrett looked at her, knowing that she was right, but he was having a hard time admitting it. She had let him know this whole time how she felt about everything in her life. She had been an open book, just as he had been with her. But the statements Andrew and her father had made at the gala had thrown him for a loop, and he couldn't get them out of his mind.

"What about your family? What if your parents did something crazy, like disowned you just because of me?"

Skylar smiled. "Garrett, my family might be very dysfunctional at times, but I don't think my parents would ever do such a thing. And my grandma would have a say in it too. She might look like a frail little lady, but she is pretty tough. She came to stay with me for a few days."

"I know. I saw the two of you down at your boat."

"If you saw us, why didn't you say something?" He wanted to see me as much I wanted to see him, Skylar thought and felt her heart leap again.

"It was a couple of days after everything happened, and I went to the boat to see you, hoping to talk to you. But when I saw you with your grandma, it just affirmed in my mind that your family was more important."

"I asked my grandma to come down because I didn't want to be by myself. She ended up bringing my brothers and sister too, and she told us the real story of our Cartwright heritage." Skylar began to fill Garrett in with the details of how her family's business truly got its start. And how her parents had met.

"But one thing she told me before she left was not to give up on you. She said that you were perfect for me. I drove by your apartment a couple of times, but your truck was gone. Other times, I wanted to call you, but I felt like you just didn't want me. I felt that you didn't want to get involved in the family drama and everything that comes with being associated with the Cartwrights."

Garrett got up and came to kneel before her. "What your ex and your dad said that night really had me thinking that I was all wrong for you. But during these last few weeks, I've been lost. I've hardly gotten any work done. All I've been able to think about is you. I never wanted to let you go. I just thought I was doing the right thing. But now, having you here with me after these few miserable weeks, I really don't give a damn." Garrett stood up and at the same time, tenderly pulled Skylar up to stand beside him. It only took a second for him to wrap his arms around her, pulling her into a tight embrace and then kissing her with so much passion that Skylar groaned. "I want you, Skylar. You are the only woman I want or will ever love."

She had longed to hear those words as she drove to Key West. The happiness that was flooding through her body was magical, and she seemed to be floating, on some kind of high.

"I know I made a mess of things, but will you take me back?" Garrett looked at her after releasing her lips from the steamy embrace.

"I don't know," Skylar said, with a stoic face. As she looked at Garrett, she saw his smile begin to thin, and his body language showed defeat. "But I drove all the way here, so it would be a shame not to try to fix things with you. You are the love of my life, and I'm not about to let you go without a fight." Now Skylar saw a broad smile on his face. "But you do have to promise me one thing."

"Anything!" Garrett said, wrapping his arms around her waist once more, pulling her even closer this time.

"From now on, this relationship is just us. Yes, I have family, and so do you. But we are living our lives for ourselves—not for anyone else. I know things will be bumpy, like they are now in my family, but if we make a promise to be there for each other *no matter what*, I think we can make this work. What do you think?"

"I think you have a deal, Miss Cartwright," he said before picking her up and spinning her around. Skylar laughed the whole time. But as she slid down his body, back to the floor, she couldn't help but take his face in her hands, gently tracing his chin and gliding a finger over his lips. His eyes closed, and he took a deep breath as she touched her lips to his once more. This kiss would heal their brokenness.

"It worked!" A girl's voice screamed, startling both Garrett and Skylar back to reality.

"Man, Abbey, you scared us," Garrett said, still holding Skylar so close that it looked like they shared a body.

"I knew it. Garrett, you can talk nonstop about fish all day long, but when you did that about a woman, I knew you were a goner. If someone hadn't done something, you would have just wasted away, asking yourself what-if questions. So, is it safe to say you guys are back together?"

Garrett and Skylar looked at each other, nodding in unison.

"Yes! I told you, Zach. He said I needed to leave the two of you alone, but I could tell by the way Garrett talked about you, Skylar, that you were special and that he was totally in love with you. He was just too stubborn to make things right again." Abbey was smiling, and Zach was behind her, his arms wrapped protectively around her waist.

"Well, I think this calls for a celebration. How about drinks at Sloppy Joe's," Zach said.

"That sounds great, but Skylar might want to rest up after her trip," Garrett said.

"Then we will go at about seven o'clock. Does that sound okay?"

"That would be fine," Skylar said.

"Zach has been letting me use the spare bedroom. Come on——you can take a nap if you want to or just rest up a bit," Garrett said, taking her hand and leading her to the room.

There was no denying that Garrett had made himself at home. Stuff, mainly piles of research papers and stray soda cans, were everywhere, and a computer was set up on a little tray table.

"Sorry it's such a mess in here. I wasn't really expecting company," Garrett said, with a wink. "But I'm sure glad to have you here."

"If I lie down to take a quick nap, will you stay with me?" Skylar wanted to feel his body next to hers to let her know that this was real and not a dream.

"I think I could use a nap too, after all the excitement."

The next thing Skylar felt was Garrett's body behind her, molding to hers. He protectively wrapped his arm around her, as though he was guarding something more precious than gold, which in Garrett's mind, he was. He was protecting the woman who now totally and completely owned his heart.

"I love you, Skylar, so much. Thank you for overlooking my stupidity. I thought I was doing the right thing for you, but in reality, I just didn't know how to handle everything that happened. Sometimes, I can be an idiot. Thank you for being the strong one and being there for me."

"Garrett, I'm not as strong as you think I am. I was only that way because I had you. When you were gone, I felt like I had lost a piece of myself. Promise you will never leave again. Please!"

"I promise, sweetheart."

"I love you, Garrett, with all my heart." Skylar snuggled a bit closer, and soon, Garrett was listening to her slow even breaths as she slept. Though he was tired too, the excitement of having her with him made it too difficult to rest. So he laid close beside her and thought about the life ahead of them.

Even though it might be rough, he wasn't going back on his promise again. He was going to be with her through thick and thin. But it wasn't much longer until he was relaxed, and slowly, sleep overtook him too.

Skylar woke up to a light snoring in her ear. Though the sound would probably have irritated most people, it made her smile. She had Garrett back in her life. Just the thought of that filled her with a joy that was hard to explain. And having him lying next to her was a pleasure that sent chills through her. She felt as if she was in a little cocoon, but if they were going to go out with Abbey and Zach, it was probably time to get up.

She slowly turned around in his arms, causing him to stir slightly. "Garrett," Skylar said softly, but she got no response. "Garrett, wake up," she said, just a bit louder but still gently.

She watched as his eyes opened and then as he realized where he was and who he was with. The smile that came to his face made her smile and blush.

"It's no wonder I was sleeping so well. You were here with me," Garrett said, caressing her face.

"I could have kept watching you sleep, but I think it might be time to get up so we can go out. It has to be close to seven o'clock, and I need to look presentable," Skylar said.

"You look perfect, like always."

"Thank you for the lovely compliment, but you are biased. I know I must look a mess."

"Once again, you look beautiful," he said, and then he stole another steamy kiss from her. He was going to have to stop, or they would be going nowhere. Plus, they hadn't taken that next step. When they did, it certainly wouldn't be in a friend's house.

They both got up and changed clothes. Skylar put on the sundress she loved so much, with her favorite sandals. When she had packed for this trip, she hadn't been sure what to pick, so she had thrown a little bit of everything into the suitcase. At the time, it seemed ridiculous, but now she was glad she had.

"I was about to knock on your door," Abbey said. "Are you ready to go? Maybe we can get there before it gets too crowded. I love Sloppy Joe's!"

"I do too, but I haven't been there in a while," Skylar said as the foursome walked out the door. As they all hopped into Abbey's red Jeep, Skylar was still on a high. Garrett was with her again, and their afternoon had been so romantic.

They found parking at Mallory Square and walked to the famous spot nearby. It was a very popular bar along Duval Street, with a colorful history. It had been in Key West since 1933, and it was a favorite of Ernest Hemingway's. But it wasn't always located where it was now. In 1938, after getting into an argument with his landlord over a one-dollar rent increase, in the middle of the night, the original owner, Joe Russell, moved everything half a block to the current location, where it had been ever since.

When the foursome walked in, the bar was already buzzing, even though it was a Sunday night. They quickly found a table next to a wall and claimed it for the evening. It felt so good to Skylar to be doing something and out of the ordinary, but the best thing was that Garrett was sitting right beside her.

Even over the loud music, they were able to have a conversation. Abbey desperately wanted to hear again every detail of how they had found each other. Then, Abbey began to tell Skylar stories about Garrett, namely how when she had moved in, he had come to dinner at her house, and she had thought it was a date. But for Garrett, it had just been a home-cooked meal with a friend. When Abbey told her how Garrett came casually dressed and talked nonstop about fish, Skylar couldn't help but laugh because she could picture the whole "date" in her mind. Garrett just sat there with his head hanging low, shaking it back and forth.

"I didn't know you thought it was a date. I'd just gotten back from being out on the water for three weeks. Having a home-cooked meal and then going to bed—my bed, by myself—was all I was after. But the way you tell it is a bit funny. Things sure have changed since that day. By the way, when are you two getting married? I already forgot the date."

"I told you the date a million times before you left—even wrote it down for you! The invitations are about to go out. It's only about three months away, and I can't wait," Abbey gushed, looking at Zach beside her.

"If I had my way, we wouldn't have waited this long, but this wedding is turning out to be a little bit bigger than we planned," Zach said, giving Abbey a quick kiss. Skylar could see that these two were very much in love. Garrett had told her some of their story a while back. They had really overcome a lot of obstacles to get where they were now. Skylar thought that Abbey and Zach's story should be a lesson for her and Garrett to give them strength through the tough times.

"I think our families are just excited to come to the Keys. We were going to go back to my hometown—Asheville, North Carolina—for the ceremony, but everyone wanted to come here for a tropical wedding. I think they were a bit disappointed that we are having the wedding in a church instead of out on the beach, like so many people here like to do," Abbey said.

"Well, it's your wedding, and you need to do what makes you happy. You don't have to please everyone else," Garrett said.

"It sounds like you could learn something from your own advice," Abbey said, taking a sip of her drink and giving Garrett a wink.

"Touché!" Garrett said, looking over at Skylar and squeezing her hand.

As they ate dinner and listened to the band, they told stories about their lives. Abbey wanted to know everything about Skylar and was fascinated that she started her own charter business. But Skylar couldn't believe that Abbey just moved to Key West all by herself, leaving her family behind. Skylar secretly wished she could have some alone time with Abbey so she could ask her how she was able to leave her family in North Carolina and still stay strong so she could follow her dreams.

As a new band started to play, more people moved to the dance floor. Skylar was having so much fun. Everyone was relaxed and enjoying the evening; it was nothing like society events back in Miami. To her, it was like a breath of fresh air.

"Would you dance with me...again?" Garrett whispered in her ear. "This song reminds me of you. It has been playing every time I listened to the radio since that night." Skylar nodded, took his hand, and let him lead her to the dance floor. The song was "Tennessee Whiskey," which was one of her favorites, and the slow rhythm was very romantic and sexy. As they stepped in among the many couples, she turned to Garrett, putting both arms around his neck, while he gently encircled her waist with his arms as they began to dance.

As they swayed back and forth to the music, Garrett actually sang a few of the lyrics into her ear, and then he softly kissed her earlobe, which sent a shocking sensation throughout her body. She began to imagine being with him in the one way they had not been. But with the turmoil surrounding them, it was not a step they should take lightly, and she was glad that they both felt the same way. But it was definitely not easy for either of them.

Though the song he liked was playing in the background, Garrett could only focus on the startling woman in his arms. At that very moment, he realized he was good enough for her, and she was the best thing for him. It was then that he found her lips, kissing her so deeply that they both stopped dancing, getting totally lost in the moment.

"So, we meet on the dance floor again." An annoying voice suddenly caught Skylar's attention. There was no way this could be who she thought it was, but as she opened her eyes and looked around, a feeling a frustration and anger began to fill her. It was Andrew.

Garrett was as shocked as Skylar. What was Andrew doing here in Key West? Did he follow them, or was someone reporting their movements to him or Skylar's father? This was ridiculous. "I guess we do. It looks like you've found someone new," Garrett said, motioning to the woman Andrew was dancing with.

"This is Lucy. We just met, didn't we, sweetheart?" From the way the couple clung to each other, it was apparent that Andrew had been drinking but was not yet drunk. But as for the girl, that was a different story. All she did was smile and giggle every time Andrew said something. "I'm here for a guys' weekend away. A few of us are staying over at the Pier House in the Dockside Suite. I bet your boyfriend here can't give you that kind of a view, or anything else, for that matter. What a waste."

Garrett moved toward Andrew, but Skylar grabbed his arm. "He's not worth it, Garrett."

"I'm not worth it. Honey, I'm worth more than you ever will be. Do you really think your little boat business has a chance in hell of succeeding? Don't kid yourself. Even with Mommy and Daddy's money, you would never have been my equal. And now, you are with this loser. He's nothing in our world, Skylar. Maybe if you just told your parents you're sorry, they might let you back into the business. That is, if they have a business for you to come back to." Andrew's laugh at the end of his statement sent Lucy into a fit of laughter too. But not Skylar.

"What are you talking about now, you asshole?"

"Wow, such language from a refined Cartwright. But then you have been hanging around sailors." This time, Garrett held back Skylar.

"Andrew, you are completely full of crap. You aren't worth anything! Your dad is, but with the way you have been acting,

I'm surprised he hasn't disowned you. You are nothing but a freeloader, finding any way to have money except the honest way. You've never worked a day in your life, but one day, you will have to, if you can.

"As for my business, you know nothing about it. You might say you sell yachts, but we know you don't do a damn thing. You are just all talk. At least I work. Even when I was selling real estate, I was working. I make my own way—I bought my own properties; I have my own rentals, and so much more. If you think my family is messed up, you need to take a look at your own. And I don't have to rely on Mommy and Daddy to pay my way. You are pathetic. I feel sorry for you, even though I shouldn't. But I will say this. Don't you *ever* say another word about me or my family, and that includes Garrett." By now, their conversation was taking center stage. None of them had noticed that the band was on a break or that their voices were loud enough for all to hear.

"And what are you going to do about it? You are just throwing out empty threats." Andrew laughed.

"Mine aren't empty," Garrett said as he moved to stand in front of Andrew. When both men were standing facing one another, Garrett towered over Andrew. And Skylar could tell by the sudden look on Andrew's face that Garrett was making him think twice about his choice of words.

"You don't mess with my family, and Skylar is part of my family. All I will say is that you need to leave her, me, and her family alone—no jokes, no threats, and no rumors. Keep your mouth shut. There are several ways to make a man's life miserable when he hurts those you love and I know quite a few. I will promise you this: you don't want to mess with me." Garrett's tone was so menacing, and Skylar had never seen this side of him. It was as though a protective giant had come to her rescue.

"And there's one more thing: Skylar is more of a success than you will ever be. You could actually learn a thing or two from her, but that silver spoon is jammed so far down your throat that you will never be anything more than a jerk." Garrett gently took Skylar's hand and led her off the dance floor. The strangers who had been looking on during the conversation still stared at Andrew and the completely drunk girl at his side.

"A round of drinks for everyone," Andrew called out, but no one took him up on the offer. What had just taken place even dumbfounded his friends. Skylar, Garrett, Abbey, and Zach went back to their table, watching Andrew and his group from afar. The drunk girl was all over Andrew, and he seemed to be enjoying every minute of it. Skylar found it disgusting.

"Of all the bars, restaurants, and places in the Keys, we meet on a dance floor again," Skylar said when she finally calmed down.

"Well, from the looks of it, I don't think you will have to worry about him anymore," Abbey said, patting Garrett's arm.

"Between the two of you, I think you put him in his place, and I don't even know the guy," Zach said, smiling. "That was a pretty good bar fight, even if there was no blood!"

"Zach!" Abbey said, but she couldn't suppress a giggle. Then Skylar followed suit, laughing, and Garrett soon joined them. But Skylar secretly said a silent prayer that she wouldn't have to deal with the likes of Andrew Danforth anymore.

28

After spending the night and most of the next day in Key West, they were heading back to Key Largo. Skylar had stayed with Abbey, while Garrett stayed with Zach, so the girls were able to chat more, promising to spend time together when they could. The two couples were able to have a nice brunch and walk around Key West before Garrett and Skylar started the journey back home. Skylar really liked Abbey and Zach and couldn't wait till they could all get together again.

Skylar followed Garrett up Highway 1, wishing they could have ridden back together, but it wasn't possible with two trucks. But it would only take an hour and a half, and they were going to his place for a dinner of takeout pizza, like old times. Skylar didn't care where or what they had for dinner as long as they could go back to their little routine. Her ringing phone brought her out of her daydream.

"Hey there!" she said, after seeing Garrett's name pop up on the phone's screen.

"Did you bring your swimsuit?"

"Are these the Keys?" Skylar said, laughing.

"Okay, don't be a smarty. Let's go swimming at Sombrero Beach before we head back. I haven't been in a while," Garrett said excitedly.

"It's getting pretty late. Is it even still open?"

"It should be. If not, I pretty much know the park rangers there. I want to check something before heading home, and maybe we can take an evening swim."

"Go swimming at night?" Skylar asked nervously.

"Yeah! It's great. Don't you go swimming when it's dark?"

"I have, but it feels weird. I like to be able to see what is around me. Maybe I watched *Jaws* a little too much as a kid!"

"Well, you will have me around to protect you; you don't have to worry about that," he said, with a smirk in his voice.

Skylar followed Garrett's truck down a winding road that led to a beautiful beach on Marathon Key. She had been here several times with her friends, but it had been quite a while.

"I need to change in case we go swimming," she said as soon as they were out of their trucks. But as predicted, the park was closing soon, so Garrett went to talk to the person in charge while she changed clothing. As she was coming out of the bathroom, he walked up, with a smile on his face.

"I knew the ranger. I told her I'm checking the sea turtles' nests, so she just asked that we park the trucks outside of the gates." Skylar watched Garrett. He was definitely in his element, like a kid in a candy store. In a flash, he had towels, his camera, some paper, and a pen all tucked into a small bag. She loved watching him like this. The way he followed his love for sea turtles was something that had attracted her to this wonderful man. Even though they had spent time together on the boat, this was another part of his world that she had not yet participated in, and it was exciting.

"Let's walk down the beach first to see where the nests have been marked off. Then before we leave, we will check them once more. Turtles are more active at night."

The beach was beautiful as the sun began to set. As they walked along, there was an abundance of nests toward one end of the beach, each was designated with a marker to make sure that the public knew to avoid the area. Garrett looked at the many nests and smiled.

"Let's go take that swim now," Garrett said and quickly pulled off his shirt. Skylar stood admiring his muscular chest and arms—those same arms that wrapped around her each day. Oh, how she had missed them, and him, for these last few weeks.

"Are you sure? If a piece of seaweed or something wraps around my leg, I might scream," she said, really meaning it, but Garrett just laughed.

"I promise you will be fine. We aren't going out that deep at all, and if it bothers you too badly, we can just sit in the shallow water and relax. It's just nice having you all to myself on a deserted beach." Garrett grinned wickedly.

"You better behave yourself, Mr. Holmes. You know I'm not that kinda girl," Skylar said quickly, batting her eyelashes at him. But she couldn't resist the laugh welling up inside of her.

"I promise to be the perfect gentleman," he said, thinking that the words he spoke weren't quite truthful, especially as he watched her take off her T-shirt and shorts, revealing the same coral bathing suit that hugged her in all the right places.

They walked hand in hand into the water till they were about waist-deep. Garrett could feel Skylar's hand trembling slightly. "How about we stop right here?" he said, submerging himself up to his chest and gently pulling her close until she could sit on his lap underwater. She put her arms around his neck, feeling safe and secure in his embrace.

"This is nice," Skylar said. "I love the water, the moonlight, and you. I don't know if I can ever thank Abbey enough for calling me. If she hadn't, I would have spent the weekend doing paper work and binging on Netflix and ice cream. That's how I seem to handle unhappy times."

"I guess I owe her too. Though I never thought she would sneak into my phone, I'm glad she did. I was just running away. I wasn't running from you, but I honestly felt like suddenly I didn't belong. I was so conflicted—my feelings for you never changed, but I wanted what was best for you."

"You are what is best for me. But we don't have to talk about it anymore. Remember, we made a deal. We are in this together, no matter what."

"No matter what," Garrett said as he smoothed the hair back from around her face. Then he traced her lips with his salty finger, and she kept still, mesmerized by his tender touch. She leaned in to him for another kiss, something that neither of them could seem to get enough of. Desire and hunger filled the kiss, for both of them. But they knew taking their relationship slowly was key, especially with circumstances the way they were. But it didn't take a physical act to prove that they were genuinely in love with each other, and nothing could take that away from them.

They swam around for a few more minutes, and Skylar finally felt brave enough to swim a little way on her own, feeling free and relaxed. Garrett was soon beside her, turning over on his back to float and look at the sky above. Soon they were both floating and stargazing.

"Are you ready to go?" Garrett said. He didn't want to break the mood, but he knew that it was getting late.

"Yes, and no. I'm hungry, but this is better than eating pizza and watching TV," Skylar said before returning to shore.

As they were drying off, Garrett looked toward the turtle nests and saw something moving along the beach.

"Come on!"

"What's wrong?" Skylar asked, suddenly anxious.

"I hope this is what I think it is," Garrett said excitedly.

"What are you talking about?"

They walked slowly toward the shoreline where they had seen the turtle nests, and suddenly Garrett laughed. "Look!" he said excitedly.

Skylar peered into the darkness. In the moonlight, it appeared as though the beach was moving. She could finally see little things scampering across the sand. Before she could find out what they were, she was behind Garrett for protection.

"What are they? Will they bite? Are they coming this way?"

Garrett laughed softly. "They are hatchlings. The eggs have hatched, and the baby turtles are heading to the water."

Skylar suddenly stepped around Garrett, and they both slowly walked closer. There were so many small baby turtles doing their best to get to the water, even though some seemed to be heading the wrong way, toward the trees. Skylar bent down to look, and then she picked one up to help.

"Don't touch them!" Garrett said quickly.

"But why? This little one is heading the wrong way."

"If they don't crawl on their own to the water, they can't imprint with the beach where they were born. If they make it to adulthood, which only one in a thousand does, they usually come back to the beach where they hatched to lay their own eggs." She watched Garrett gently guide the little hatchling back toward the water by using a small stick to block its path.

Skylar was in awe as she watched all the turtles make their way to the sea. She had always heard of this but had never seen this awesome sight in person.

"Wow. We were here at just the right time." Garrett was still stooping, watching the turtles, and Skylar could hear him counting too.

"There are probably about one hundred hatchlings. That's pretty good."

"This is amazing," Skylar said, continuing to watch as Garrett stood up and put his arm around her.

"Welcome to my world. I love this. I have had a special place in my heart for sea turtles since I became interested in marine biology. Most of my friends that studied with me were all about dolphins and sharks, so they would make fun of me sometimes. But I love that turtles are slow but steady. They might not be fast, but they still reach their goals because they are persistent. To me, that is a great life lesson."

Skylar looked up at him and knew that he was right—taking things slow but staying on course was important. Then as she looked down at the last of the little turtles to enter the water, she realized she had just learned a life lesson from nature—be persistent, especially when you know your goal and your passion. And don't let anything get in your way. That was what she was going to do with her life, with her business, and most of all, with Garrett.

29

The next morning, Skylar heard a horn honk outside, and she quickly grabbed her tote bag and lunch for the day. Garrett was here to pick her up. He had a lot of paper work to do, but he decided to work on the boat with her while they took a morning scuba trip and an afternoon snorkel tour. Right now, he wanted to be with her every second, if he could, and since he had his notes and computer with him, it would be easy to work on the boat. As for Skylar, she couldn't be happier.

"Good morning, my love," Garrett said as soon as she reached the truck. He had gotten out and opened her door for her, helping with her bags and then giving her a sweet good-morning kiss.

"Now, this is my kind of limo service." She giggled as she slid into the seat.

"And you're my kind of passenger, if I do say so myself!"

They pulled into the parking lot at the same time as Max. When he saw both of them getting out of one truck, there was a shocked expression on his face that both Garrett and Skylar saw immediately.

"It looks like you guys had a great weekend!" Max said cheerfully. "And thank goodness. I wasn't sure how much longer I was going to be able to be around Skylar. She has been pretty depressing to be with out on the boat."

"I wasn't that bad!" Skylar said defensively.

"Are you kidding? You were awful, but I will say you put on a pretty good act for the tourists. How ya doing, Garrett?"

"I'm much better now," he said, looking over at Skylar.

"Man, don't get all mushy on me. You are a guy—you aren't supposed to do that. We are the cool ones, remember?" Max said.

"Max, when you are my age, you don't really give a crap what anyone else thinks. And when you really care for someone, you always let them know." Garrett quickly reached over and hugged Skylar to his side. Max walked ahead of them, still with a bounce in his step, but he was shaking his head, as if everything Garrett was doing was against his code of conduct as a guy.

"It's an age thing," Garrett said, looking at Skylar.

"I'm glad you are just the way you are."

As they walked down the dock, Garrett finally decided to broach the one subject that he had avoided during the whole weekend, not wanting to spoil their reunion. "I want to ask you something. We talked this weekend, and you told me what is going on with your parents, but you didn't tell me how you guys are going to handle the situation. Please don't take this wrong, but with your family being as prominent as they are in Miami society, shouldn't you have some kind of plan in place to help with the rumors and idiots like Andrew?"

Skylar knew Garrett was right. "Truth be told, I have kinda stuck my head in the sand on this. I was leaving everything up to Harris, Mara, and Chase. After what Andrew said and Dad's remarks at the gala, I really didn't want to have anything to do with them." But Garrett could tell she wasn't being completely truthful. The look on her face and the tone of her voice told a very different story.

Garrett took the bags and placed them on the boat, and then Skylar climbed on board. "I know that's not true, Sky. I can tell by your body language. I also know it's not true because that's not the kind of person you are. I know you are tired of dealing with the games you have had to put up with all your life, but you are finally making that move toward independence. Hell, you are already there! But don't separate yourself from your family. You will regret it one day. Even with all the difficulties right now, they will always be an important part of your life."

Skylar looked over at him to see a far-off look in his eyes, as if he was remembering something. "What about your family? We've never talked much about them."

"I only have my mother and her husband. My father left us when I was very young, so my mom raised me by herself. She finally found a really nice guy when I was just about to graduate from high school. If she hadn't, I don't think I would have been a marine biologist. I wanted to take care of her, like she took care of me. But Gene, her husband, treats her well and I couldn't have asked for a better stepfather. They have been down here for a few quick trips and might be coming again soon."

"Why haven't you told me more about your mom and stepfather before? And when will they be here?"

"She just never seemed to come up. Plus, I grew up so differently from you. She and I lived from paycheck to paycheck. And even though I would never know it because you look at life so differently than your family does, you had money at your disposal.

"As far as a visit goes, they are going to let me know the dates soon. I told them I only have a small spare room, but they said they don't mind," Garrett said quietly.

"Are you embarrassed by your past?" Skylar said quietly.

"No, of course not. My mom worked hard, and so did I. I just wasn't sure how you would feel about it."

Skylar went up and curled one arm around his waist, and her other hand caressed his cheek. "If your mom is anything like you, I will love her. And I already admire her. It takes a lot of guts and determination to raise a child on your own, and I think she did a fantastic job," she said, looking at him with pride. "When she gets here, I'm going to tell her myself, and if they want, they can stay in the spare room at my house. It is a tad bit bigger than yours." She smiled at him sweetly.

"I knew I loved you for some reason," Garrett said, hugging her tightly.

"Hey, if you guys are finished, I think our scuba class is here," Max said, once again shaking his head and laughing.

"Hey, get used to it, Max!" Skylar said loudly, with a big grin on her face.

The day turned out to be nice, as far as Skylar was concerned. There was a beautiful blue sky above, southern Florida's turquoise water surrounded them, and the gentle ocean swells made for a relaxing ride to the reef. As the scuba class dived during the morning and the snorkeling group had fun in the afternoon, Max watched and helped. Skylar did some work on her iPad, and Garrett started working on the next report that was due. Every now and then, she would look at him, and she felt so blessed to have found this man—someone she could see herself staying with always. While growing up, she had somehow convinced herself that because of her weird ways, she would never find anyone who would like her. She was definitely not like the other girls she had grown up with. But now, she had found that man who was her other half.

It seemed as though the next few days were identical. The routine stayed the same: they boated during the day and spent the evenings together, either at Skylar's place or Garrett's. They had mentioned going out to eat, but both wanted to stay home, just the two of them.

As they were about to sit down to a dinner recipe that Maggie had taught Skylar—beef stew—her phone rang. She picked it up only to see whom the caller was and saw Mara's name on the screen. A feeling of dread came over her.

"I have to answer this," she said to Garrett. "It's Mara, and I haven't talked to her in over a week."

"No problem."

"Hey, Mara. How are you doing?" Skylar said, with hesitation in her voice.

"I was wondering how you are doing, but I also have some news." Skylar sat down, feeling that she wasn't going to like what she was about to hear.

"I was just getting ready to have dinner with Garrett. I'm going to put you on speakerphone," she said before Mara could ask a question or protest.

"Hi, Mara," Garrett said, smiling at Skylar.

"Uh…hi…Garrett. I guess what I heard was true then," Mara said slowly.

"What did you hear?"

"The Miami rumor mill is at its finest. Supposedly, you had a run-in with your ex in Key West at Sloppy Joe's. Did you and Garrett threaten him?"

"That asshole!" Skylar said loudly.

"So, it's true," Mara almost screamed into the phone. "I tried to tell you what an idiot he was when you were dating him. I always wondered what you saw in him."

"I'm wondering that too." Skylar was mad and had definitely lost her appetite. And she could tell Garrett was unhappy from his white-knuckled fists.

"But I'm so happy for you two!" Mara said in delight. "Garrett—just don't mess with my little sister. You promised me that, and you broke it. Don't do it again because I will personally come and find you!"

"Mara!"

"Sorry, Sky, but I'm your big sister, and that's what big sisters do."

"Then why didn't you stand up for me in high school?"

"Because that was not what we did back then," Mara said, with a laugh in her voice. "I was calling you about this because Andrew is really making Garrett out to be a thug or something. I also called about Mom."

"What's wrong?" Skylar asked, suddenly forgetting about her dreadful ex.

"She came home drunk last night. Honestly, none of us can believe she made it home without being pulled over for drunk driving. When she got home, though, she pulled into the driveway and drove straight into the garage—without opening the door—and into the cement column. Grandma said it shook the whole house. She thought they were having an earthquake!"

Skylar only looked at the phone in disbelief. "Mom has got to get help," she said, now with concern in her voice. Garrett reached over and took her hand, stroking the back of it to help her calm down.

"Can you come to the city tomorrow? I know you have charters, but we are going to talk to Mom and Dad. This has gone on long enough. If they aren't going to take charge of the situation, then we will, or we have to try at least."

"Actually, tomorrow is fine. It is a paper work day for me. What time should I come?"

"Dad usually gets home around five thirty. We figured we would all be at the house at five o'clock."

"I'll be there," Skylar said reluctantly.

"I know you didn't want to come back here for a while, but this is different. I really wouldn't ask you, but we need to show a united front."

"I'll be there too," Garrett suddenly said.

"I'm not so sure that's a good idea, Garrett," Mara said shyly.

"Why not?" Skylar said defensively.

"Dad is just Dad. I'm just not sure how he will feel."

"If I'm coming, so is Garrett. We aren't hiding anymore, Mara. I don't care what our friends think. I am who I am, and Garrett is a part of my life." Skylar felt good as she finally stood up for herself and the man she loved.

They could both hear Mara sigh. "Well, don't say I didn't warn you."

"We can handle your dad now; believe me. We did pretty well taking care of that huge mess at Sloppy Joe's with Andrew; that is for sure. Now that I know that he is talking trash, he will regret it," Garrett said. Skylar looked at him, puzzled, wondering what Garrett intended to do.

"Do you have something planned?" Mara asked.

"Is he still engaged to that girl I was introduced to on the night of the gala?" Garrett asked.

"If you mean Alicia, yes. I think the wedding date is about two months away."

"Poor Alicia! Especially after what we saw in Key West!" Skylar exclaimed.

"Well, I didn't think you needed any more…um…news at that time," Mara said, choosing her words very discreetly, knowing that had been when Garrett left Skylar.

"So, anyway, what's the deal with Andrew? How can you put him in his place?"

"I'm working on it. I don't like to be the bad person in a situation, but all I'll say is karma is a bitch," Garrett said firmly.

"I'm liking you more and more, Garrett. I'll see you two tomorrow." With that, Mara hung up the phone.

"What do you have up your sleeve?" Skylar asked when they were finally able to sit down to eat dinner.

"I'm working on it, but I think it will definitely take the wind out of your ex-boyfriend's sails, for sure."

30

Taking the familiar trip to Skylar's parent's house brought back some bad, stressful memories for Garrett. As they got closer to the Cartwright mansion, he still felt as if he was entering a world he didn't belong in. But now he felt that he and Skylar were on a united path. He decided he would draw on her strength and follow her lead as long as her family treated them fairly. If not, he would protect both of them, even if it meant possibly alienating the family. But his intuition told him that scenario seemed unlikely, and he hoped and prayed it was.

"Are you ready for this?" Garrett said as he parked the truck along the edge of the round driveway in front of the house.

"I think so. I have tried to convince myself during these past weeks that this just isn't my world, that Key Largo is now my home, and it is. But this is also part of me; whether I like it or not, this is my family, and I love them, warts and all."

"That's the girl I fell in love with," Garrett said, leaning over and giving her a kiss of encouragement. But she needed more and took it, not releasing him till she heard a tapping on the side window.

Chase was standing there, with a grin on his face. Even though the window was open, neither one of them had heard him approach the vehicle. "You know, Dad could be here any-time now. Mom is taking a nap, we think. Mara is waking her up now, unless she is in a drunken stupor."

"Then I guess we'd better go inside. Is Blair here with you?" Skylar asked.

"No. Our relationship isn't at that level yet to involve her in this kind of family matter. This is pretty serious, and I don't know what will happen tonight. Just be prepared for any-thing," Chase said, walking with them into the house.

When they entered the family room, Harris was watching TV with their grandma. Skylar immediately walked over to the older woman, giving her a hug and a kiss. "I brought someone along with me." Skylar motioned for Garrett to come over.

"I told you so. He's a bright boy. And he knows a smart, beautiful woman when he sees one. Just this time, young man, don't you hurt my granddaughter."

"I promise," Garrett said, but the older lady motioned him to come closer.

"Then give me a kiss on the cheek to seal that promise. I haven't had a kiss from such a handsome young man in a long time. It will give me something to talk about with Marie!" Grandma said, making everyone laugh.

"Marie is Grandma's best friend. They still get together every week, like they have for the last sixty-two years," Mara said, coming into the room and hearing the tail end of the conversation.

"That's what I call a real friendship," Garrett said, admiring the Cartwright matriarch then giving her the kiss she requested.

"Mom will be down in a minute, but she doesn't know everyone is here. I told her I had something to show her. I don't think she has been drinking, but I can't tell."

Just then, they all heard the front door open, and Jonathan Cartwright came around the corner and stared at his children.

"What are you all doing here?" he said, scanning the room, with his eyes landing on Garrett at the end.

"Dad," Harris said. "We've come to talk to you and Mom. I think there are some things we need to discuss as a family."

"I don't know what is so important to bring you all here in the middle of the week, but this certainly isn't a family occasion," he said, looking over at Garrett. Skylar didn't miss the look and took charge.

"Dad, whether you like it or not, Garrett is part of this family because he is with me. We are together, no matter what you feel or think is best for me. I'm a grown woman, and I know I'm with the person I'm going to spend my life with."

"Well, when you have a ring on your finger, then you can say he is part of the family. But not until then. And if the rumors are true, you both have some explaining to do about your actions in Key West."

Skylar was now getting irritated with her father. Why couldn't he just trust her for once? Why did he assume the worst? He hadn't always been like this, so what had changed?

"The real story is that Andrew basically verbally attacked us in Key West," she said, motioning to Garrett. "He was dancing with a very drunk blonde. He made some very derogatory remarks, and I just set him straight. When he got nasty with me, Garrett stepped in to defend me. As for Andrew, he is not as well-bred as you think he is. I think his fiancé, Alicia, would love to hear the real story about what happened down there, and she should know that her perfect boyfriend was having a liaison with another girl." Skylar watched her dad, who was contemplating everything she said. Then he sat down in a chair very wearily.

"If what Skylar says is true, then I thank you, Garrett, for taking care of my little girl. But there is no proof. I want to believe you, Sky, but with the way you have been acting, I just don't know anymore," Skylar's father said.

"I've been myself, Dad, just as I have since I was a little girl. When I was younger, you always thought it was sweet that I wanted to save the whales, go fishing, or hunt for shells on a beach instead of going shopping at the mall or attend balls and expensive luncheons with everyone else. Now that I'm an adult, why do I suddenly have to fit into a mold? I know now that I honestly never will, but I'm still your daughter, and I love you and Mom very much.

"What I want to know is when you are going to be truthful with us," Skylar said, looking directly at her father. "Grandma told us the real story about how you grew up. Also how you and Mom really met. We don't understand why the two of you would hide such a thing. Are you ashamed of your pasts? We also know about the affairs, and Mom's drinking has been very obvious to everyone."

"Well, Jonathan, it looks like our children know all our little secrets." Sadie Cartwright descended the stairs, a drink in hand. As she reached the landing, she stumbled slightly, but not enough to lose her balance completely. "Is this why all of you are here—to chide us? If you are, then every one of you can leave because it is none of your business. This is between me and your father." She sat down in the chair opposite her husband, locking her eyes on him and never once looking at the gathering of people around her.

"Well, Mom, you and Dad have made it our business. You know how you guys were so upset about Skylar's relationship with Garrett. That is nothing compared to how upset you'll be when every person you know finds out that you both had affairs and that you have a drinking problem, Mom," Harris said more loudly than he had intended.

"I still don't see how this is your concern. Your father and I are working on a few things, isn't that right, dear?" Sadie said in a very monotone voice, arching one eyebrow, while gazing over at their father. Jonathan Cartwright remained silent and stone-faced.

"We, as your children, are involved. People are asking us questions or avoiding us. This could possibly hurt the business," Harris said.

"The business is fine, Harris. You need to stop worrying so much," their father said, still showing no emotion, as though he didn't care.

"Dad, how would you know? You haven't been to the office in over a week!"

Everyone sat silently as they waited for the volleying between father and son to continue. Except this time, their father said nothing; he only looked down at his hands.

"So, where have you been all week? Is there someone new?" Sadie asked as she took another drink. But what happened next surprised them all. Chase took the drink from his mother's hand, smelled it, and threw the glass across the room. It shattered on the tile floor.

"You accuse Dad of seeing someone while you can't stay away from the liquor. We all know what happened the other night. You're damn lucky you made it home in one piece since you were driving drunk. We've seen the car and the damaged column in the garage. You must have paid someone a pretty penny to get a new garage door up so quickly. Thank goodness you or no one else got hurt."

Though shocked by what her youngest child had done, Sadie only sat for a moment before she started laughing. "How dramatic, my little one. And I can stay away from the liquor, as you so eloquently said. Sometimes it just helps since living with your father is a bit difficult."

"You should try living with both of you!" Grandma Cartwright suddenly said. "First of all, you should both be ashamed of yourselves. These children came here to help you, nothing more. And it's because they love you, despite what you have put them through. While growing up, they had to do everything you said, or you acted like you would disown them. They still loved you, enough to follow in your footsteps, even if they didn't want to." With that last statement, Grandma Cartwright lovingly looked over at Skylar.

"Do you know how blessed you two are? Most kids would have rebelled, but not yours. Now they are here because the two of you are acting like little kids throwing temper tantrums. Affairs! Drinking! It is all ridiculous, and if your father could see this, he would be pitching a fit. For once in your life, listen to them. Don't make this only about yourselves, because some of the things you do have an effect on us all."

Everyone was silent, looking at each other. Skylar was the first one to speak.

"Our sole purpose when we decided to come here today was to help both of you. Dad, we want you to see a counselor. And, Mom, you need to see one too and possibly go to AA meetings. One of us will even go with you, if you want."

"You can't make me see a counselor. I can figure this out on my own!" their dad said defiantly, standing and starting to pace the room.

"Me, go to AA." Their mom laughed. "That will be the day."

"We aren't kidding. You both need help. Because what you are doing right now isn't working; it is even dangerous," Mara said, looking at her mother this time.

"No children of mine are going to tell me what to do," Jonathan said, with anger in his voice.

"Well, then you leave us no choice. We are all leaving the business. You will have to find people to replace us starting next Monday," Harris said as calmly as he could.

"There will be no more family dinners on Sundays, and Grandma is coming to live with me. We will be packing her stuff this weekend, and she is leaving on Sunday," Mara said.

"That is actually wonderful. Now I can get rid of that hideous garden on the side of the house."

"Mom, this isn't a joke!" Skylar practically screamed at her. "We are serious. We are a family, or at least, we were. We are so fortunate to have each other and everything around us. I mean, have you actually given it any thought at all? Grandpa worked hard to build the business. He trusted Dad and his brothers to carry on, and now you look to us. Something has broken in this family, and it needs to be fixed. It doesn't matter what the outside world says. We care about you and Dad. If we have to make threats and changes to get your attention, we will."

"I know I'm not a part of this family. I'm just here to support Skylar—" Garrett started, but he was quickly interrupted.

"Then keep your mouth shut!" Jonathan said.

"No, I won't. You have material wealth, and that is fine. But you have four kids who actually give a damn about their parents, kids that love you and only want to help. Do you know how rare that is? I do. I didn't grow up like this. My mom and I barely made it from week to week. The kids I grew up with— once they were grown, they left their parents, not caring what happened," Garrett said.

"Well, isn't that what you did?" Skylar's father said sarcastically.

Garrett took a deep breath to calm down before continuing. "No, I didn't. My dad left us when I was young, and when

I graduated from high school,, I was going to stay in Savannah to help my mom out. But right before I finished school, she found a wonderful man, and they have a terrific relationship. So I went on to college and she encouraged me to go out and explore the world, to follow my dreams. That is why I'm here in Florida. No, I don't make money like you do. I certainly don't have all the things you do. But I have love, with my mom and her husband and now with your daughter," Garrett said as he reached for Skylar's hand. "And that is what your children are trying to give you right now. It's like you have this great gift right in front of you and don't even know it."

When Garrett finished, no one said a word. Then suddenly, Grandma Cartwright stood up, walked slowly over to Garrett, and placed one hand on his cheek. "I knew from the moment Skylar brought you into this house that you were a good man. You remind me of a time in my life that was simple and loving." She then turned to everyone else. "This family has so much, and that is because of the hard work of those that came before you. Straighten this mess out, Jonathan and Sadie. You have a lot to lose. I'm going to my room now. I think everything that needs to be said has been." They all watched as she slowly made her way to the hallway that led to her room.

The rest of them sat silently for what seemed to be an eternity. "Well," Harris said, looking at both of his parents.

"These are just empty threats. You children couldn't make it on your own."

"You really don't think we can. Dad, I've built a successful boating business in less than a year. Before that, using what *you* taught me, I bought and sold real estate, making money on each transaction. I put that money back into investments and rental properties," Skylar said.

"I've done the same thing, except I've been investing in the stock market after learning about it from a my friend's dad. I've been working in real estate because I felt like you needed help. Plus, I enjoyed working with the people. But I'm comfortable. Walking away would be easy for me, but you would have to step in pretty quickly to learn what I've been doing," Harris said.

"Paul and I are also fine, Dad. Again, I don't think you realize how much you taught us. We've made investments, and even though Paul is teaching at the high school, which he loves, he has a successful Internet business that allows us a lot of freedom. We have just chosen to keep things simple for Lyla and because we love that lifestyle," Mara said quietly.

"I've got substantial savings, but I've been building a side business in photography. I haven't told anyone, but I'm actually doing quite well. I've even been approached to publish a book based on my photos," Chase said.

"Well, it seems like you all have your little ducks in a row. That is fine and dandy. But there is no way in hell I'm going to an AA meeting." Sadie was now fully alert, and her cheeks were red with frustration.

Mara and Skylar both went to sit beside her. "One of us will go with you. You aren't in this by yourself, unless you want it that way."

Sadie had tears in the corners of her eyes as she finally let her guard down. It seemed as if her whole body just slumped into the chair and she released the boulder she had been carrying. "What have I done?" Sadie said in barely a whisper. And then she looked at her husband. "What have we done?"

For the first time, their father's face started to show some emotion. His face softened, and he bent over to put his head in his hands.

"I never meant for any of this to happen. The affair was so long ago, and it only happened once, I promise. But everything changed from that point for your mom and me. Things were never the same. Then she had an affair, and I couldn't blame her. It's such a mixed-up mess."

"We should have talked more when you told me what happened. Instead, I started drinking. It was only a little here and there. Then I got drunk one night and made the mistake of being in the wrong place. You had been with someone so turn about is fair play, right? I was just trying to get even, like you owed me something. And when you didn't get upset, I couldn't figure out why. That's when the alcohol became my drug of choice. I've lived in this high-society world for a long time now, always feeling like I had to fit in, but I never did. Your dad told me when we married I would be just fine. I might have played the part, but I never felt fine inside. And now I don't know how to fix it."

Skylar took her mom's hand. "This is a start. You are talking to Dad and to all of us. Everyone makes mistakes. What we learn from them is what counts. That is what you always told us when we were growing up. Now it's time for you to take your own advice. Seeing a counselor isn't a bad thing. I think sometimes, we all could use one."

"Sadie, I'll go to a counselor as long as we go together. And if you need to go to AA meetings, I'll go too." Their father sounded defeated but also as though a burden had been lifted off his chest. "To tell the truth, I'm glad this is all out. Hiding a secret, pretending that everything is fine, is a horrible burden. I was so worried about what other people would think that I forgot about those that really mattered to me."

"It doesn't matter what people say, as long as we stick together. We are the Cartwrights, and we are strong. And you two are the strongest people I know," Mara said, and her brothers and sister agreed with her.

Before they knew it, Jonathan stood up and walked to his wife's side. He took her hand, encouraging her to stand up in front of him. "I'm sorry. I've done so many things wrong. I've shut you out instead of letting you in. We've gone this far; let's not lose what we have. I know there is a lot of work ahead of us, but we were a pretty tough team once. I think we can do it again."

They all held their breath, wondering what their mother's response would be. She still seemed angry.

"It couldn't hurt for us to see someone. And despite these years of growing tension, I still love you. But I can't say I trust you. And now I know you feel the same about me. It looks like we have a steep road ahead of us." Jonathan embraced his wife, and she actually hugged him back. The children looked at each other with hope in their eyes, thinking that maybe, just maybe, this would repair the family's damage and, more importantly, fix their parent's relationship.

"Thank goodness I don't have to move my stuff," Grandma Cartwright said from the hallway, though no one could see her. "And my garden is not hideous, Sadie. Good night."

They all started to chuckle softly, realizing that the little woman had hid in the hallway to hear the outcome of the discussion. Jonathan and Sadie hugged each of their children. But when Jonathan reached Garrett, Skylar instantly felt some tension, wondering what would happen.

"Garrett, I want to apologize. I didn't want to believe that you and my daughter actually had a relationship. I always saw Skylar with one of the boys she grew up with. But she seems to have picked a decent man. I'm sorry about the remarks I made. I said them from a place of anger, but I wasn't angry with you; I was angry with myself." Skylar's heart swelled as she watched the man she loved with all her heart shake hands with the man that had given her life and taught her to be the woman she was today.

They had done it, or at least, it was a start. The big concern was whether her parents would follow through. But at least they were talking. All the secrets seemed to be out in the open. And what made the evening even better for Skylar was the fact that her parents seemed to be accepting Garrett.

"Are you driving back to Key Largo tonight?" her mom said as everyone gathered their things to leave.

"We had planned on it. I didn't think it would be this late, but it's not a long drive," Skylar said.

"Then both of you should stay here, in the spare room upstairs. Your father and I don't mind."

Skylar looked at Garrett, and he just shrugged his shoulders. "That's fine with me. We'll just have to leave early in the morning."

"Use the room next to your old bedroom, Skylar," her mom said.

"Mom, we don't share a room. Garrett can sleep in the guest room, and I'll just sleep in my old bedroom."

"Really," her mother said, surprised. "Well, Garrett, I'm even more impressed with you now." Skylar rolled her eyes, and Garrett tried his best to suppress a grin. "Right now, let's see if there is anything for dinner."

After they ate a quick dinner of sandwiches and chips, Skylar showed Garrett to the guest suite.

"This is huge!" he exclaimed as he looked around the very ornate yet tropical room, which had a beautiful view of the lagoon through sliding glass doors. "I think my whole apartment would fit in here."

Skylar just smiled, walked with him to the glass doors, and slid them open to the balcony. "It's beautiful out here. I remember as a little girl sneaking into this room just so I could go out here and draw. Or better yet, when Mom and Dad would have parties, I could always come here and watch the festivities below." She now moved closer to him, wrapping her arms around him, and Garrett brought her closer to him.

"Thank you for everything—for coming with me and for coming to my defense. But I think what you said about family opened a huge door in their minds."

"Sometimes people just need to be reminded about what they have and what they can lose. We all take so much for granted, and nothing is guaranteed."

"I can guarantee you this: I love you, Garrett, with all my heart and soul. You are stuck with me!" she said, laughing.

"Well, if I have to be stuck with something, I sure am glad it is you." He turned her to him and took her face in both of his hands. He kissed her gently on the lips, the cheeks, and the tip of her nose, and those same little shivers pulsed through her body—the ones she could never get enough of. But when his kiss deepened and he let his hands roam down her back, Skylar suddenly felt as if he was lighting a fire inside of her. "I love you, Skylar."

As they continued to stand on the balcony, watching the nighttime activities in the houses around them, Garrett knew there was one more thing he wanted to do before they left town.

"Do you know where Andrew's office is located?" Garrett asked as he continued to look out at the scene before them.

"I have been there plenty of times. It is at the marina in the building of the yacht brokerage firm his parent's own. Why?"

"I know I wanted to leave early, but I've changed my mind. I want to pay him a visit first thing in the morning, before we head back to Key Largo, if that's okay?" Garrett said anxiously.

"Why?"

"I think we need to clear the air about what really happened down in Key West," Garrett said, with a smile on his face.

31

Garrett and Skylar walked into the office of Danforth Yacht Brokers—a nice, opulent office right on the marina. Though everything was rather quiet, a young woman greeted them right away.

"Hi! May I help you?" said the cheerful girl.

"We are here to see Andrew Danforth," Garrett said in an authoritative tone.

Skylar noticed that the girl was staring at her. "Are you Skylar Cartwright?" she asked.

"Yes I am and this is Garrett Holmes."

"I thought I recognized you. I'm Kim. It's nice to meet both of you," she said enthusiastically.

"We have come to talk to Andrew for just a few minutes," Skylar continued.

"I believe he just went into a meeting so he probably won't be available for a few hours. Let me check." Kim spoke into her headset, and she frowned when she looked back up at them. She then typed something quickly into the computer at her desk. "He says he will be right out," she said in an almost scared tone of voice.

"That's okay, we will go to him," Skylar said, knowing where the rooms were in this office, having visited several times.

"You can't go in there!" Kim yelled, but Garrett followed Skylar straight to a set of double doors, which she opened, and they both walked in. There were about twenty people sitting around a huge conference table. Skylar recognized most of them.

"You can't barge in here like this," Kim said breathlessly as she had tried to keep up with them as they walked quickly toward the room. "Mr. Danforth, I'm so sorry. I did as you requested but security didn't get here soon enough."

"That's okay, Kim. I've got it from here," Andrew said from where he sat just to the right of his father who was seated at the head of the table.

"Andrew, what is going on?" the elder Mr. Danforth said, looking sternly at his son.

"Everything is fine father. I'll take care of this." Andrew stood up and addressed Skylar and Garrett directly, while everyone in the room looked on.

"Wow, it takes a lot of guts to come here after what you have done. Everyone knows about the fiasco in Key West and, unfortunately, about your family troubles, Skylar. Some people just weren't made to live in this type of world." The arrogance in his voice made her want to lash out, but she knew what was coming, so she remained calm, with Garrett by her side.

This setting couldn't be more perfect, Garrett thought as he looked around. There would be witnesses to what was about to come, and that was what he had been hoping for.

"Andrew, I want you to retract the ugly things you have been saying about the Cartwrights and also tell the real truth about your trip to Key West," Garrett said in a firm voice.

"I have no idea what you mean. I haven't said anything that wasn't true."

"Why are you being such a bully?" Skylar said, on the verge of losing her temper, but Garrett slowly put his hand on her back, rubbing her gently to help her calm down.

"I'm just telling the truth. Maybe the bully is the one that is standing beside you. I always knew you were not made for our world, even when we were dating. Your family just happened to get lucky all these years." Andrew's smug look and snide comments made Skylar feel like she was about to explode.

"Like I said, you will publicly retract the things you have said about the Cartwrights." Garrett firmly held his tone, letting Andrew know that he wasn't backing down.

"No, I won't. Everyone here now knows they are no longer part of decent society."

"I will tell you one more time," Garrett said. "You will retract what you have said about the Cartwrights."

"I don't know if you have some kind of hearing problem, but the two of you just need to leave," Andrew said as two security men walked into the crowded conference room. But as Garrett pushed the play button on his phone, the conversation Andrew heard loud and clear made him freeze in his tracks. He saw Garrett holding his cell phone up for everyone to see. The volume was as loud as it could be. On his phone was the scene from Sloppy Joe's, showing Andrew with the very drunk blonde attached to him like a leech, his hands all over her. Andrew was boasting about his money to the whole bar, about who he was and how he could have anything he wanted. The drunken girl kept giving him one kiss after another, which Andrew returned, even though he was engaged to Alicia, whose father just happened to be in the conference room.

Andrew's face turned bright red. "How in the hell did you get this?"

"If I remember right, I told you not to mess with the family. Things will always come back to haunt you. You came back to Miami and spread some rumors and lies to cover up your mess. But here is proof to everyone that you just aren't who you say you are. This will be on the Internet in about two hours. I just thought I would show it to you first so at least you could tell your fiancé."

Skylar looked over at a man sitting near the center of the table. "Mr. Tanner, we had no idea you would be here. And we don't want to cause Alicia any trouble, but you need to know what your future son-in-law was truly up to in Key West. Alicia deserves so much better, just like I did."

Andrew came storming around the table. "You son of a—"

"*Andrew!*" A booming voice came from the head of the table. Andrew backed down quickly, now looking at all the faces staring at him. "Sir, I didn't get your name," said the elder Mr. Danforth.

"Garrett Holmes."

"Well, Mr. Holmes, it seems that you have shed some light on my son's activities. I would like to ask you not to post that video. I can assure you I will take care of Andrew's actions quickly and efficiently. Doug," Mr. Danforth said, looking to Alicia's father. "I'm sorry for this. I'm not sure what you want to tell Alicia, but I think my son has some more growing up to do before he can be anyone's husband."

Then Mr. Danforth turned to Skylar. "As for you, Miss Cartwright, you have always been one of the sweetest young ladies I've known. I've heard good things about your charter business in Key Largo. Your father has to be proud of the brilliant young lady he has raised.

"As for everyone in this room, I would rather you didn't spread gossip, but I know things will be said. I only ask that if you decide to say something, make it truthful, or don't say anything at all."

"Thank you, Mr. Danforth. And I'm sorry that it had to come to something like this," Garrett said, putting his arm around Skylar. "You have just proven to me that not all people of your stature are cruel; you are a real person, like me. You won't see this on the Internet unless things spiral out of control. But right now, I think things are settled." With that, Garrett and Skylar turned to leave the room.

As they got in the truck, Skylar finally felt as if she could breathe, and then a huge smile came across her face. "We did it!" She practically flung herself onto Garrett, who didn't mind one bit.

"Yes, we did," he said, giving her a tight hug.

"Thank goodness I asked Abbey to video Andrew that night. I can't wait to tell her we did have to use her video. She will be so excited knowing that. But it helped a lot of people today—not just your family, but it also kept Alicia from a bad marriage, I would assume. Even though I feel sorry for Mr. Danforth, knowing that his son is not who he thought he was." Garrett took a deep breath and started the truck. "I say let's go home."

"That sounds so good to me."

32

The ride back to Key Largo was beautiful and relaxing. Skylar couldn't wait to tell Mara what had happened, but she decided to save it for their family dinner this Sunday. Since Mom and Dad had agreed to seek out counseling, the children would keep coming to the family dinners unless their parents didn't follow through. And Grandma Cartwright was on the scene to make sure both her son and daughter-in-law did as they promised.

The next few days out in the boat with Skylar and Max felt like old times to Garrett. He did some work but mostly helped with the tourists and divers. He loved doing this and began wondering whether he should just teach, instead of always being in search of the latest grant or research project. He loved it here in the Keys, and he wanted to help with the coral restoration project. Plus, he had the best spot to continue his sea turtle studies. But he had never settled in one place before, and that gave him pause. He wondered whether he was ready to stick around permanently. He had always been on the move, traveling all over the world. But as he looked over at Skylar, who was helping a little boy get ready for his first snorkeling adventure, he immediately knew the answer in his heart. Garrett wanted to stay here because of her.

The ringing phone in his pocket brought him out of his daydream. He looked down to see his mother's name on the screen.

"Hi, Mom! To what do I owe this pleasure?" Garrett said sweetly, with a smile on his face.

"Can't a mom call her baby for no reason at all?" said Linda Norris, Garrett's mom.

"Of course you can! We are just getting ready to go out on a snorkeling trip."

"Are you still dating that girl? Skylar, right?"

"Yes, Mom," Garrett said, as though he was a ten-year-old giving a report.

"She better be treating my baby boy right."

"I promise she is," Garrett said happily.

"Goodness, I don't think I need any details. Your voice says it all," Linda said, with a laugh. "I need to ask you a question. How would you like a visit from your mom? Gene and I want to come down there and stay for a few days. Last time we were there, you were in Key West. Do you have any room for us at your new place?"

"Mom, if you guys come, I'll make sure to have room for you, or I'll buy you a hotel room. I'm just glad you are coming. When will you be here?"

"We'd like to come in about three weeks. Is that too soon?" Linda asked cautiously.

"Mom, that is perfect!" Garrett said, so happy that he would be able to see her and Gene, especially after what he had just witnessed the Cartwright family going through. But most of all, Garrett couldn't wait for his mom to meet Skylar.

"We will talk more over the next few days. But I can't wait, and Skylar will be anxious to meet you too. I love you, Mom, more than you know!"

"I love you too! Tell Skylar I said hi." And with that, the phone clicked off.

"Wow, that must have been some phone call. What has made you all smiley?" Skylar said as she walked up to him. But he picked her up in a big hug and twirled her around..

"You always make me smile! But that was my mom on the phone. She and Gene are coming for a visit. It seems so long since they have been here, and now they will get to meet you." With that, he kissed her once more. "She wants to stay with me, but my place is so small. Can I take you up on that offer of your spare room?"

"Of course—you know that! But I just need to fix it up a bit. I've been meaning to pick up a few things at Shell World that will make the place feel really cozy and tropical. Now I have an excuse to go shopping," Skylar said excitedly.

"Like you need an excuse to go buy things for the house." Garrett looked at her with his eyebrows raised, and she gave him a small punch in the arm.

"You know what I mean."

"You really don't mind if they stay with you?"

"Garrett, they are your family. They are always welcome at my house. But right now, I think it's time to get this trip started. Is everyone ready to go snorkeling?" Skylar asked the people on board the boat. They all shouted back with a big yes, and within minutes, she, Garrett, Max, and their passengers were on their way to the beloved reef for another ocean adventure.

As she had promised herself, Skylar kept the news of what they had done to Andrew to herself till she and Garrett were at the table eating Sunday dinner. Harris said he had heard some rumblings about Alicia and Andrew calling off the engagement without explanation. They were all shocked when they watched the video for themselves, and they laughed that the arrogant Andrew had finally met his match in Garrett Holmes. But better news came from their parents.

As they had promised, Jonathan and Sadie had sought out help. They actually went to a counselor together, in Fort Lauderdale, where they could go without being bothered by the gossips around Miami. They also both went to an AA meeting, and after talking to the counselor and someone at the meeting, they determined that Sadie had been abusing alcohol, but she was not an alcoholic, though if she didn't stop the path she was on, she would be. When she quit drinking, she had no withdrawal symptoms, except for finally facing the fears and anxieties that she had been covering up with her drinking. There was a delicate line, but she was doing fine without the alcohol, and she told her children that for the first time in a while, she was feeling like her old self. Skylar's parents still had so much to work through, but she felt as if she was getting the parents she remembered from childhood back, even though her mother had been playing a part instead of fully admitting to growing up poor. But Skylar knew that little by little, all her family members would grow from this experience.

"Garrett and I do have some news for everyone," Skylar said as they passed around plates of key lime pie.

"You're getting married!" Mara screamed out.

"No! My gosh, Mara! Garrett's mom and husband are coming for a visit. They will be here in a few weeks. I would like to bring them to Sunday dinner, if it fits their schedule."

"That would be great," Jonathan said. "Garrett, could I talk to you in private for a moment please?"

Skylar looked at her dad and then at Garrett. She had no idea what her father wanted, but she hoped he wasn't going to lecture.

"I'll be okay," Garrett whispered in her ear before he got up and followed Skylar's dad onto the patio outside.

"I owe you a huge apology. I've been such an ass toward you. And you have been nothing but gracious to our family and protective of my daughter. Thank you," Jonathan said, shaking Garrett's hand. "What you did to protect this family by confronting Andrew—all I can say is thank you again."

Skylar and Mara both watched from a window in the corner, where the men couldn't see them.

"What do you think they are talking about?" Skylar asked quickly.

"I don't know! But at least it looks friendly and not as if they are about to punch each other."

"What are you two doing?" Chase said, coming up behind them and talking so loudly that both women jumped back and hit their heads together. Then Chase looked out the window. "That's what you get for spying on someone," he said, laughing and walking away.

Skylar and Mara peered out the window again only to see both men walking toward the door. They scrambled to get back to the couch as quickly as they could, and Skylar wondered what her dad and Garrett had said.

"So, what did Dad say out on the porch?" Skylar had barely been able to contain herself, but she had waited till they were heading back toward the Keys before asking.

"Actually, he apologized for all the negative things he had said about me."

"Well, thank goodness. Did he say anything else?"

"No, not really. He thanked me for taking care of you, but I told him you pretty much do that all on your own," Garrett said, giving her hand a squeeze.

Skylar was hoping for more news, but she wasn't really sure what she had expected. It was just such a shock to see her father and her boyfriend talking in a civilized manner, and it had made her so happy. Things were finally starting to look up, after all the turmoil around them.

33

"Oh, my gosh. This is just beautiful," Linda Norris said as everyone looked in all directions from atop the Seven-Mile Bridge. "The water's color is amazing. It's no wonder you like it here so much," she said, standing beside her son. It was only the second day of Linda and Gene's week-long vacation, and Garrett loved having his mom beside him. In the distance, he could see Gene and Skylar walking along the bridge, his wonderful girlfriend giving Gene a very detailed history of the old bridge.

"She seems like a really sweet girl. I'm glad you finally found someone in your life that has passion and drive, just like you do. You really deserve it."

"Thanks, Mom. Do you ever hear anything about Cecelia?" Garrett asked quietly.

"No, do you?" Garrett's mom asked.

"No, but with the way I travel and do my research, I didn't really figure I would ever hear from her."

"Are you truly over her now? Don't you dare put this girl through any pain or heartbreak," Linda said sternly.

"I am over her, and I knew it the moment I met Skylar. I felt like one door closed and another door opened. But I haven't told Skylar about her. Not yet." Garrett looked down at the aqua-colored water below and sighed deeply.

"Why not?"

"I don't know, but I plan on talking to her tonight. There is a little swing at the end of her road. It's a beautiful place to sit and watch the sunset. I think tonight, if it is okay with you and Gene, she and I might take a walk down there so I can talk to her. I don't want to hide anything from her. Not now."

"I think you have guarded your heart long enough. It is time to let someone in and share your life. Skylar is special, I can tell just by looking into her eyes. That doesn't come along every day, so grab it with both hands, and hang on to it. It's worth all the ups and downs, which will come along, believe me. But you have someone by your side that will stick to you like glue. That is a beautiful gift, Garrett. And I don't think she will be anything like Cecelia." His mom looked at him with such tender eyes, and he knew she was right. He gave a hug and whispered, "Thank you."

Suddenly, he heard someone say, "Turn around!"

There Skylar was, her camera in hand. "Stand together so I can get some pictures." Skylar started snapping away, taking so many pictures Garrett knew she would run out of memory on her phone at any time. "Okay, Gene, you go and join them." Once again, she took an array of pictures. Garrett was indulging Skylar. It almost felt as if he was on vacation with a little child, but in truth, Garrett loved every minute of it. And the fact that his mom approved of Skylar made it even more special.

Garrett had asked his mom and Gene what they had wanted to do during their stay here so all kinds of trips were planned for the week, with a picnic boat ride saved for Friday that would include Skylar's parents. Skylar had carefully planned the whole week, even hiring a boat captain to take her diving and snorkeling trips that she had already scheduled. She wanted to make sure that Garrett's parents had the time of their lives.

They returned home, and Skylar quickly put dinner in the oven to cook while they all took baths and cleaned up from the day. She enjoyed having people in the house. Garrett's mom was all that he had said she was, and more. Skylar asked all kinds of questions about Garrett's childhood, and Linda told story after story; most of them were funny and made Garrett blush and hang his head, while Skylar soaked up every memory.

"Hey, let's show Linda and Gene the swing at the end of the road. It's going to be a fabulous sunset," she said excitedly to Garrett.

"Sweetheart, I think Gene and I are going to turn in. With everything we have planned this week, I think I need some sleep. Today was simply beautiful, and the dinner was lovely. Thanks for letting us stay here." Linda came over and gave Skylar a motherly hug. "Now, the two of you go out there and enjoy that sunset for all of us."

"I think you are making quite the impression on my mom," Garrett said just as they reached the swing. Garrett sat down, and Skylar nestled into his arms.

"I hope so. I think she is so sweet, and Gene is wonderful. They make such a great couple. But I'm amazed at your mom—what she went through when you were younger, your father leaving and raising you on her own by working two jobs. She's a remarkable woman. It's no wonder you are such an awesome guy!" she said, reaching up and giving him a sweet kiss on the tip of his nose.

As they sat in the swing, taking in all the beauty around them, Garrett broke the silence. "Skylar, there is something in my past that I haven't told you about. I wanted to make sure the time was right before I said anything, and after talking to my mom today, I'm ready to tell you." Skylar quickly sat up and looked at Garrett, who suddenly had a far-off look on his face.

"What's wrong?"

"Nothing is wrong. There is just something that I think you should know about. No, it is something you have to know about for our relationship to continue."

Skylar felt the hair on her arms suddenly stand on end. The prickly sensation gave her a dark feeling that she quickly wished away, but it didn't go anywhere. "I'm listening."

"When I was twenty-eight years old, I met and fell in love with a fellow biologist named Cecelia. At first we just worked together, but we became good friends and then more." Garrett halted at that, giving Skylar time to take in what he had said.

"After being together for a few months, we found out that Cecelia was pregnant. I was elated, but I could tell she wasn't. She acted happy, but I knew something wasn't right. We planned to get married and stay in Savannah, where both of us could teach, and we could raise a family. But I could tell she was putting up a facade. We planned the wedding for a month later, and we had everything in place. But a week before the ceremony, Cecelia disappeared for a day. No one could find her. When she finally contacted me the next day, she told me over the phone that the wedding was off and that she'd had an abortion. I was devastated. I loved her and the baby. I was so happy that I was going to be a father. I had this nice little scenario in my head of us being the model family— Mom and Dad were teachers and had two kids. But she wasn't ready and had other things in mind. She wanted us to travel the world and do marine research in different countries. One of her goals was to do research on each continent." Garrett stopped talking, reliving the memories in his mind. "I'm sorry I didn't tell you until now."

"I'm sorry that you went through that, but why wouldn't you tell me?"

"I don't know. Maybe I was afraid you would leave me too. I've been in a few relationships since then, but it has always been hard. That fear is in the back of my head that the other person is going to leave. My dad left us, and my mom was alone for so long. Cecelia left and took away my child. I think that fear is one of the reasons I walked out of the gala that night after hearing what your dad said. I felt like after everything that happened, you would probably leave me too." Garrett sat quietly for a moment, staring out at the water. "It was easier to just throw myself into marine research, learn everything I could, and be the Fish Man. Maybe that is one reason I talk so much about my work." With that last sentence, he chuckled slightly. "I hope you don't think less of me for not sharing this with you sooner."

Skylar looked at Garrett, who was still staring off into the distance, over the ocean. She could almost feel the pain he was experiencing as he told the story, even though she knew his love for Cecelia was long gone.

"Garrett, I'm not going anywhere, unless you ask me to leave, or you leave me. Like I've told you since the moment we started seeing each other, I'm in this for good. Do you remember? You are stuck with me. I only wish I could take away some of the pain you have gone through. Until lately, I don't think my siblings or I truly knew what it was like to go through so many of life's ups and downs. And you and your mom have been through so much. I'm just glad that now we have each other to hold on to for support when things are not so great and also to celebrate every day."

Skylar changed positions in the swing, putting her legs over Garrett's lap. This way, she could be closer to him and talk. "I love you more than I can ever say. You are truly special, and I'm so glad you picked my boat. First of all, you helped me pay off the silly thing. But secondly, I got to meet a wonderful man. Thank you for sharing your past with me, but is there anything else I need to know?"

Garrett laughed. "No, that's all from me. I think my mom has already told you the other stories. And I'm sure if you keep asking, she will keep coming up with things to keep you entertained at my expense." Skylar laughed, but she was also tracing her fingers on his lips. The sensual feeling made Garrett caress her neck and run his fingers through her beautiful brunette hair, which was hanging down around her shoulders instead of up in the ponytail she usually wore.

"I love you, Skylar."

"I love you too!" she said softly.

34

The rest of the week was like a whirlwind. Garrett and Skylar wanted his mom and Gene to see everything in the Keys, but there just wasn't enough time. So they picked a few places that were must dos.

They spent the next day in Key West, leaving bright and early in the morning. It took them a bit longer to get there than was planned, as Garrett's mom wanted to stop so often to take pictures, but they didn't mind. Seeing her and Gene happy made the trip priceless for Garrett. He had always wanted to do something like this for his mom because she deserved so much. When they got to the city, they immediately parked at Mallory Square and took the Old-Time Trolley Tour around the city three times. It seemed as if each trip was different, and they even got off a few times to see the Hemingway House and the Southernmost Point buoy then to have lunch at Margaritaville. After a bit of shopping along Duval Street and watching the sunset at Mallory Square, it was time to head back home. Everyone but Garrett slept in the car. He had never felt this way before as he looked at the sleeping trio around him. It was like he had a real family—as he had always dreamed about.

The next day they took another day trip to Bahia Honda Beach. Even though there were other places they could have gone and things they could have done, Linda insisted on going because she had read it was one of the best beaches in the United States. Linda loved the beach, as her son did; it was one of the reasons they lived so close to the shore in Savannah. But Bahia Honda was like no other beach she had been to before. The water was clear and peaceful, and before Garrett knew it, both his mom and Gene were in the water and swimming around, like two little kids. Garrett and Skylar could only laugh, and suddenly Skylar was stripping away clothes, revealing a bathing suit he had never seen before: it was a two-piece bikini in a stunning aqua color that showed more of her than the world deserved to see. But he couldn't help but admire her as she slowly walked toward the water, looking back at him with sultry eyes and motioning him to follow, which he did, like a puppy dog on a leash. The water was warm and relaxing. After all the stress they had been through during the last months, these family moments felt like little gifts of fun that he wanted to treasure forever.

The next day was spent deep-sea fishing off Islamorada, since it was the sport fishing capital of the world. Gene loved deep-sea fishing, and Skylar knew just the boat he should go on. But she bowed out of going so she could get some paper work done. She watched the trio sail off with her friend, knowing that they would have the time of their lives. As she drove home, she decided to go to the marina to make sure the boat was ready for tomorrow's trip, especially since her parents were coming along. They had never been on her boat, except for the night that her dad showed up and interrupted her very first date with Garrett. There were no trips scheduled for today, so she was able to just sit on the boat and think for a while.

So much had happened. As she looked back, she was amazed at what she had been through. Her business was now thriving. Her family had been broken into pieces by secrets, but now they were working toward putting everything back together again. Her ex-boyfriend had been out to destroy not only her but also anyone else who got in his way. Garrett's crazy intern had been hell-bent on revenge for something Skylar didn't even do. And she had also met the man who had stolen her heart.

As Skylar considered the dark time that Garrett had revealed to her the other night, at first she wasn't sure what to think. Should she be upset at him at waiting so long to tell her all the details? She thought she should, but she couldn't. He wasn't being mean or malicious by not telling. He had thought he was protecting himself, but to her it only confirmed the strength of their relationship since he felt he was finally able, after all this time, to share that story. So instead of upsetting her, it made her feel even more secure in the love they shared. Skylar didn't feel as vulnerable anymore about revealing her feelings and being open about how she felt. All of this only verified that he loved her as much as she loved him.

The paper work was done, and dinner almost ready when the trio walked in from their fishing trip.

"We decided we are going to change clothes and go to the Shrimp Shack. They have the fish we caught today, and they are going to prepare it when we get there," Garrett said in a rush.

Though Skylar's dinner was almost ready, she quickly put everything into containers, and they headed to the famous little restaurant in Islamorada. The restaurant was well-known for fixing your own "catch of the day" in several ways, which the locals loved. And Skylar had always enjoyed their food and atmosphere. As she sat with everyone that evening, she couldn't help but smile at what an amazing week it had been so far. Was this possibly the "simpler" life her Grandma had always referred to in the stories she told? If it was, Skylar was loving every minute of it.

When Skylar woke up on Friday, she quickly got up and fixed coffee for everyone. She knew Garrett would be over shortly, as he had been ever since his mom and Gene had arrived. Today, they were all going on the boat for a picnic. Skylar was nervous about her parents meeting Linda and Gene. She wasn't sure what to expect when they were together; the families came from completely different walks of life. Skylar knew her parents were making progress from the reports she got from her brothers and sister.

They were all meeting at the boat at ten o'clock and then heading back to the Holiday Isle Sandbar off Islamorada, where Skylar and Garrett had run into Andrew's friend Ben.

She was still a bit nervous about everyone being together and just prayed that the day would turn out alright.

"What a beautiful boat," Linda said as she climbed aboard. "And you bought this all by yourself. And you're the captain." She looked over at Garrett. "You better hang on to her, son!"

"I plan to, Mom," he said while smiling broadly at Skylar.

"Is there room for two more?" Skylar recognized her father's familiar voice and turned to see both of her parents standing on the dock.

"Come aboard! There's lots of room on here," Linda said. "I'm Linda, Garrett's mom, and this is my husband, Gene."

"I'm Jonathan, Skylar's dad."

"And I'm Sadie, her mom."

As their parents shook hands and introduced themselves, Garrett and Skylar just stood back, amazed that they didn't have to say a word. Everyone seemed to be talking as if Skylar and Garrett didn't even exist, and this made them both happy.

"Are we ready to get underway? There is a little island out there that is waiting to be explored," Garrett said.

"I've never been on a sandbar before," Linda said. "Well, at least not one out in the ocean. Everything here is so different than in Savannah, even though I love it there. Does it take long to get there?"

"It won't take too long, and the scenery on the way is beautiful. We just have to be careful because the water is shallow in places, so following the channel markers and buoys is essential. Just sit back, and enjoy the ride."

Skylar steered them out of the marina and into open water. Both sets of parents sat in the back of the boat, talking, as Skylar and Garrett piloted the boat.

"I think everything is going well so far. What do you think?" Garrett said over the noise of the wind and the boat's motor.

"I think so. I wasn't sure what to expect with my parents, but they seem to be doing well. Let's just see how the picnic turns out."

As they pulled up, there were already about thirty boats surrounding the island.

"Is it usually like this?" Linda said as she looked around in amazement.

"This is nothing, Mom. Some days, there are hundreds of boats out here, and it's just one big party. Some people actually call this Islamorada's own little beach. It's beautiful, isn't it?"

"It's stunning! I can't get over the color of the water or how you can see to the bottom and see all the fish. It's no wonder you have been down here for so long. I don't think I would be able to leave either. And now that you have a special someone, I don't think you will be moving home to Savannah anytime soon." Linda just grinned at her son, who blushed at the comment.

"Skylar, let's anchor right here. The depth of the water is just right and we can still get to the sandbar, if anyone wants to walk around." Soon the anchor was in the water, and they were enjoying the sights and sounds around them. Steel drum music was coming from a nearby boat, and someone with a grill on the sandbar was cooking hamburgers, which they could smell all the way out on the boat.

"I wonder if they would fix one of those burgers for me," Skylar's dad said as they pulled the food out of the cooler. Skylar had brought big sub sandwiches, potato chips, potato salad, a fruit tray, and chocolate-chip cookies. They had filled the second cooler with water and various drinks, but they didn't bring alcohol for Sadie's sake.

Because of the boat's layout, Skylar was able to lay two thick cotton blankets on the floor of the boat, and everyone had room to sit and eat. They each took a cushion from the side benches, and they put the food in the middle of the blanket. And even though they were sitting on the floor, they could still see the surrounding activity and hear the music.

"I feel like I'm at a big beach party," Sadie said as they were eating their sandwiches. "I've never been here before. Have you, Jonathan?"

"I have, but it was so long ago. I really haven't done anything like this in years. It seems that work took precedence over everything. I haven't had any fun in quite a long time. And this feels really good." Skylar watched in amazement as her dad leaned over and gave her mother a kiss on the lips. It was simple and sweet, but in her eyes, it was monumental. She hadn't seen affection like this from her parents in years. She really couldn't remember the last time she had, and suddenly, she felt tears at the corners of her eyes.

"Are you okay?" Linda asked, looking at Skylar.

"Oh, yes. I think I got some sunscreen in my eyes. That stuff stings pretty badly," Skylar said to cover up her watery eyes. But as she looked over at Garrett, he just smiled and blew her a kiss. He heard the exchange between her parents and knew exactly what was going through Skylar's mind.

As they nibbled at the fruit and chocolate-chip cookies, Skylar suddenly wanted to go take a dip in the ocean. "I think it's time for a swim, even though I know we are supposed to wait till the food settles. But the water just looks so good!"

"I agree," Linda said quickly. "I want to walk on that sandbar and take pictures too. They are never going to believe me back home unless I have pictures."

"Well, sorry, ladies, but no one is going anywhere just yet," Garrett said, making the two women sit back down. "I have something I want to say." Skylar and Linda quickly took their seats, looking at each other wondering what was going on.

"First of all, Mom and Gene, this has been a wonderful week. Spending time with you here on my turf has been amazing. The times you have been here before were so quick that we never had a chance to enjoy the islands. I'm so glad you came, and thank you, Skylar, for letting them stay with you. My spare room, or should I say closet, would have been just a bit too cramped."

"We would have made do. But thank you, sweetheart," Linda said, patting Skylar's shoulder.

Garrett then turned his attention to Skylar's parents. "Mr. and Mrs. Cartwright, thanks for coming with us today. I'm glad that we all get to spend time getting to know each other. You have an amazing daughter, and I feel so blessed to have her in my life." Garrett suddenly took a deep breath and turned to Skylar.

"Skylar Cartwright, from the moment I saw you, I knew you were special. I couldn't believe you were the captain of that boat, being a girl." He gave her a wink. "But I gave you a chance, and you did a pretty good job." Skylar looked at him and stuck her tongue out, like a little kid. "But every day we spent together, the more I got to know you. You are the most kind, caring, and loving individual I have ever met. I never thought I would fall in love again, but you changed all that. So now..." Garrett said, reaching into his pocket and pulling out the most beautiful diamond ring she had ever seen. "Will you do me the honor of becoming my wife?"

Skylar was in complete shock. The happiness spreading through her was like a wildfire, and though no words would come, she nodded "yes" while the tears flowed down her cheeks. When she reached to hug him, she finally found her voice. "Yes. Yes, I will marry you." She pulled back, and he placed the ring on her finger and made it official. Then he gently took her face in his hands and kissed her ever so tenderly. They were so caught up in the moment that they had forgotten their parents were watching.

"My baby is getting married," Linda said, getting up and hugging her son.

"You are going to make a beautiful bride and more importantly, a wonderful wife. We are so proud to call you our daughter." Both of Skylar's parents embraced their daughter. There were smiles and tears all around.

"Now we have a wedding to plan," Sadie said, looking at Linda.

"Yes, we do! This will be so much fun," Linda said excitedly.

"Let us just be engaged right now. I want to absorb this moment fully. Happy doesn't begin to describe how I feel right now," Skylar said, looking up at her husband to be.

"I love you so much, Garrett. You have made me one very happy woman!"

"I can't begin to tell you how you have changed my life. I love you more and more each day. So now we can make this official."

"Most definitely," Skylar said, pulling him into another romantic kiss under the tropical sun.

EPILOGUE

Everything looked to be in order, as usual. All the gear was ready for the day. The boat was booked for two snorkel trips, and both were completely full. Skylar checked the gear one more time, then the passenger lists to make sure everything was as it should be.

"What are you doing?" Max said as he came aboard the boat.

"Just double checking everything. I know you are more than capable of doing it, but old habits don't go away very easily. Where is Jack?"

"He pulled into the parking lot right after I did. He should be here any second. Do you need any help?" Max said as Skylar climbed out of the boat.

"Nope, I got it. I'm going to check on the *Gypsy Queen* now. Call me when you get back," Skylar said to Max, and he gave her a thumbs-up.

As Skylar walked up to the other boat, she couldn't help but smile. This was the second boat in her business and it was like a dream come true. Once again she was able to find the same boat style as her first, the *Sea Gypsy*, used but in good shape. Getting her ready for paying clients had taken a little time and money but the boat had already made more than enough money to pay off the repairs and now the profit was going toward paying on the loan. It was fully booked for each day this week and the captain of the boat, Beth Lockhart, had been a wonderful find.

Beth had grown up at a marina her family owned in Marathon Key. But when her parents wanted to retire, her brother took over the business and Beth decided she was going to travel for a while. That was until she ran into Skylar one day at a local bar and grill during the lunchtime rush. The two women happened to share a table while waiting for their take out food and before she knew it, they had agreed Beth would come to see Skylar's new boat as it's potential captain. And even though Beth hadn't traveled like she had planned to except for going about fifty miles from her home, she fell in love with the boat and agreed to be the new captain. Since then she and Skylar had become best friends.

"How's it going Beth?" Skylar said from the dock, seeing her friend at the captain's helm.

"Everything is fine and ready to go. What are you doing here?" Beth asked.

Why was everyone asking her that question? This was her business, her dream, floating in the water in front of her. Skylar couldn't just sit by and let everyone else do the work. It didn't feel right.

"I'm just double checking everything. You know—passenger lists, equipment—the usual," Skylar said.

"I have it all taken care of, I promise," Beth reassured her.

"I know. Just miss going out to sea."

"I understand. When the third boat gets here, you can go back to being captain, okay? Right now, Max and I have got it covered."

"Where do you think you are going, Mrs. Holmes?" She heard a voice and looked up to see her husband walking toward her.

"I'm just checking the boats. Both are fully scheduled this week, and I'm making sure everything is in order."

"You know that is what the captains do, right?" Garrett said as he came up behind her and put his arms around Skylar's expanded waistline. "They are capable of checking the gear, the weather, and passenger lists. That is why we hired them, remember?"

"I know, but it's hard to stay on shore when I'm so used to being out on the boat. I just want to go out on the water for a little while. Please?"

"It's only a couple more weeks then our little girl will join us. Maybe instead of taking her for a ride in the car, we can take her out on the boat instead," Garrett said, flashing that smile that still made Skylar's heart melt.

"I like that boat idea. I want her to love the water as much as we do. As far as waiting a few more weeks, she can come anytime. I can't even see my feet anymore, and the store keeps running out of Popsicles."

"Well, your feet are just as beautiful as the rest of you, and as for the Popsicles, you are the first woman I know who craved only Popsicles during her pregnancy. I wonder if Taylor will love them as she is growing up," Garrett said, turning Skylar around to hug her, still able to get close despite the size of her baby bump.

"As long as she loves the ocean as much as we do—that's more important. But if she doesn't, I don't want to hold her back from her dreams. But right now, let's just enjoy every minute we have together and not rush things. I know I said I'm ready for her to come, but I like this alone time with you too. Since you aren't going out in the boat today, let's stay home and watch movies. I know I'm supposed to be walking and exercising, but I just don't feel up to it."

Just then, Skylar felt something wet trickle down her legs. "Well, I guess we need to make other plans."

"What do you mean?" Garrett said.

"My water just broke!" Skylar said excitedly.

"What?"

"I said my water just broke. We need to get my stuff from the house and go to the hospital."

"Really...we are having a baby today." Garrett was dumbfounded, so shocked that Skylar could have pushed him over just by barely touching him.

"Garrett, I really have to go!"

"We are having a baby today!" Garrett yelled so loudly the whole marina could hear him.

"We might have a baby here on the dock unless we get going," Skylar said, looking at her husband and smiling, even though she suddenly felt a contraction that almost took her breath away.

"Max, you are in charge, and I'll call you," Skylar said. Suddenly, people were all around, trying to help them. When they got to the truck, Garrett helped her because she felt another contraction coming on.

"I love you, Garrett."

"I love you too, sweetheart. Are you ready to meet our baby girl?"

"I can't wait!"

ACKNOWLEDGEMENTS

It's hard to believe that this is the third book in the "Florida Keys Romance" series and I would not have been able to bring it to life without so many people who have helped me along the way.

Most of all, to my wonderful husband, Jeff: thanks for all the support you give me as I pursue my love of writing. Once again, letting me talk out scenes and ideas non-stop, giving me time and space to write, fixing meals so I could continue to work and so much more. You are my rock and I love you more and more each day.

To my mother, Irene Slusser: You probably knows all my stories better than me as you have been my sounding board, part-time editor, beta reader and more. You have been with me when I get frustrated but also when I would breakthrough a particular part of the story that would challenge me. I couldn't have done any of this without you.

To my father, Sonny Slusser: You have been such a great supporter of my writing endeavors and the best marketing rep I could ever have. Your solid business advice and complete support of my writing is such a treasure to me.

To my accountability partner and best friend, Donna Gauntlett: You have yet again kept me on track as I wrote this book. You have been there for me both professionally and per- sonally which is truly a precious gift.

And to my wonderful readers——you are simply the best. You encourage me to write more each and every day. Your support means more than I can put into words.

Big hugs and lots of love to each and every one of you!

Miki

WELCOME TO THE FLORIDA KEYS

I guess you can tell by now that I love the Florida Keys. There are so many wonderful places to see, things to do, and wonderful food to eat. The island vibe is alive and well from the moment you cross the bridge into Key Largo and throughout each Key as you drive and reach Key West.

There are several places I mention throughout Garrett's and Skylar's love story and I wanted to make sure I gave you a list so when you visit these fabulous islands, you have a few places you can check out!

-The Lorelei Restaurant is a great place located on Islamorada. The food and service is wonderful and if you love outdoor dining, this is the place for you.

http://loreleicabanabar.com

-Mangrove Mike's Café on Islamorada is a terrific little place where you will feel right at home. Great food and it definitely has the island touch.

www.mangrovemikes.com

-The Islamorada Shrimp Shack is a very unique restaurant with very tasty food and the fact that they will actually fix your "catch of the day" after you have been out fishing is exciting! Plus, they have some wonderful Key Lime Pie––yummy!

www.islamoradashrimpshack.com

-The Holiday Isle Sandbar is a hopping place you can only get to by boat. Very popular with locals and tourists and a great place to have a party surrounded by the beautiful waters of the Keys.

www.mapinit.com/islamorada/c#!/124-holiday-isle-sandbar/

-The historic Seven Mile Bridge is a must see and if you are traveling to Key West, it is part of your ride. There is a small area to park that will allow you to walk the old bridge. To learn more about the history, check out:

www.friendsofoldseven.org/bridge/

-The John Pennekamp State Park is the first undersea state park in the United States. If you love to snorkel or dive, this is a wonderful place to go.

www.pennekamppark.com

-Sloppy Joe's Bar on Duval Street in Key West is a local tradition. It has a colorful history which is quite interesting.

www.sloppyjoes.com

-Old Towne Trolley Tours is a wonderful way to get to see the sights of Key West while learning its history from the fantastic tour guides.

www.trolleytours.com/key-west/

-Sombrero Beach is a beautiful spot to put your feet in the sand and go for a swim on Marathon Key. Just remember it is a turtle nesting beach for Loggerhead Turtles.

www.ci.marathon.fl.us/government/parks/city-parks-and-beaches/

There is so much more to see, do and experience in the Florida Keys that I will be putting together a resource page on my website. You can check it out at:

www.mikibennett.com

When you go, I hope you fall in love with the Florida Keys as much as I have!

Miki

ALSO BY MIKI BENNETT

From the "Florida Keys Romance" Series

"The Keys to Love"

Divorcee Maddy Sumner is ready to work on creating the next chapter of her life. Adjusting to a newly empty nest and coping with chronic health issues, she's desperately in need of some time to rest and regroup.

So, she embarks on a much-needed vacation to the Florida Keys, with the help of her best friend Riley. There, she catches the eye of Jason, the mysterious neighbor across the street, who finds himself captivated by the beautiful woman in the rental house on the water.

When an emergency situation causes Jason and Maddy's lives to collide, it isn't long before the pair discovers meaningful feelings for one another, secured even more deeply by a whirlwind trip to Key West. But when a set of painful circumstances from the past emerges, will complications put an end to this blossoming romance?

"Forever in the Keys"

After attending a wedding in the Keys, twenty-eight year-old Abbey Wallace decides to pack up everything she owns and move to Key West. The budding artist loves the vibe of the city and hopes to become an artisan at Mallory Square.

Abbey quickly settles into island life, finding her dream job, a beautiful apartment, and begins making new friends. However, her mean-spirited neighbor, Josie, poses a real challenge. But, Abbey persists at building a friendship, determined to find the real reason behind the older woman's disagreeable attitude.

For Zach Isler, Abbey is more than just a co-worker. He is totally enamored with this interesting woman but Abbey is afraid to admit her attraction to him. Then a sudden life altering incident makes her re-examine her emotions for this handsome man.

Book Two in the "Florida Keys Romance" series, *Forever in the Keys*, explores friendship, romance and the excitement of life's second chances.

ABOUT THE AUTHOR

 Miki Bennett lives in Charleston, South Carolina with her husband, Jeff and her little dog, Emma. She is the author of the "Florida Keys Romance" series which began with her debut novel, *The Keys to Love* and followed with *Forever in the Keys*. She has an intense love for the beach and goes to the shore as much as she can. When not working on her latest book, she enjoys creating paintings and experimenting with new art techniques in her studio. She also has a love for the newest gadget and is known as the family computer geek.